C0-EFL-781

LETTING GO

*To Cynthia
Thanks for all
the support*

"2006"

LETTING GO

By
Bethena Smith

E-BookTime, LLC
Montgomery, Alabama

Letting Go

Copyright © 2006 by Bethena Smith

All rights reserved. No part of this book may be reproduced or transmitted in any form or by any means, electronic or mechanical, including photocopying, recording, or by any information storage and retrieval system, without permission in writing from the copyright owner.

This is a work of fiction. Names, characters, places and incidents either are the product of the author's imagination or are used fictitiously, and any resemblance to any actual persons, living or dead, events, or locales is entirely coincidental.

Library of Congress Control Number: 2006921455

ISBN: 1-59824-134-6

First Edition
Published February 2006
E-BookTime, LLC
6598 Pumpkin Road
Montgomery, AL 36108
www.e-booktime.com

Contents

Acknowledgements 7
Introduction - Looking for Prince Charming 9
The Affair 17
Love Shows No Mercy 25
Jean Lets Charles Go 31
Ken's Secret Life 41
Charles Lets Amy Go 50
The Blood Test 62
Brad Walker 70
The Kisses 81
Charles Wants to Come Home 84
Brian's Test Result 95
Ken Breaks Down 101
The Funeral 113
Love at First Sight 123
Beth and Brad Make Love 132
Amy Lets Ken Go 141
Amy Tells Her Parents About Charles 147
The Engagement 154
Earl Comes Home 160
The Wedding 166
Charles Gets the News 182
The Missing 188
Ellen Gets Desperate 207
Beth Gives Up on Love 222
The Engagement 228
Who's Jamie's Father? 238
The Fire 248
The Courtroom 261
The Wedding of a Princess 268
Ellen Plots Her Escape 272

Acknowledgements

I first want to thank God for giving me such a vivid imagination that I could write this book! God is good!

I would like to thank my husband for his suggestions, encouragement and understanding while I made my dream a reality. He said to me one day, "You should right a book about "Letting Go" and moving on." Well, I took his advice and the book was written two weeks later. Thanks to the love of my life, my husband Isaac.

I want to thank my daughters Cameren and Nadia and my niece Shardey for all their patience and words of encouragement. And to all my family who advised me on doing the right thing, thank you.

I had the pleasure of having two editors, Belinda Buggs and Wini Knotts. They took my words and gave them life. "I love you both!" One more great thanks, to my publisher Gean, for taking time with my book.

One more thank you to my AAFES family of friends who tested the waters and advised me to keep on rowing.

I discovered in a short time that being a great author does not always entail knowing big words; it's comes when you write from the heart. Every word of "Letting Go" comes from the heart. I hope you enjoy reading it as much as I enjoyed writing it.

Introduction

Looking for Prince Charming

When the marriage or relationship is over, please let go! My name is Beth, and I will be telling you most of the stories in this book. Some of the stories will make you laugh, some will make you cry and others will make you mad as hell. A lot of you will think this book was inspired by true events. The characters will possess traits similar to your friends, sisters, brothers, co-workers or even you. The truth is most wives, husbands, boyfriends and girlfriends are someone else's ex. Once you get involved, you have to deal with all the baggage that comes along. The truth is most ex's aren't looking for anyone else. They're holding on to the past; which makes the current wife, boyfriend or girlfriend' life a living nightmare.

Here you are trying to build a life and all they want to do is tear it down piece by piece. Where do you go from here? That's the million dollar question! The truth is we have to fight! I don't mean literally. We sometimes have to fight in court over child support, alimony or even over our personal items. Ladies, you don't even want half the stuff you're fighting over; you're just angry and mad that he left you. You want him to pay and suffer for walking out. Right! So ladies and men let's get serious. The world is not going to stop rotating and throw you off just because your man or woman left.

You have got to face being left with a little more dignity than you had in the past. Some of you would rather see him or her dead than have him leave you; especially if another person is in the picture. That shows you how much you've attached yourself to these individuals. Let go! Cut the string! Walk away! Run if you can! In the end he or she will always come back!

We have to show more self-control. The bottom line is we can't accept being left. It would mean nothing for us to walk out on them. The ex's aren't authorized to leave us; they're our bread winner! What gives them the right to walk out on us? There were many times when I wanted and wished my husband Earl would leave me, but he didn't. Earl liked the freedom that marriage offered him. It gave him a sense of pride. Earl had two or three women at his disposal depending on how his week was going. Yes! Earl would brag about having other women, telling me if I didn't like it I could leave!

This was when I turned things over to God. The only way to win a battle like this is through the Almighty. I brought prayer back into my life. I prayed quite often those days asking God to deliver me from the darkness and pain that this man had dropped me into.

I didn't give up on life; there were many times when I, wanted to take his, but I figured he wasn't worth it. There are moments in most of our lives when your man can push you too far, and I was there. I would almost lose control on occasion, but I refused to let this man take my freedom. You ladies know exactly what I'm saying. You get so mad you can't see straight. The damage you could do in the flicker of an eye. Anyone who has had a cheating boyfriend, girlfriend, wife or husband can understand what true pain is all about. It's the pain that is buried on the dark side of the heart and when that pain is awakened someone usually has a high price to pay for waking it up. There were times when I wanted to wake Satan and have him take Earl to the dark side.

I knew from the beginning that I had married the wrong man. I was looking for my Prince Charming, and found the Prince of Darkness! You see, when I was nineteen I started praying for him. But God was taking too long; I wanted a husband now! I was ready! I had no patience and went looking for myself.

If you ever ask God for something and you don't wait on him you may get something or someone you didn't bargain for.

That's what happened to me. I had a man that had no clue about marriage or fidelity. I married the first man that asked me. My time clock was ticking! I was getting older every second; I was already nineteen. I had dreamed my whole life of marriage

Letting Go

and kids. I had no clue what lay ahead of me. But I soon found out that my marriage would be nothing like I had dreamed.

Since I was determined to marry the first man that asked me the mistakes rolled in faster than I could roll them out. I won't go too deeply into the details, but I have a few stories to share with you. I was looking for Mr. Right. Well, I found him, and his name was Earl Taylor. He was several years older than I was; but age was nothing but a number, right? Wrong! Age has everything to do with it when your nineteen and haven't got a clue of what life is all about! You're just beginning to learn, why bring a total stranger into your life at this point?

Earl was popular and his family had status in our community. My mom was ready for me to say "I Do". Earl wasn't available at the moment, because he was dating three other young ladies at the time. Earl was going to be my husband as soon as the coast was clear; I needed him to hurry! I waited on no man! He succeeded and we married three months later. Not enough time people! Not enough time to know my new husband! The marriage started off rocky, but I was determined to stay Mrs. Taylor, and hold tight to that title! In my home town having a title was everything.

Well, there weren't enough opportunities in our small town for rising stars like Earl and myself so I encouraged him to join the Marines. They were looking for a few good men and he qualified, right? Just between you and me; I wasn't the only one he fooled.

Our first duty station was Ft McClellan in Alabama. Earl was always in the streets, never home. I was often left home with our new daughter Marie, who was six months old at the time. I can remember several nights a week he would go out to meet the boys. I often asked if I got a sitter could I come along. The answer was always the same. "It's just a bunch of guys hanging out, you would be the only female there." I would cry of loneliness for my husband while he was out with the boys.

On one particular night when he didn't come home I was terrified, so alone and far from home. One of my friends and I searched the base for Earl. We called around to police stations, hospitals and emergency rooms looking for him. What, if he was dead in a ditch somewhere? We were in Alabama, worse things have happened in the south. I never guessed Earl was in jail. Earl was arrested for being in the wrong place, at the wrong time, with the wrong woman, and in the wrong position.

That's when I learned my first lesson about the "boys". They were always pretty young girls with boy names, like Bobbie, Jessie, and Sammie, if you know what I mean. That was my first class on infidelity, and I can tell you it left a bad taste in my mouth. He had been hanging out with Bobbie for several weeks. They were finally busted by the law when they were caught in an unauthorized position with their pants below their knees.

God has a way of working things out for you; all you need to do is wait on him. Let's just say, Bobbie's husband Carl didn't hang around for lesson two! Carl left after the first lesson was over.

I had to hang around. I wasn't strong enough to leave yet. I needed to be financially able to support myself and my child before I left. I had to stay and try to live through the trauma. This was the beginning of a life with no future. In the few weeks that followed I was left in a daze; my heart was broken. He had reduced me to less than the person I started out to be. I asked God, "Why me?! Why did Earl have to have this woman? Why not a sister? How could I compete with what she had to offer him?"

She was the one woman a young black man that grew up in the south wasn't allowed to have up until now; but now she was his for the taking. I couldn't compete with the color of her skin. I was just a little too dark, so she was in and I was out. She had long flowing hair down her back and her eyes were as blue as the sky. She was beautiful. She was everything Earl had ever wanted, but what about the promises he had made to me?

He had promised to take care of me until death do we part. This was not the marriage I had dreamed of all my life. Just when you think you're winning life has a way of playing tricks on you. I was dealt a rotten hand, and I would have to play it out. I would have to rethink my position as a wife. The game was the same old game that all men played! All I needed was to learn the

Letting Go

rules and I too could play the game; the game of who can sleep with who and not get caught. Earl was already winning. I needed a reverse card to get me back in position if I wanted to win at this game. After all, he was my husband. The one I had to have. The one I went out and rounded up for myself. I was being cheated out of a happy life and Earl knew he was cheating! Earl just kept on stacking the deck! I had married a player! This whole experience had left me drained and incomplete as a woman. Who was I?

Every night I went to bed knowing he would be in another woman's arms while I lay alone in our bed with no arms to hold me! I knew there had to be a better life than this. I prayed to God to please help me; and not let Earl and his lies destroy what I had been given, my child. Well my life didn't change much. Earl kept on running around and I kept justifying being married by looking in the direction of other men for love and attention; what my husband Earl had refused to give me. No, I wasn't proud of what I was doing but it is a cruel and hard world out there and no one ever promised me that my marriage was meant to last. That was my own misconception! You have to understand; I was nineteen years old and full of hopes and dreams that I had found my "Prince Charming". Earl would make me his princess and rescue me from my captors, who at that time were my small home town and strict parents.

No one should ever learn that hard of a lesson at such a young age. It wasn't the affair that had broken my spirit. It was the fact that Earl had "fallen in love" with this woman! I couldn't accept the fact that he didn't love me anymore. After I found the letters I knew the marriage was over. We had since been transferred to Europe. Earl and Bobbie were claiming their undying love for each other halfway across the planet.

Why did he wait until now? How can you have an affair and fall in love? Aren't affairs supposed to be all about sex; about not getting enough at home and needed more? The smart ones should know when to pull out of a relationship; when the woman starts speaking of love! Right! But what happens when the man starts speaking of love?

What do we, as wives, do then? We let them go! Well my husband didn't go! He wanted to, believe me, but he wasn't just obligated to me he was also obligated to Uncle Sam and Uncle Sam had given him a military bonus for two more years of Earl's time. You can't just take Uncle Sam's money and run, otherwise he would have left me in a heartbeat! So he stayed. That fool had dragged me all the way to Europe and decided he wanted someone else. Guess what? He didn't get her! He had to settle for me! Why not? I had settled for him! I was not going to come to Europe and get dumped! I hung in there and stuck to my marriage vows. The few I could remember. "Until death do you part" was the only one that came to mind! I wasn't going to let him go! Not just yet! He was going to have to pay for his freedom!

I tried to focus on life and my daughter Marie; she would have to be my reason for living and going on with this charade of a marriage. My parents didn't raise a quitter! I lived through one affair after another. I learned to adapt to my husband's way of life.

I was expecting our second child when I learned he was sleeping with our baby sitter. He wasn't picky about who he slept with as long as it wasn't me. He came in late one night with passion marks on his neck. I had to know where they came from so I asked, "Earl, why are there passion marks on your neck?"

"Oh yeah, I was working on the car starter and rested it on my neck," he said.

The average woman might have been able to control herself, but I was several months pregnant. Earl shouldn't have been surprised at what happened next. I picked up the nearest knife and threw it at him, barely missing his head! "I will not be treated as though I'm stupid! Cheat on me yeah, but don't play me for a fool! Someone may get hurt!"

Earl tried to stay clear of me for several weeks after the knife incident. I wasn't trying to kill him, but I had said "until death do you part"!

I knew this woman didn't want Earl. Neither did I for that matter. All I needed was time to master my career and stand on my own. I wasn't going to let Earl take anything else from me,

Letting Go

he had taken enough. Earl had already stolen my faith in marriage and any future we may have had together. Earl would always belong to every other woman, never to just one. I was more than prepared to share him. I just hoped he was prepared to share me when the time came, and believe me it was coming.

The overseas trip left me with permanent scars! The scars I'm sporting are hidden in my heart! I still cry at night, and I'm still very lonely for a man's touch but I have learned to be patient. I'm waiting on God to make every thing right this time. Prayer does change things. You are about to see just how it works.

Earl and I are back in the states and now we're stationed in Washington DC.

I was lucky enough for my employer to transfer me along with Earl. Something tells me that this place is going to be lucky for me and my girls. I have a great job and I received a promotion along with my transfer. I started working on Bolling AFB two weeks after getting settled. My new position gave me the opportunity to manage several employees. That wasn't the problem; the problem came from trying to manage my life. All I needed was time, and in time, I would master my personal life just as well! We moved into post housing and my job was within walking distance. Post housing was not very appealing, but I was state side. I would have to be patient and wait on the house to come. The best news came when Earl received orders to Korea for the next year on an unaccompanied tour. That was music to my ears. Things were already looking up! This would be my first chance at freedom. Even as a married woman, I felt freedom coming!

If you really think about my life it's very sad. When a woman's husband is leaving she should not be celebrating, she should be crying and thinking of the loneliness and the hard nights when he's not there to hold her. Not me. You can't miss what you never had! I was happier than two peas in a pod! Marriage can do that to you if you let it!

With Earl on his way to Korea, and the girls settled in school, I needed to start work on me. I needed a lot of work. I would have to rebuild myself from the inside out. I knew my life was going to change, that things would never be quite the same again. I was ready for whatever life had to throw at me.

My new position on base gave me exposure, something I had never had before! I had the pleasure of making friends. Friends I would share the rest of my life with. I was dedicated to my girls, Marie and Michele; they were my reward. I knew my marriage was over; I wasn't fronting that fact. I felt complete for the first time! All I needed was God, my kids, family and friends. We celebrated birthdays, new births, and anniversaries; suffered through bad marriages, divorces, cheating husbands, and funerals. Our lives were full of happiness and sorrow. I had so many wonderful friends; we were like family. Jean was one of my closest friends in the world. The day we met we knew we were kindred spirits, sisters for life. We were closer than any blood sister could ever be. Jean was my confidant and I was hers.

The Affair

The day Jean discovered her husband Charles was having an affair was one of the worst days of her life. I was the expert in our little group of friends since I had weathered some of the worst storms ever to hit a marriage. I was the one that could tell if he or she was unfaithful just by their habits. So when Jean came to tell me that Charles was having an affair, I wasn't surprised. I knew the moment he had started his love affair. She was my best friend; you never tell your friends anything that could change their marriage status from married to unmarried. Not if you want to keep your friends. I didn't want to take a chance on losing Jean's friendship. I knew if Charles kept on sneaking around, sooner or later he would get caught. They always do.

I only wished Charles would come to his senses before she found out. Jean was every man's dream wife. She did everything for him. Jean cooked, cleaned, ironed, and made sure he had his slippers waiting and his bath drawn when he got home. She even ironed his uniforms. Charles was envied by his friends for having the perfect wife. Charles lost his greatest love when his life changed direction. This is my best friend Jean's story! I'll try and tell it as it happened. After all, we both lived it.

It was to be their 5th anniversary celebration. Jean had started getting things ready early in the week. Jean was expecting something magical to happen to her on this big day. Well what she received was far from magic; it was more or less on the verge of a nightmare. Jean had waited up for Charles that night as it was their pre-anniversary dinner. Charles had always made special plans for the two of them; tonight was another special night. Jean hurried around the house fixing dinner and making everything perfect just the way Charles likes it.

Charles hadn't made it home and it was already 6:30pm so Jean was getting a little worried. She tried calling the office around seven, but there was no answer. She was thinking he might have stopped by the Mall first. It was Friday the 13th and the traffic could be a monster. Jean then tried Charles' cell phone, still no answer so Jean left a voice message. She had been worried earlier in the week because Charles had been working late hours. He'd been out of town these last months on business trips almost every other week.

Charles had been so tired lately that he hadn't approached her in months about making love. When Charles had first mentioned to Jean that he would be traveling more often she was upset, she wasn't used to Charles being away from home. It took her a while to get used to the idea of him being gone so much.

Of course Charles reminded Jean that he had a job to do for his country and if he was going to get that promotion they talked about so often he needed to get the exposure these trips offered. Jean tried not to complain whenever Charles had to leave. She continued to support his every effort and Charles assured her he was doing this for the both of them.

Jean was thinking back about how much she worshipped Charles from the moment they met. Jean knew their love would last a lifetime. She felt sorry for her friend Beth, she had never found true love, and she'd married young and foolish. Beth married a man she hardly knew. Earl was definitely not the man for Beth. Charles, on the other hand, had given her everything she ever wanted except kids.

They had tried the first year of their marriage and Jean had a miscarriage. Her doctor told her to wait a few years and try again. Her doctor also mentioned adoption as an option for the two of them, especially if they wanted to start a family right away. Jean was ready for kids, but Charles wasn't going to even consider adoption. He went on about how he wanted to have his own kids and he couldn't raise anyone else's kids, he couldn't love them the way he would love his own. Jean was heart broken. Charles knew how badly she wanted kids, yet he refused to share her dream through the adoption possibility. They could still have a complete life through adoption but he wouldn't even discuss the issue.

Letting Go

    She would bring it up again tonight after dinner. Jean realized while sitting there waiting on Charles that she had let him make all the decisions for both of their lives. Jean had noticed that Charles was becoming more and more involved with his job and less involved with her. Beth had asked if Charles had taken on a part time job since she never got to see them together. Jean had never wondered if Charles was being unfaithful to her, until now. Where could he be? It wasn't like Charles to stay out so late at night and not call. Jean thought that maybe she should call some of his friends to see if they knew where Charles might be. She knew that would probably create gossip about Charles and their marriage and Jean hated gossip. She would just wait a little longer. He should be home soon.

    Jean didn't know what to think; maybe she should call Beth. She would know what to do. No, she didn't want her friend to know Charles may be involved with someone else. This was all so stupid! Charles would be home shortly with a very good explanation as to where he had been. She would be patient and wait. She didn't want to think about the possibility of losing her husband. He was the glue that held her together. She would have to get a grip, and fast. Charles will be walking through that door and everything will be just as it should be. She would have to keep telling herself that. But Jean had a bad feeling that something was wrong. She had wanted to ask Beth if she thought Charles might be cheating, but she was afraid of what Beth might say. Jean loved her friend dearly but they never talked too much about Charles. Charles was not as popular as Beth's husband Earl. Whenever they talked openly on the subject of cheating husbands, Earl was at the top of the list. Charles was always doing special little things that showed how much he cared for her. Jean had no reason to suspect him of anything. He was perfect.

    Beth had gone with Jean shopping earlier in the week at Macy's and found the perfect dress for her big night. It was black with a halter back and a split that was totally indecent with matching shoes and purse. She didn't care; she wanted to look her best tonight. She even purchased matching underwear. She had showered and dressed in less than thirty minutes. She was ready to party!

Jean didn't really care where they went tonight as long as they were together. But, deep down, she really wanted to go to the park where Charles had proposed marriage five years ago. Jean remembered the park so vividly. It was located in the heart of Washington DC. There was a statue there called "The Awakening". She said it always made her sad when ever she would look into his face. It was a huge figure of a man that found it very hard to wake up and get to his feet. Well that's where she really wanted to go! Jean ran one last comb through her hair before returning to the kitchen to check on dinner. Charles will be coming home shortly; he hadn't called to say he would be late. Whenever he was going to be late he would always call her in advance. Jean's excitement was growing; she couldn't wait for Charles to get home. "What is taking him so long to get home?" Jean thought.

Charles was still at the office. He looked up at the clock on the wall. Charles knew Jean was expecting him home on time. He was already over and hour late. Tomorrow was their 5th anniversary and she would be expecting a big night tonight. He wished he could change things and spare her the pain that she was about to experience. He hadn't made any plans for her tonight or any other night; their marriage would more or less end tonight. Charles was sure of that. Things had changed in the last three months. He had met someone and she was waiting for him at this very moment. Charles wasn't sure when things had gotten so serious between him and Amy. He was in love with a woman that made his heart weak from just saying her name. She would be the next "Mrs. Charles Brown!"

This was a different kind of love, something he had never experienced with Jean. He was sorry he didn't love Jean any more. It's hard trying to love two people; one always gets the short end of the stick. Jean would be the loser in the end. Charles had to get home soon and tell Jean about Amy. Amy had asked to speak with him before he left tonight. She told him it wouldn't take too long.

Letting Go

Amy knew tomorrow was Charles' anniversary, but what she needed talk to him about couldn't wait any longer. Amy wanted to tell Charles she was pregnant and he was the father. She was in love with him and she was sure he loved her. They were going to their special place tomorrow after he told Jean tonight about their relationship.

It was important that he knew this information before he spoke to Jean. It could change things for both of them. She was thinking of the first time she and Charles made love, back in December, three months ago. It was the most exciting night of her life. They had been working on a special project all week. The whole office had gone out to celebrate except her and Charles. They were the last two in the office. Charles had already cleared his desk and was ready to go.

He and Amy usually left about the same time every day. He waited on her as he had done so many times in the past so they could walk out together. They both went to push the elevator button at the same time, their hands touched, and neither one wanted to release the other's hand. They pushed the button together. The touch had sent fire through Charles' body as if he had been hit by lightning. His manhood had hardened to a painful size. This woman always drove him crazy.

They entered the elevator. Amy pushed the off button to stop its motion. They were the last two in the office and no one else had a need for the elevator tonight. Once the elevator stopped Amy turned to Charles and said, "Isn't it time you kissed me?" Charles's mouth was over hers before the last word was off her lips. He was breathless. He was already past the point of no return. It was so strange that he hadn't imagined at what point he would make his move. They were in each other arms before the door closed completely. Charles had wanted to do this from the moment they met.

Her mouth tasted of sweet honey. Charles couldn't get enough. Amy began taking his clothes off. Time seemed to stand still; neither of them could find words to match the moment. Amy was full of desire and Charles was eager to give her what she needed. They moved in rhythm together; their bodies were heated with the fire of a thousand candles. Charles had lost control to this beautiful woman, he was hers for life. How would they go back to their lives after experiencing the passion that had captured them?

From the moment they stepped into the elevator their lives changed forever. Where would they go from here? They managed to dress and make plans to continue this at a later date. That was the first of many nights that filled both of their lives with passion.

"Amy, are you ready to go? Are you alright sweetie?"

"Yes I'm fine Charles! I was just thinking back to the first time we made love."

"Oh yeah! The elevator!"

"Charles, do you need to call Jean before we leave?"

"No! I'll try her later."

Charles knew he was wrong but at this point he really didn't care. He was where he wanted to be. Jean deserved so much more than he was able to give her. Amy had captured his heart and where the heart is the man will follow. Amy and I hadn't planned on falling in love, it just happened. We had spent so much time on different projects at work that we became instant friends. I started sharing things with her that I couldn't even share with Jean. Tomorrow is February 14, the day I asked Jean to marry me five years ago. What has happened to us? Here we are five years later and I'm preparing to ask her for a divorce on the same day I had asked her to be my wife! Love has a way of working itself out sometimes; it's never what we expect. I will tell her the truth tonight. Charles headed out the door. The drive to their love nest was thirty minutes from where they lived. Amy would follow in her car.

Charles had tried to fight his feelings for Amy so many times before but it was bigger than the two of them. Amy had gotten under his skin and into his heart. He knew Jean would be waiting on him when he got home. He would have to deal with Jean later; right now he belonged to Amy. Charles arrived a few minutes before Amy, entered the hotel room, and was coming out of the bathroom as Amy walked through the door. "Hi darling. What's going on? Are you feeling ok?"

Letting Go

Amy sat on the bed facing him with her head buried in her hands. She felt like such a fool! Things were great between them, but now she might lose him because of what she had to tell him. The tears starting falling down her face.

Charles was afraid she was about to tell him she was leaving him. He had never seen Amy cry before and it tore his heart out. "Sweetheart, whatever it is we can deal with it together. I love you and there's nothing in this world that will change the way I feel. Please stop crying! I'm here love, I'll always be here." Charles held her close as the tears ran down her face.

Amy knew her life would change the minute she said the word "pregnant". She had to tell him that he may or may not be the father of her child. She already knew how he felt about raising another man's child. She couldn't expect him to gamble on his marriage. "Charles I'm pregnant. I found out last night. I didn't know how to tell you. There's a fifty, fifty chance you're the father. I can't guarantee you're the father, but it's been months since I've been with Ken. He was never home and when he was home his mind was a thousand miles away."

Charles took his hand and lifted Amy's face up to him. "Do you know how long I've waited to hear those words? I'm going to be a father! Amy that's wonderful! Are you alright?"

"Yes, Charles, I'm fine."

Charles couldn't believe what he just heard. He was going to be a father! All his life he had dreamed of a family and now his dream would finally come true. He would have everything he ever wanted in life. "Amy, can I get you something? It's late you should be resting. I want you to go home and get some rest this minute!"

"Charles I'm not going anywhere until you make love to me."

"It will be a pleasure!"

Charles took Amy to a new plateau filled with the passion of life. They laid in each other arms discussing their future without their spouses, and the future of their unborn child.

Amy told Charles she was sure Ken wouldn't be surprised about the divorce. They barely saw each other anymore. "I will have to tell him about you as soon as he gets back into town. He's been away ninety five percent of the time. I haven't missed him at all Charles. Ken hasn't touched me since we've been sleeping together. He acts as if he wants me to leave! What are we going to do now Charles? Charles, you're already married and so am I."

"We will have to a get a divorce and then get married. Amy do you love me?"

"Of course I love you Charles!"

"Then why can't you see the big picture? We will be together and raise our kids as a family."

"Charles what about Jean? This will destroy her. You have always told me that she worshipped you. How can you walk away from a woman like that?"

"I love you Amy! I've loved you from the moment we met. I have studied your face, your walk, your smile. I know when you're sad by the way you hold your head. I know when you're having a bad day by the tone of your voice. I have never been able to tell those things about Jean. I'm not saying I never loved her, I'm saying I've never loved anyone like I love you. I never wanted Jean to act as if she was my mother. I have a mother! I need a wife!"

"Charles, Ken will be back on Saturday. I'm not prepared to tell him about the baby just yet, but I will tell him I'm leaving."

"I'll call you in the morning. We both need to get home. I still have to face Jean and it's already three thirty. There's just no way that I will be able to discuss this tonight with her. It will have to wait until tomorrow. I know it's going to be hard trying to sleep in that house tonight without an explanation as to where I've been."

"I bet it will be!" Amy laughed and said, "Good luck!"

"I'm going to need it!" Charles said.

They both laughed, kissed goodnight and promised to talk later that afternoon.

Love Shows No Mercy

Jean had fallen asleep when she heard Charles' key in the door. She was startled. She hadn't realized the time. "Charles, is everything all right? What happened to you? I was worried sick! Did your car break down?"

Jean was still trying to focus when Charles walked past her, heading upstairs to the bedroom.

"No! The car did not break down and I'm fine!"

"Charles, where have you been? It's four in the morning!"

"I was out with a friend!"

"I thought you might have been in an accident. Why didn't you call Charles?"

"I lost track of time Jean!"

"Is that all you're going to say, "you lost track of time"? I would like an explanation Charles!"

"Not tonight Jean!"

"Yes Charles, tonight!"

"Jean we will discuss this in the morning. I'm going to bed, it's late!"

"You think you are going to walk in here over twelve hours late and go to bed without an explanation and expect to sleep in this house tonight? I don't think so!"

It was as if someone else had taken over Jean's body and she had no control over her actions. Jean followed Charles up the stairs to the bedroom. "I called the office around seven and I didn't get an answer. So what time did you and this friend go out, and who was this friend Charles? Anyone that I know?"

"No Jean, you do not know her, she is a white co-worker!"

"Was it a life threatening situation, Charles, that couldn't wait?!"

"OK Jean! I wanted this to wait until tomorrow, but I guess we can discuss it now!"

Jean listened carefully, not knowing what was happening to her life. She was having trouble breathing. Her air was coming out short in her chest, she had to control herself or she might pass out. She wanted this man standing in front of her dead! Who was this guy? This was not her husband telling her he was leaving her for another woman, and a white one at that! What's with the brothers and these white women? Jean pulled herself together. She had to ask the right questions and get to the bottom of this. She had to find out where she went wrong. Of course it was her fault. "Ok Charles, please repeat it once more for me. I'm listening."

"Her name is Amy. We've been seeing each other for several months now. One day we just started talking."

"Charles, the only Amy I know that works in your office is married. Is this the same Amy?"

"Yes! What does her being married have to do with anything? Amy and I have a lot in common. We share some of the same marriage problems."

"Charles! Why is this the first time I'm hearing that we're having marriage problems? Did you ever think the problem might be you Charles? Your lack of interest in your wife may be the problem!"

"I told her you couldn't have kids and that I refused to adopt. The more we talked the more I started looking forward to seeing her."

"Does she have kids Charles?"

"Yes, she does. I'm sorry Jean."

"Well, Charles, that's an understatement."

"Jean, I never meant to hurt you. But I should tell you that Amy is pregnant. That's why I was out so late tonight. We were discussing what to do next. Amy was thinking about an abortion because she didn't know if I would be able to be with her. I want to be a part of my child's life."

"What are you saying Charles, that you want to leave me and marry this woman? Hello Charles, you already have a wife."

"Yes! Jean, what I'm saying is that this is my baby, I want to be with its mother and she wants to be with me. She is going to leave her husband."

Letting Go

"Does her husband know she's pregnant?"

"No he doesn't. She hasn't told him yet. He's currently out of town on business."

"How many months is she pregnant Charles?"

"She's three months Jean."

"So this has been going on for a while. Charles if you were determined to cheat why didn't you use protection, or is this what you wanted to happen?"

"Deep down inside I was hoping that something like this might happen. It's been no secret that I've always wanted kids Jean. When you couldn't have any I had almost given up hope of ever being a father."

"I've had a void in my life also."

"Yes, I know, but Jean you're not the only one that has suffered from not having kids."

"But, Charles, we had a chance to adopt kids. That would have filled the void in both our lives."

"It's not the same Jean. I want my own flesh and blood running through my kid's veins. I'm sorry Jean, I should have told you this a long time ago. I didn't want you to feel any more incomplete than you already felt. This is my chance to experience having children of my own. If this baby turns out to be mine I will be in its life. I know the price I have to pay and I'm willing to pay the price."

"Well Charles, I guess you have pretty much made up your mind."

"It's really up to Amy now."

"Do you love her Charles?"

"Yes Jean. I've loved her from the moment we met. She's perfect. Her face, her smile, her walk, the way she talks, her entire being is perfect."

"Does her husband know that you're black?" No Jean he doesn't.

"Well, maybe I need to pay him a visit when he returns home."

"I think he has a right to know you're black Charles. Don't you?"

"Amy will be telling him everything he needs to know!"

"Maybe I should tell him his wife is pregnant by my "black husband".

"Jean, I want you to stay out of this! This has nothing to do with you!"

"What do you mean this has nothing to do with me? Are you that stupid, Charles? Maybe you are if you think that! This is my life you're screwing with! I refuse to let you make a laughing stock out of me! How will I face my friends and family, Charles?"

"I don't care about your friends and family! You're not the only woman whose husband has ever left her! This is between Amy and me so stay the hell out of it! Am I making myself clear Jean?"

"Very clear Charles. So, if the baby isn't yours will you be able to raise another man's child? I know how you feel about raising other people's children."

"I love Amy more than I have ever loved anyone in my whole life."

"Thanks a lot, Charles! That really makes me feel good."

"I'm just being honest."

"Where was the honesty when you were sleeping around with Ms. Barbie? OK Charles, what's your next move?"

"I want a divorce Jean! Amy and I will be married, as soon as possible. I will move out in the morning."

"Charles, it is morning now."

"I know my timing couldn't have been worse, *but love shows no mercy!*"

"You're just full of wisdom tonight, aren't you Charles!"

"I guess those are words I'll need to remember."

"Come on Charles, I'll help you start packing. There's no need for you to spend another night in this house. Your life has changed direction! I really don't care where you go, but you have to leave here. Whatever you can't take now; call me later and let me know where you're staying and I will send the rest of your things."

Jean was amazed at her calmness. She had no idea where the strength came from. I guess the old saying is true that the wife is always the last to know. Jean needed her friend Beth to

Letting Go

be with her. There was just no way for her to get through this alone.

She would give her a call later in the day, it was much too early. All she needed to do right now was to survive the night. Jean was having and out of body experience. She couldn't believe Charles had just walked out on her. This kind of stuff only happened in the movies. This was no movie, this was her life. Jean managed to get through the early morning. Her prayers had lasted almost the entire night. She felt it was her fault Charles had left her. Maybe she should have been more like Beth. Men seem to love women they can't trust a lot more. Jean kept hearing Charles' voice in the house. Jean had to come to terms with the fact that her marriage was over. Charles had taken her love for granted. He had discarded her like a pair of used shoes that didn't fit any more. Her heart was hurting. Jean would have never believed that Charles could hurt her the way he just did. How would she make it through life without him? He was her sunshine on rainy days, he was the stars in her sky. He was her everything.

Charles had taken a car load of his things and left. Charles couldn't believe Jean had asked him to leave tonight. He was sure she would understand how things like this happen. He didn't start out to hurt her. He had just fallen in love. How wrong could that be? He would give Jean time to adjust to everything. He would look for a house tomorrow for Amy and himself.

Jean, had made the decision to let Charles go, not like she had a choice in the matter. He was determined to be with his baby's mama. How stupid does that sound? Jean didn't sleep at all. She was trying to figure out when Charles had started cheating and why didn't she know. Why couldn't she tell?

She called Beth. She went straight to the point. "Charles left me last night."

"What? You have got to be kidding me! What in the world happened Jean?"

"He fell in love with someone named Amy who worked with him at his office. I asked him to call me once he's settled in and I will forward all his mail and calls to his new address. I didn't let him see me break down, Beth. I wouldn't give him the satisfaction of knowing he took my life away from me. Beth, I'm alone. My husband just walked out like we were friends instead of husband and wife. How could he be so cold Beth? I will never forgive him for this."

Beth knew Jean had been crying. She was trying to be strong for Jean. She wanted to cry herself. Charles had been her everything. Now he was gone.

"He took a part of me with him Beth."

"I know, Jean."

"I now understand what it feels like to not be truly needed and wanted by your husband. I know you told me so many times how Earl cheated and ran around on you. I somehow felt that you didn't cater to him enough that's why he was cheating on you. I'm sorry, Beth."

"I see it doesn't really matter what you do, a man is going to be a man first and a husband second. I should have been more compassionate when it came to you and your feelings about Earl. Can you please forgive me?"

"Sure girl. I never gave it a second thought. I forgive you for thinking I should be more like you Jean," Beth said. "I'm sorry this has happened to you. If you need me to come over I will get Carol to watch the girls and be right over."

"Thanks Beth, I'll be OK. I have to get used to the fact that my husband doesn't love me, that he has never loved me the way I deserved to be loved. It's going to take some time to get over finding that out."

Jean Lets Charles Go

Charles called the next day all pumped up and asked me if I was ok. "Yes, Charles, I'm wonderful under the current circumstances," Jean replied. "It's just that I need to re-examine my life to see where I failed you as a wife."

He reassured me that I was the perfect wife and that he was to blame for everything.

"Yes, you're right you are to blame. Maybe I should have been more creative in bed." Jean said.

"You were great in bed Jean. It just wasn't meant to be; you deserved someone to love you for you and who you are. You're a good woman Jean, don't ever forget that! I'll come by later and pick up more of my things. I'll try and be there around three. I found an apartment not too far from work."

"That's fine Charles I'm happy for you and Amy. You know Charles, today would have been our 5th anniversary!"

"I know Jean! I'm sorry it had to happen when it did. But, I would be lying if I said I'm sorry it happened because I'm not!"

By the time Charles came back Jean had gotten all of his things together. Charles asked for a bedroom set from one of the guest rooms. Jean had avoided him as much as possible because the last twelve hours were wearing on her and Jean refused to let him see her pain. She had been up half the morning crying!

Beth has such strong faith in God; will He pull me through also? Jean wondered. Was her faith strong enough? All she needed to do was to pray and trust in God. She knew that. Jean had never questioned her faith in God before. Was she so weak now that she would doubt the one that had never forsaken her? She was more tired than she realized. Beth had told her on so many occasions how she prayed and asked God to help her through the pain that Earl had always seemed to put her through. Jean knew she would survive also!

Jean went on to work on Monday; she refused to take any time off. She would never wallow in self pity. Jean figured she wasn't the first women that ever had a man leave her and wouldn't be the last. It seems that lately a lot of our friends are going through turmoil in their relationships. Our black males are converting to white females. We would have to roll with the punches. All this time Jean thought Charles completed her. She never realized that she didn't complete him.

Jean went through the week on prayer alone; nothing else seemed to be working for her. By Friday she had decided to talk to her parents and explain to them how she would spend the rest of her life without Charles.

Her mom cried enough for the both of them. Jean assured her that she was fine. Her dad just said, "He'll be back. You'll see." Jean told her dad that she had moved on mentally which was more important than moving on physically at this time.

In her heart she knew Charles and her would never be man and wife again, she had already accepted that.

Charles had picked up the last of his things from Jean's place and moved them into his new apartment. He had already called Amy and asked her to stop by to check out their new home. Charles noticed she hadn't seemed very excited on the phone. Charles wanted to make sure she and the baby were ok.

She assured him that they both were just fine. "I'm just a little tired," she said. "Ken and I were up all night talking." Amy agreed to meet Charles at the new place in an hour.

Charles rushed around the place in excitement trying to make it look as inviting as possible. Amy had to make a few stops before meeting Charles. She wanted to stop by her parents and drop off the girls and some birthday presents for her mother. That would give Charles a little more time to complete the house. Charles couldn't remember the last time he had ever been this excited about anything in his whole life. He had resolved to accept this baby even if it wasn't his, that's how much he loved Amy!

What had he done to Jean? He felt really bad that he had hurt her. That wasn't the plan when it all started. He and Amy were only friends talking about family and friends and how they

Letting Go

both felt incomplete with their relationships. Amy often complained that Ken left her alone with the kids. They were talking about having another child but things changed so fast. She said Ken came home one day saying, "Let's wait on another child. I'm working on a new job that will keep me traveling most of the time, at least the next few years." He needed a year or two so they had postponed having another right away. Charles remembered the elevator moment. He had felt the attraction so intensely! They both knew it was just a matter of time before something happened between them. Charles was the only man other than Ken that Amy had been with. He had often dreamed of their living together and celebrating wedding anniversaries and birthdays together. Charles was definitely in love. If this was a dream he never wanted to wake up!

He couldn't wait to take her to bed in their new place. There would be no disappointment. He had tasted the lips of her body and he knew where to touch her to make her moan. He would send small kisses down her spine and watch her wiggle like a worm. He had memorized each and every inch of her. He had done things to Amy that were unmentionable. She had always left him wanting more. He couldn't get enough of her. They knew at that moment they both had crossed boundaries that weren't to be crossed. They would both be forever lost in each other's soul. Their lives had changed forever. Amy was so open and inviting when they made love that each time was like the first time. He got excited just thinking of her. She would be here soon. They were in love and the world could accept them or not, Charles really didn't care. They were going to be together. Charles felt he was the luckiest man on earth. He had a second chance to be a father and a loving husband and he wanted things to start as soon as possible.

Amy was not looking forward to seeing Charles. She was confused about her life. She was so preoccupied she almost missed her turn. She'd been driving this way for years. What was happening to her? Why was she so worked up? She would be giving Charles a chance to get back with his wife. That would be a good thing. Amy had seen Jean several times at the Post Exchange and on the base. She looked like a reasonable person.

She would forgive him! She didn't start out to ruin Jean's marriage, it just happened. Amy felt sorry for Jean. She was wonderful and after all the things Charles said she did for him, I don't understand why he needed to reach outside of his marriage for anything. Nevertheless; he reached out to me and in return I took hold and was prepared to weather the storm until last night!

Amy told Ken the details of her relationship with Charles; that he was a black co-worker and they had been sleeping together for several months. She wasn't planning on telling him about the baby until later, but Ken wanted to know every thing. He felt she was holding something back. She told him about the baby and about moving in with her lover Charles! She explained what happened and how it started and what lead her to Charles in the first place. Ken was hurt and disappointed, he hadn't seen this coming. They had been married since high school and had always been there for each other. It was only lately that he was distracted and had let her down. They were voted most likely to succeed in high school. People envied them, even some of their family were jealous of their marriage. He was a well known contractor and she was a consultant for the military. Amy was torn apart about her feelings for Charles. He was so different, not just his being black. He was interesting and so much fun. He wanted to become a General in the military. He had so many dreams. He was a beautiful person and a perfect specimen of a man.

She tried to explain Charles to Ken the best she could without hurting him any more than she had already. "The night we made love I thought my body had taken wings and flown. I had never felt the passion this man sent through my body. My fingertips left my fingers; I was transformed from that moment on. I'm sorry Ken. This is how he made me feel. Charles gave me attention, something you had forgotten that I needed. He was real; he made me the center of his universe. Now that I think back I can imagine how his wife must have felt. He was giving me his all, there couldn't have been anything left over for her. But that wasn't my concern. That was Charles's problem! All I knew was I had to have him!"

Letting Go

After she had told him everything about Charles he was still willing to hold on to her and her baby! He wanted to keep his family together.

Charles was wondering what was taking so long. Amy should have been there already. Charles was beginning to think something might have happened to her. He was wondering had things changed. Amy sounded distant on the phone, maybe Ken was home and she couldn't talk. That would be over soon! He had so many plans for them. They would become man and wife as soon as they both were divorced.

He hadn't told his parents yet, he wasn't sure how they would handle Amy being white. It won't matter to his father; it was his mother he had to worry about. She was going to have a fit. They thought of Jean as their daughter. Charles remembered telling her that Jean had had a miscarriage and couldn't chance getting pregnant right away. His mother was so wonderful and understanding, she had come over to assure Jean that things would be just fine. As long as they loved each other they could get through anything. Charles made a mental note to call his parents after Amy got settled in.

Amy reached the house about thirty minuets late. She knew she was running late. Charles would be frantic. That's the kind of man he was. Amy knew Charles would be worried. He worried all the time about her and the baby. Charles was at the door when Amy drove up. He ran to the car and wrapped his loving arms around her as if she was a child that needed help with her very first step. Amy was taken aback for a moment and then she realized that this was why she loved this man so much, that she would always love him.

Charles could see Amy wasn't looking as happy and cheerful as she usually looked. He needed to get her inside to rest. He had to make sure she took care of herself. She was his whole life now, she and the baby. Charles insisted she lay down first and get some rest, that they could talk later. After all, they had their whole life ahead of them to talk.

Amy apologized to Charles for being late; she had taken longer than she had planned. She needed the extra time to think.

35

She had to think of a way to tell him that they would not have the life they had talked about.

Amy made a promise to Ken and she was there to keep that promise. She couldn't betray her husband a second time. Charles wanted her to rest! Amy refused. She didn't have time to rest. "Charles, Ken is waiting on me, I have to get back." Charles was confused. "Please sit down Charles! I'll try and explain everything!"

Amy sat across the table from Charles; she could see the confusion on his face! Earlier when she had driven up she had noticed a gleam of happiness in his eyes. She was about to take that gleam away and replace it with gloom and throw him into a world of sorrow and sadness. They both had been so happy when they had found true love. They knew that whatever lay ahead of them they would face the challenge and win. Now she was backing out on her part of the deal. The tears had already formed in her eyes. She was crying and Charles was at her side.

"Whatever it is we will handle it together," he said without thought. "Is there something wrong with the baby?" Charles asked. "Did you decide not to have it, that you don't want it?" His heart began to beat faster! "What's going on Amy? Are you leaving me?"

She nodded her head yes! Tears had begun to fall, she was losing control. Why was this so hard? She knew this was what had to be done. Yet the pain was still there. She truly loved this man. Charles looked as if someone just gave him a week to live! How was he going to handle this, he wasn't capable of dealing with this degree of pain! Amy knew he would be lost after today. She had to make him understand why. He meant so much to her! How could she destroy his world like this? What would happen to him?

Amy faced Charles and told him that her husband refused to let her go and the child she was carrying had a fifty percent chance of being his. Her husband was willing to accept it even if it was not his. "I know that's a big gamble, but I have to think of my position and my parents." Amy was trying to get Charles to listen to her. Her family would never understand her reasons for leaving Ken. "Charles, you're a wonderful man but you're not

Letting Go

the man that I was promised to. Ken has promised to do better and not leave me alone so much."

"We also discussed going to counseling." It was very hard for him to accept that she had slept around and stepped over the racial line. Amy was repeating what Ken had told her. "Charles, Ken says he still loves me! He promised to love me forever! My husband is a wonderful man and he took me for granted and I took his neglect and used it to have an affair. I can never say I'm sorry enough to make up for what I've done to him. I hope in time he will forgive me. Last night I told Ken that I had to meet with you and explain that what we had wasn't real, it was sex and only sex and I had got caught up in the moment. My actions caused you to leave your wife for the dream of us sharing the rest of our lives together. I could never let him know that I loved you from the moment I laid eyes on you. I couldn't tell him that you took me to heights that were unnatural and made me feel a completeness I have never felt with him. I can only hope you understand Charles. I wish things were different. Maybe it's not too late to ask Jean for forgiveness and tell her you made a mistake."

"But Amy, I didn't make a mistake; you're the one making the mistake. You just told me that you're not in love with your husband, that you love me."

"Yes, Charles, I do love you but I'm Catholic. We have to do everything to make our marriage work! I have to at least try Charles! Please try and understand. What would I tell my parents? They're from the old school, they don't believe in divorce."

"Tell them the truth, that you and Ken aren't in love anymore and that people get divorced every day. If they love you Amy, they will want what's best for you."

"Charles, it's not that easy. I've told Ken that I'll at least try. I have to Charles, I owe him that much."

Amy was crying again, her heart was in such pain. She was trembling and Charles tried to comfort her but his heart was hurting also. How could she do this to them? They belonged together.

'I know we made promises to each other but I'm in no position to keep mine. I will always love you Charles. What happened to us was a dream. There's no way this could have lasted, it was too perfect from the beginning."

"I will be leaving the area; Ken is going to ask for a transfer to Japan. If it comes through we will be leaving the first of March. Please believe every word I ever said to you was real, it came from the heart. Charles, we rushed into things not realizing the consequences of our actions. It wasn't just you and I, there were other people involved. We should have been more careful, we had promised ourselves no one would get hurt. We broke that promise, also. I will not be able to see you again Charles, it wouldn't be fair to Ken. I won't let him down again. What I've done most men would never be able to live with, yet my husband still wants me. Ken made a promise to God for better or worse. This will be his way of keeping his promise. I have to leave Charles!"

She hated seeing the pain that he was in and knowing she was the one responsible for it. "Ken's probably wondering what's taking so long."

"Amy, please don't leave me. I can't let you go; I've waited my whole life for you. Please don't ask me to give up the best thing that ever happened to me."

"I'm sorry, so sorry, Charles, please forgive me. Neither one of us realized the price we would have to pay if we continued to see each other. I have more at stake than you. Charles, I already have two kids that mean more to me than anything or anyone in this whole world. Ken will divorce me and take my kids if I continue this relationship with you. He said he would be left with no choice. I couldn't bear that."

"I'm sorry Amy; I wasn't aware of your motive for staying."

"I didn't want to tell you that Ken was using the kids as a hold over me. I had to tell him that it was sex and that I wasn't in love with you or he would have made my life a living hell. He knows the kids are my life. He even threatened to take this one once it's born."

"We can fight him Amy!"

Letting Go

"No Charles, you're a black man and my kids are white, no judge in his right mind will give us custody, plus my husband's family has money and they don't mind spending it. I really need to leave Charles. I will always love you. No matter where I'm at or who I'm with I will love only you."

Amy was tired; her long blond hair draped her face as she looked down at the floor. She couldn't face Charles; knowing that if she looked into his eyes she would change her mind. She wanted to take him in her arms and make the pain go away; Charles had given up everything to be with her. The tears were blurring her vision; she wiped her eyes and kissed him good-bye.

Charles turned his head so that Amy couldn't see the tears in his eyes. This was the woman he had been waiting for all his life. Now she was leaving with what could be his only child. He wanted to hate her but how could he when she was trying to keep her kids. He watched as she drove away. Charles was a man and men don't cry he kept telling himself. He couldn't believe this had happened, he was in shock. She had left him just as fast as she had come into his life. Where would he go from here? Charles was beside himself. He couldn't think, he needed to figure out what would be his next move. This wasn't happening to him, not Charles J. Brown. He was a man! Women didn't leave him, he left them. Charles couldn't believe the passion and intimacy they had shared, it went so deep, and way beyond words. It would leave the both of them breathless every time they made love. Now she had told him she was taking all that away along with his child. This can't be happening. Charles wondered how he would continue to breathe without her.

Amy drove home with tears streaming down her face. How did she let this happen to her? She could barely see the road. She needed to get control of herself before Ken saw her. She would have to answer all his questions, with little or no emotion. She would tell Ken that Charles was very special to her.

She phoned her mother on the way back home and asked if she would keep the girls overnight. She told her mom about the baby, she was overjoyed. Amy promised to call her later.

Ken was wondering what was taking so long. Amy should have been back long ago. He was getting worried. Ken never really understood what had happened to his marriage. One day they were talking about another child and the next she was telling him she was leaving him for another man. Some black guy that worked in her office. Ken was still trying to piece it all together. He wasn't sure asking her to stay was in their best interest. He didn't know if he could make things work but he would give it a try. All he knew was that he couldn't let a black man raise his kids.

Ken's Secret Life

Ken was hurt that Amy didn't come to him when she was in need. He was her husband and that's what husbands do, take care of their wives. Ken knew he had been leaving her alone quite a bit lately. He had no time for foolishness; he was dealing with his own demons! When Amy had asked to speak to him at the airport he had a sinking feeling she had discovered his secret life. She had mentioned that they needed to talk in private. She had dropped the girls off at her mother's house on the way to the airport. Ken had no idea of what could be that important. His mind was racing trying to think of what Amy wanted to talk to him about. Whatever it was it needed his full attention. He was getting worried. Had she found out about Brian?

How did she find out? Wasn't he careful enough? Didn't he always tell her that she was number one in his life? He tried to tell her he loved her at least once a day or whenever he would call home. Maybe someone had seen him and called her with information about where he'd been these last few weeks. How could she know? Ken was beginning to sweat! What will I say to her? Will she be able to handle what I've done? How will I tell her that Brian, my best friend, had been my lover for the last two years? She will never be able to handle that kind of news. How will I tell her I'm in love with another man?

He was ready to leave her but he wanted it to be on his terms, not hers. He had planned on telling her for months now. That he had been living a lie all his life; and that he and Brian were moving to Japan. They had accepted two open positions that would be available in March. He hadn't mentioned it to anyone. Ken was really worried; he didn't want his parents to know any of his personal life. That would be one of the worst things a man could do to the people he loved the most. His parents would surely die from shame if they found out. He would have to make Amy understand that this had nothing to do with her. He knew from the moment he was born he was not like the other boys. His parents pushed him into sports and girls; so he hid behind a mask. He never would have been accepted by anyone if they knew the truth. Now if his wife knows, sooner or later everyone will know, including his parents.

Ken wasn't sure how this would play out. He knew that if Amy knew about Brian their marriage would surely be over. Ken wasn't sure he wanted to save his marriage but he knew he had to do something and do it fast. She would be here soon to pick him up. What do I say and how do I say it? Ken had to cover his state of panic... If she knows about Brian, our secret is not a secret anymore and our plans will have to change. I will have to consider taking Amy to Japan. We will leave the area and start over if Amy will still have me. I'll have to call my CEO on Monday and get my orders changed. I will see if there are any other positions out there that I may qualify for if she is not willing to go with me to Japan. She would have to consider leaving her job which she truly loved. Taking the girls out of school would be a task. Brittany and Sandra really loved their school. Everything could be managed with very little effort except for one thing. Telling his and her parents that they would be moving across the world and taking their grandkids with them. Neither set of parents would like that too much. Ken would first check with his boss about the position and go from there. He had made such a mess of things. How did he let himself get so far off track and how did she find out?

Ken thought back to his secret life with Brian. He really cared a lot for him but they would never be more than closet lovers if they stayed here. It would be hard giving him up if that's what he had to do. He hoped it wouldn't come to that!

Ken had met Brian at their company picnic over two years ago. He was the star of the company basketball team. Brian was the most beautiful black man Ken had ever laid eyes on. He had dimples that took up half of his cheeks when he smiled. Ken also noticed that all the ladies from the company were fussing over him, trying to get and hold his attention but Brian seemed oblivious to their presence. Ken and Brian played on the basketball team and had gotten into minor conversation. Brian

Letting Go

was from New York. He had just been transferred in to take one of the top accountant positions. They became friends immediately. Ken liked Brian because he was easy to talk to. They were working in the same office and were assigned the same contract which required Ken and Brian to work closely together. They often talked about family and friends and great loves. Brian never talked about his great loves, while Ken spilled his guts often. Several weeks passed and Brian asked Ken for a ride to work. He had to put his car into the shop for a tune-up.

Ken had agreed to pick Brian up at 5:00 a.m. so they would have enough time to go by the gym before heading off to work. They often met there and worked out for an hour or so before going to work. Ken enjoyed his time with Brian. Ken arrived at Brian's around 4:45 a.m. Brian was running late! He had already told Ken the door would be open. Ken had never been in Brian's neighborhood; it was nicely covered with palm trees and had the northern architecture common to the area. Brian's street was surrounded by trees. Brian's home sat off the main street on a secluded lane. The home was beautiful. Ken walked up the winding driveway to the main double doors.

The door was open just as Brian had said it would be. Ken walked into a large living room, neatly decorated and well organized. Ken didn't have many friends that were this neat. Brian's place had a touch of class. He was impressed! He would have to find out who decorated his home. Amy could use some help! Ken continued to wander through the house. He didn't hear the shower running nor did he realized that he was walking into Brian's bedroom.

Brian was trying to hurry. He knew Ken would be there soon. He jumped out the shower and realized he had been in such a hurry he had forgotten to bring his towel into the bathroom with him. It had been left out on the bench in his bedroom. Brian walked into the bedroom with ringlets of water dripping of his body when he noticed Ken was standing in his bedroom door.

Ken didn't move. He had been watching Brian through the glass doors as he showered. Ken knew it was Brian because he had studied his body from his head to his feet. Every inch of him would be forever etched in his memories! Ken's excitement was bursting out of his pants! He could barely contain himself! Ken's eyes moved from Brian's ebony chest to his manhood. My goodness this man is breath taking, Ken thought. Ken eyes returned and locked on Brian's.

They weren't even aware that they both were in motion until they stood toe-to-toe, in front of Brian's bed. Ken wasn't sure whether or not he was breathing. All he knew was that whatever happened from this moment on he would relive this part of his life over and over again.

Brian was speechless! He had no idea Ken felt this way. How did they get to this point? Was Ken inviting him into his world? His next move was very important. He didn't want to scare Ken off, he was so important to him. From the first day they met Brian had deep feelings for him but he would never have acted on his feelings without encouragement from Ken.

Every second was longer than the last.

Ken didn't know what he should do now. He wanted Brian to take the lead, but he worried that this could be Brian's first time also. They would have to take their time and teach each other.

Brian reached over and took both of Ken's hands and brushed them with his lips one at a time.

Ken released a soft moan when Brian's lips touched his hands. He felt the softness of Brian's body next to his. Ken had never experienced such a rush in his life. Brian felt like silk. Ken took his hands and placed them in Brian's. He would let Brian lead him. Ken closed his eyes with delight. This had to be right! Nothing wrong could ever feel this good; this was who he was and this was how he was meant to live his life! He would stop running and face fate head on! He was gay! He took Brian into his arms and they kissed with such longing it was as if a floodgate had opened and they would both drown in the sea of their passion!

Brian guided Ken to the inviting bed.

Ken wasn't sure if he walked or floated, he only knew he felt the waves of the river under his back. It was a waterbed! How amazing was this going to be?! This would be another

Letting Go

adventure for Ken because he had never been on a waterbed before. Brian now straddled Ken's chest, Ken's clothes had been removed. Ken's chest was covered with deep brown hair. As Brian ran his fingers through his chest hair Ken felt tiny sensations run up and down his spine. He was on the verge of totally losing control. Brian was caressing his nipples, which stood erect just high enough to place his entire mouth over them. He had been transformed into someone else. He had to come back to reality; he was a married man and this was not his life. This should have been his life, but he had made the wrong choice and he would forever live a lie. Ken was totally lost; he had missed out on so much. He would never be able to touch his wife again! Ken lost himself to desire, he erupted into total submission. This had never happened to him before!

Brian acknowledged Ken's defeat and gave up into the height of full eruption himself!

Ken and Brian made love throughout the morning and well into the evening, stopping just long enough to catch their breath and get a bite to eat. They had both called in to work, reporting car trouble and an accident. They had enjoyed a full day of making love. Brian was Ken's teacher, he taught him everything he needed to know to give and receive pleasure. They were totally exhausted as they lay in each other's arms and slept way into the night.

Ken knew he would leave there a changed man. He had said things to Brian that he hadn't understood himself. All he knew was that Brian belonged to him and he belonged to Brian!

On the way to pick up Brian's car the next day they discussed where they would go from here. They had feelings for each other. They would have to keep their relationship on the down low for right now.

Brian wanted to tell Ken his secrets; that his last lover had died of AIDS. He wanted Ken to know everything. That his last lover had the virus before they got together; and that he had been tested and had moved before his test result came back. He would have to track them down now. He wanted Ken to know everything about him. There were to be no secrets between them, but this just wasn't the time; they would have plenty of time to discuss that later. Brian had told Ken he didn't have to worry about them not using protection. They had made love in such a rush that there was no time for it. Ken hadn't worried, he had been very careful with his past lovers. Plus things had happened so fast. One minute he was touring the house and the next he was living his dream!

Whenever Ken thought of the first time he and Brian were together he relived that moment over and over. He knew fate brought them into each other's lives. From then on he wanted nothing else from life, not Amy, not anything. He only wanted Brian, nothing else mattered. He didn't want to live without him.

They had just come from spending another long week together in New York where they had a place. Brian had lived there before he came here to Washington DC.

Ken was worried for no reason! All this time he was thinking Amy had found out about him and Brian and here she was having an affair with a black man herself! "How ironic is it that we both chose to sleep with a black man?" he thought. Ken started laughing when he realized the irony of the whole thing. He had even rehearsed his speech to her from the airport. Now he will never need it and she will never know that he is sleeping with their best friend Brian! Ken had made his mind up to tell Amy he was leaving after Valentines' Day. He and Brian were, tired of sneaking around! Going away on trips was the only real time he and Brian had spent together. How could she leave him for a black man when he had already left her for one? What on earth would give her the idea that I would let her and her lover raise my kids? Ken had to wait and see what happened with Charles before he told Brian about the mess he was in. They would have a big laugh! They would have to postpone their trip for now! He would have to wait until Amy has the baby before he could leave her. He only wanted to make sure that Charles and Amy would never be together. Ken knew his place was with Brian and he was not going to give that up for anyone! Ken had made plans to see Brian after he got settled. He would have to hurry and call him. They both had been so happy that they were leaving for Japan next month. Brian was getting things ready and would be expecting him tonight. Ken would have to let him

Letting Go

know he would be late. He was waiting on Amy to return from her lover's place.

Amy knew Ken would be waiting! Charles would probably run back to Jean. Amy didn't like the thought of him being alone. She hoped Jean would take him back.

Ken had gotten impatient waiting. He had plenty of time to think of his plan of action. He was so sure she had found out about Brian. Since she hadn't, there was no need to bring him into this situation. He would work things out. He would take Amy to Japan with him and Brian. This would put some space between Amy and her lover and Brian and I can still be together. He was not going to live without Brian in his life! He was such a large part of his life. They weren't just lovers, they were best friends. Brian was always at Ken's home and doing things with the family. He would never, ever, live without Brian's love. They had shared so much. The only time he felt complete was when he was with Brian. They had found what everyone searched their whole lives for and never came close to achieving. They had found true love. Ken refocused his attention on the situation currently facing him. He would have to deal with Amy and her lover and that would not be easy.

Amy's car pulled into the drive way. She had dried her eyes from the crying. She had to lie to Ken about her feelings for Charles. Amy sat in the car for a few minutes; she needed to compose herself before going in to see Ken. He would expect her to walk away without scars, without ever looking back. She would never be able to mourn her loss. Charles had saved her, now she had to walk away from him. As Amy entered the house she found Ken waiting by the door.

"Well how did he take it?"

"He'll back off and leave me alone Ken. He only wants what's best for me and the baby."

"Amy, were you in love with this guy? I want the truth."

"I cared deeply for him, Ken. Charles and I spent a lot of time together. You were gone so much I was lonely and he was there as a friend and a companion. Ken, we didn't plan on hurting anyone, we just got carried away. I will start packing as soon as we get the orders."

"What about the baby, Amy?"

"What do you mean 'what about the baby?' I'm having this baby and if he's Charles' he will never know. We'll be half-way around the world in Japan. He will forget me in time. Today we said our final good-by. He will not try and stop me!"

"What happened with his wife?"

"I don't know Ken. I guess he'll try and get her back."

"Do you think she will take him back? He hurt her pretty bad!"

"If she does she will never be able to trust him again."

"I guess you got something there! Can I trust you Amy?"

"Yes, Ken, you can trust me! Charles was the only guy I have ever been with other than you. I have no desire or wish anymore to look to another man for what I need. I hope you can remember that Ken. I do want to apologize for all the heartache I've caused you. I know you would never hurt me the way I hurt you. I will spend the rest of my life making this up to you. I have a doctor's appointment scheduled for Tuesday. Would you please go with me? I have to get the official pregnancy test done by our doctor."

"Sure, Amy, I'll go." Ken wondered how she could have been stupid enough to not use a condom when she slept with Charles!

He was getting tired of pretending he cared so much about her falling for Charles; it didn't matter one way or the other if she loved him or not because he was in love with Brian. He needed to call Brian! Brian was expecting him tonight. But there was still a fifty percent chance the baby was his. The one night he had gotten drunk and made love to her was the only reason he might be the baby's father. Ken wasn't turned on by Amy. She was a part of his past life. His new life consisted of Brian and him. He had no desire to ever make love to her again. He would be gay for the rest of his life! He had told Amy he would accept this baby regardless of the outcome, but if it turned out he was not the father it would be hard to keep his word. Ken noticed that Amy had seemed happier these last few months. He was sure that had something to do with Charles. He wished things were different. She deserved so much more than he would ever be able

Letting Go

to give her. He decided to speak with Brian and let him know the Japan trip was going to be with a third party, Amy. She would be going with them, her and the girls.

Ken left the house soon after Amy got back home. He told her he needed to pick something up from the office. Amy asked if it could wait until tomorrow. Ken never answered to anyone; he wasn't about to start today. See you later," he said as he closed the door behind him.

Charles Lets Amy Go

Charles was so torn up after Amy left their place. He was still trying to pull himself together.

Jean didn't want to hear from Charles. Why was he calling me? He and Amy should be busy planning their life and decorating their love nest. She almost didn't answer the phone. Jean had no reason to face Charles ever again. She wanted to close this chapter of her life. Jean had received Charles' call on Saturday night asking if he could stop by and talk. She wanted to know what they had left to talk about. He didn't want to go over anything on the phone. Jean felt she knew too much already. What else could there be?

Charles arrived around 6:00 pm. He looked drained, as if he hadn't slept all week. She hadn't spoken to Charles since he moved out. He seemed smaller somehow than she remembered. He walked into the living room and sat down. She asked, "Is everything alright Charles?

"Sure Jean!" he answered. "Life is full of surprises!"

"You are telling me! What's going on?" she asked.

He didn't say anything for a couple of minutes and then said slowly, "Amy has decided not to leave her husband. Ken wants her to stay and work things out with him."

"Did she tell him about you and the baby?"

"Yes, Jean, she told him and that doesn't matter. They took wedding vows and Ken wants to obey them. He loves his wife dearly and blames himself for her infidelity. He was gone a lot and he feels he let her down. The baby could be his! He's willing to take a chance."

"I'm sorry, Charles. I know how much you were looking forward to a life with her and your hopes of having a child."

Charles never looked as small as he did at that moment. He began to cry, the tears fell like an open stream down his face. Jean wasn't sure what was expected of her. Just a few days ago

Letting Go

she had felt a similar pain. Jean's heart went out to him for she knew the pain he felt was real. She went over and placed her arms around his small shoulders and let him cry until there were nothing left.

He said, "I'm sorry Jean. I didn't mean to lose control. I don't know what came over me. I've been driving around for hours trying to figure out where things went wrong. We were making wedding plans one minute and the next she's telling me she was not going to leave him. I didn't know where to go! I know this is the last place I should have come, but I needed to see you Jean."

"That's fine Charles; you're welcome to stay here until you pull yourself together. Charles, you should know by now that life isn't always fair. It has a way of playing tricks on us. You told me once that *love shows no mercy*. I guess this is a prime example of that, isn't it?"

"Ken will be asking for a transfer from the area. He wants to go to Japan. There's an opening in his company there. If the baby's mine I'll never know! What should I do Jean?"

"Let her go, Charles! She doesn't belong to you, she never did! She has a husband and you have to respect him, even if you didn't respect me. Charles, the only advice I have for you is prayer!" Jean explained to Charles about prayer. "Charles, prayer is what helps me deal with your leaving. I'm sure it will help you deal with your grief over Amy."

Charles held his head down in shame. He destroyed one relationship to build another one. He had lost more than Jean's love, he had lost her respect. She would never see him as the man he once was.

Charles got up and walked out the door and on to a new life full of uncertainty. He left as a broken man; he knew Jean had moved on. Charles realized that he never really thought or cared about her feelings and the pain his leaving would cause her. All he could do now was face the facts; that he would have to build a life without either of them. He had gambled and had lost everything. What could he have been thinking of? His whole life he had dreamed of the life he had with Jean and he went and simply threw it away. He had nothing. Amy had broken his spirit. Men are strong creatures, they're leaders not followers. Charles had lost his direction, in addition to losing his wife and lover. Now he was going to feel the pain that Jean must have felt when he left her! "Pay back is a bitch!" Amy was never his anyway; after their last conversation he had realized that.

Charles had to pick up the last of his things from Jean. Charles knew he didn't stand a chance of coming back into Jean's life. She had closed the door. Sometimes women have such an ugly attitude when they discover their man cheats, but not Jean. She was so determined to be the best at everything. She was a good sport even when her husband left her. She would never ask him to come back because deep down she knew she would never be able to trust him again. Jean was focused on what she wanted and it sure wasn't Charles.

Beth was trying to make sense of what Jean had told her about Charles. He was in love with another woman and she was pregnant. Jean was in such pain; Beth wished she could help her friend. Sometimes, no advice is the best advice. Jean was holding up better than most people. She would be there just in case Jean needed her.

Jean came into work on Monday. She was very private about her personal life. Everyone kept their private lives out of the work place. I was the only one that knew the pain she was going through. We would discuss what ever was on our minds together and no one would be the wiser. We would have to suffer together now. Charles had shown her that she could never surrender her heart completely too any man. That we should always hold some love in reserve for a rainy day. I often told Jean this and she would laugh at me. Well, now she sees what I had been trying to tell her all along!

Earl had always tried to hide his affairs; he just wasn't that good at it. At least Charles was man enough to come out in the open with his. I decided long ago that my marriage to Earl wasn't worth losing any more sleep over. I've cried my last cry and shed my last tear. I'm just killing time until something better comes along.

Jean and I saw him at the same time. He walked into the store as if he owned the place. Who was this guy? And where

Letting Go

had he been all our lives? He was dressed in a crew neck, black, long-sleeved Jordan polo shirt, with black dress pants and wearing a pair of high-gloss shoes. He had to be important! He looked the part he was playing, and we both wanted to play on his team. He simply took our breath away. He stood every bit of six feet four inches and was built. We didn't realize we were staring until another employee tried to get our attention. Good looking guys just always seem to avoid us. It's not that we're not in the receiving area; we just never got to see them. I moved from my current position so I wouldn't be spotted. I only wanted to look! Looking has never caused any damage to one's heart has it? This guy was too fine!

Jean moved out to assist him with the uniforms items. I would have to keep my distance because it had been a long time since I'd seen someone look that good. I wasn't to be trusted; plus I was still so-called married. I knew he had to be also; the good ones are these days. After Jean finished helping him, she walked back to my hiding place to give me the news.

"Yes, he's married and has one child, a son named Jamie who is two. His name is Brad Walker. He's the new manager of Housing and Development. He's also a Colonel in the Air Force, with one of those cross service agreements or something with the Army. He lives in Maryland!"

"Jean, how did you get all that information in such a short time?" Beth asked.

Jean said, "I asked and he answered. I also got his phone number at work if you want to call him when his merchandise comes in."

"No thank you! I'm staying clear. I have enough of my own problems! I wouldn't know what to do with a guy who looks that good."

"Come on, I saw the look on your face when he walked in; I was looking and so were you."

Beth said, "There's nothing wrong with that! I have no intention of ever flirting with a married man again. Do you remember what happened the last time, Jean? No? Then let me refresh your memory. His name was James. He was married, and drove a black Mercedes Benz."

"Oh Beth, I remember him. I introduced you to him and his wife Stacy."

"Yes you did! That was a disaster! His wife Stacy was in the office every day looking for him. She thought he was planning to run off with me until she found out it was her sister he was planning to run off with. The girl scratched up all the cars in the parking lot because she wanted to make sure she got my car. I just happened to be off from work that day, thank goodness."

"I'm sorry, Beth, please let's not talk about that mess."

"I should have known better than to flirt with a married man anyway, but Earl wasn't paying me any attention. It wasn't long before the flirting got out of hand and James made a pass at me. Maybe I shouldn't have called Stacy and told her. It's hard for women to believe another woman when she tells her that her man wants to be unfaithful. But I would believe you Jean, if you told me that Earl made a pass at you."

Sure, you would have believed me because you know Earl; he will make a pass at anyone.

"Yes, you're right, bad example," said Beth. "Jean, Stacy was your friend so you should have told her. I was trying to give her a heads up."

"I heard James was messing around on her for a while. That she was already having problems with other women," Jean said.

"But it wasn't with me!" Beth proclaimed.

"I didn't want to be the reason her marriage broke up. I didn't want to add to her problems. There's nothing to worry about, you weren't interested in him anyway, Beth."

I know, but that was something to think about, men only want sex; and more sex. They're not looking for a good woman; they're looking for free sex with no attachments. Jean, now that we're talking about free sex; what are you going to do about Charles since he went out and had free sex and fell in love?! Why do our husbands have to fall in love?" Beth asked. "Didn't they read the handbook on free sex and how to handle it before they got married?! Let's get Earl and Charles a copy and let them read the guidelines on free sex and cheating husbands!"

They both had to laugh!

Letting Go

"Will you let Charles come back home, Jean? Since Amy is out of the picture are you ready to jump back into bed with him?" Beth asked. "I know he's still your husband."

"That's just a formality!" Jean said. "Charles said some pretty ugly things to me not to mention he may have gotten Amy pregnant. He didn't even think enough of me to use protection, Beth. Not that we were sleeping together anyway. I may have caught him in a weak moment and we had sex, but we haven't made love in months, Beth!"

"I'm sorry Jean! I didn't know."

"How could you have known? I didn't tell anyone. I wanted people to think Charles and I were happy. Charles never really cared about me, Beth. He told me he had been looking for Amy his whole life and that she completed him. How could I ever forget those words, Beth? When the man you vowed to love forever tells you another woman completes him. All those years I was fooling myself, girl. I should have seen this coming!"

"I was so busy being perfect I forgot to be real. Amy was real. That's what Charles was looking for, a real woman. Beth, you know I really feel sorry for Charles at this point; he did me a favor by leaving me. I'll find someone else, and the next time I'll be a little wiser and a lot smarter. When the next guy says he loves me, I'll have to say, 'Prove it!' Charles left me just a little bitter."

"Charles lost everything trying to be something he's not. He lost Amy, his baby and me," Jean said. "Beth you should have seen him. He looked so broken hearted and alone he made me want to cry for him!"

"I bet he didn't cry when he left you. Jean, how can you feel sorry for him after the way he treated you?" Beth said angrily. He left you with no warning, no nothing. He just walked out. He didn't care if your heart was broken or if you died!" Beth said, getting angrier by the second.

"That's not true, Beth!"

"What part is not the truth Jean? Charles was thinking of himself and being with Amy, his white prize! That was his only concern. I think he got just what he deserved and I'm going to

55

tell him that the next time I see him! I'm going to say; Charles you made your bed hard, now lay your tired ass in it!"

"Calm down Beth, Charles is suffering!"

"What, like I care? And I guess you're having the time of your life! He walked out on you Jean, and don't forget that!"

"He had a lot riding on Amy, after all, she was his soul mate," Jean said.

"Well, I guess he wasn't Amy's soul mate; if he was then maybe Amy wouldn't have left him," Beth said.

"Beth, I guess we haven't met ours yet," Jean said. "You can bet Earl is not yours. What about the new housing officer? Maybe he's yours, Beth!"

"Jean, don't be ridiculous! He's already married and I'm sure the way he looks his wife has him on lockdown!"

Beth realized what Jean was saying later on that night. With Earl in Korea and she by herself for a year she could rediscover who she was and what her purpose in life was. Let her hair down and have a little fun, she thought. That may sound good, but I still have Marie and Michele to think of and keep her grounded. Plus, Brad Walker looks dangerous. I don't know if he's the kind of guy that likes to have flings. Plus, I'm not really ready to start something that I can't finish.

The next few weeks went by slowly. Jean and I talked daily about our tall, dark, and handsome stranger. We hadn't seen him around. Charles called Jean; pretending he cared about her welfare now that he was alone. Jean assured him that she was fine and that she was a survivor; that it would take more than him to break her. Charles wanted to know if she had considered selling their beach house. Since the house was in both of their names it should be sold. Jean told him she would speak to her lawyer and let him know. There was no need to have a vacation home with no one to vacation with, Jean had said to Beth. Jean had noticed something in Charles voice and had asked him if everything was ok. He said he was coming down with a cold that he couldn't shake and that if he wasn't better by the end of the week he would go in to see one of the doctors on post.

Jean said she made a quick retreat by wishing him well, and hung up the phone before he asked her to come over and take

Letting Go

care of him! Jean hated he was calling her so often. Every since Amy and he split he been trying to cling to her. She needed to cut all the ties she had with him. As soon as the divorce was final she would consider leaving the area; there was no reason for her to stay other than the girls and me. Her parents had retired to Florida, she would move closer to them. She still had some feelings for Charles; they were married for 5 years. You don't just stop loving someone because they stop loving you. Beth had learned that long ago. Now Jean would have to learn it also; the first lesson is always the hardest! It will take her some time but she has plenty of that these days. And she has me; we can suffer together. But Beth knew her friend would choose to suffer alone in her own way.

Brad, came in the store on the following Monday to check on his order. Jean had just placed it on my desk for me to call him.

Jean approached Brad and said, "Your timing is perfect. Your order just came in. I was just asking our manager if she wouldn't mind calling you. I was backlogged with other projects. Your merchandise is on her desk. Just walk through the main office. Her office is the one on the right."

Beth was glad she had worn a dress today. Dresses showed off her long slender legs. As she looked into the mirror checking her flawless makeup and hair she could never understand why Earl had cheated on her with all those women when he had a woman that looked the way she looked. She had the full package. Total strangers often told her that she was gorgeous. Beth knew she was attractive, but she never thought of herself as gorgeous, or even beautiful. Earl never said any of those things to her. She had seen Brad come into the store. Beth had worn her hair loose today; it hung down her back and around her face. She hoped it would hide the excitement in her eyes at seeing him. She wasn't sure why she was being fussy over her looks today. She never really cared after the morning started because she usually held up pretty good. Beth wasn't sure she was ready to face the man that had been invading her sleep every night since she first laid eyes on him. She would wake up in a hot sweat. Now here he was standing in her doorway looking more intimidating than she had ever imagined. Beth knew this man spelled danger and they hadn't even met. Jean said that Brad would be a test to see how well I was glued together.

"Hello, I'm Brad Walker, nice to meet you."

"I know Sir!"

"Well then, you have the advantage. I don't think we've met."

"No, we haven't. I'm Beth Taylor. Nice to meet you Mr. Walker."

"Please, call me Brad. No one calls me Mr. Walker."

"All right Brad. Your order just came in today. I was dialing your number as you walked through the door. Mr. Walker, I'm sorry, I mean Brad, Jean tells me your managing the Housing Office here on post."

"Yes, that's correct."

"And that you're also a Colonel in the Air Force."

"Correct again! Since we're playing twenty questions, I have one for you. Are you married Ms. Taylor?"

"Yes Brad!"

"You're not wearing a wedding ring?"

"No, I'm not. I haven't worn a wedding ring since the first time my husband cheated on me. I'm sorry, I didn't mean to be so blunt. Is that too personal for you?"

"Not at all!"

"He's stationed in Korea at the moment. "I have two daughters, Michele is five and Marie who is nine. I heard you have a son."

"Yes, he is two his name is Jamie. You haven't worked here long have you Mrs. Taylor?"

"Will you please call me Beth?"

"I like Beth; it has strength and power."

"It was my great grandmother's name. We shared the same birthday. She died when I was very young."

"I'm very sorry to hear that Beth."

"Thank you. I've been here for almost a year. I haven't seen you in here before last week."

"There's little need to come into the uniform store because I don't get to wear my uniform that often. I'm here now to replace

Letting Go

some of the brass on it because it's old and tarnished. I'm replacing it rather than polishing it."

"That shows you've been in the military way too long." She liked this guy; he was so easy to talk to. Beth didn't want the conversation to end. Brad was more handsome than she had remembered. He had a cleft chin. You didn't see that everyday on brothers. Beth's hands were sweating profusely. She dried them on her dress before reaching and shaking his hand goodbye. He had a nice firm grip and held her hands a few seconds longer than needed. Beth decided to escort Brad to the nearest register so he could checkout. Beth offered her services in helping him find anything else he may need to complete his uniform, but he had everything he needed for now.

Jean had made her way to the front to see if Brad had gotten everything.

"Thanks, Jean, for all your help."

"My pleasure, Brad!"

"Tell me ladies; are you two coming to the annual ball this year?" Brad asked.

"I don't think so. We're not in the partying mood this year."

"It could be good for the two of you."

"No thank you."

Brad promised to call if he needed anything else.

The moment he left Jean was on Beth with twenty questions. "What do you think? When will you see him again?"

"Slow down girl! He's too much for me, Jean! Plus he's happily married. Jean, at this point I'm not interested in any man, especially not a married man."

"Beth, did you forget who you are talking to? I saw you sweating and in the mirror before he walked into your office."

"OK, so he's all that and a bag of pork rinds dipped in hot barbeque sauce! But he's married!"

"Yes, but is he happy?"

They both laughed.

"You're married also, or did you forget?"

"No, Jean, I haven't forgotten. I'm only married on paper and in Gods eyes. Would you please tell Earl the next time you see him that we are still married? I think he's forgotten."

Beth left work early that day because she wanted to take the girls out to eat at their favorite restaurant before going home. They loved McDonalds. Beth didn't notice Charles' car pulling up in the parking lot. The girls were finishing up the last of their Happy Meal when she heard someone calling her name from behind. "Hello Charles, how's life treating you these days?" Beth asked.

She wasn't sure what he wanted, probably just wanted to ask her about Jean. He made small talk about work and then asked about Jean. She told Charles she was doing great, that she's a fighter. "Jean had a few bad days but I'm there for her. She'll be ok in time. How about you Charles, will you be ok? I heard you didn't get the girl!" Beth felt he deserved everything he was getting for the way he treated her friend. He looked like he had been hit by a car, no, maybe a transfer truck. He had on wrinkled clothes and his shoes weren't polished. She felt sorry for him. At that moment he needed a friend but she couldn't help him. She was too busy helping her friend heal her broken heart! "He needed more help than any normal man could give him, he needed God," Beth thought.

"Are you sure you're ok Charles?" Marie and Michele were staring at Charles.

"Mama, is Uncle Charles ok?" Marie asked. Marie asked the question as if Charles couldn't hear her.

Charles, looked at his niece and said, "Yes sweetie I'm fine! I'm just fighting a cold. I'm going to my doctor in the morning. Thanks for asking about me."

"You're welcome Uncle Charles," Marie said. She then turned back to her sister and joined her in playing with their Happy Meal toys.

"Charles, this is not the end of the world," Beth whispered.

"See you later, Beth."

"See you, Charles."

Beth had never seen Charles look so bad. She would have to call Jean and let her know what a fine mess he'd gotten himself into. He was headed down hill faster than a rolling stone!

When Beth tried to call Jean she wasn't home, she was meeting with realtors about selling the house in Florida. She

Letting Go

called her back later that night and told her about running into Charles at McDonalds and how bad he looked. Jean told her she had already noticed it; she had seen him the over weekend.

"Jean, you're not thinking of going back to him are you?"

"No, Beth, I'm not! He just needed someone to talk to, that's all. I'm still his wife and I still care about him."

"I know Jean, you're a good woman. He lost more than a wife when he lost you, he lost his best friend."

"Did Charles mention Amy?" Jean asked.

"Not to me Jean."

"That's sad," she said. "He hasn't heard anything from Amy since she left him."

"What does he want to hear from her Jean? Does he want her to come back?"

"I guess so, Beth. He didn't say. He made her a promise that he would let her go, so he's keeping his promise. I think Charles was hoping she would have come back already; but since she hasn't he is facing the truth that she never really loved him in the first place."

"You're probably right, Jean. Don't let him make you his wishing well! I wish I hadn't left you... I wish I could take all those things back... I wish..."

"Ok, Beth, I get the message," Jean said, stopping Beth in her tracks. "Let it go, Beth!"

"I'm sorry, Jean. I got carried away!"

The Blood Test

Ken went to the doctors with Amy just as he had promised. They were sitting and waiting on her test results to come back. Amy was wondering what was taking so long. In the past it had only taken her five minutes to give blood and she would have the results back in thirty minutes. Amy knew Ken had reservations about the baby, that was understandable, but he had promised to love it no matter what. Amy hadn't heard anything from Charles. She thought he would have at least tried to call her by now.

Charles was so broken the last time she had seen him. She hated herself for what she had done to him and his family. She knew she was totally responsible for his leaving his wife. Now he and his wife were probably both alone. If they could only make their way back to each other the way Ken and she had. It would be hard but in the end they would at least have each other.

Amy was so deep in thought that Ken had to touch her to let her know they had called her to come back into the examining room. Amy was worried, but why should she be worried? She had already done this twice before. This would be a piece of cake.

Amy's doctor called her Mrs. Robinson. He never called her that. He had always called her by her first name. "What's going on Dr. Rose? You're frightening me by calling me Mrs. Robinson. Is there something wrong with my blood test?"

"Amy, I would like for you to take another test. We're not sure but your test may have been exposed to something in the lab that interfered with the result. I'd like to perform the test myself and I will call you when the result comes in on Thursday. Amy, don't worry. Everything will be just fine, it's probably nothing."

Amy was worried! What had happened to the first test she had just taken? Why was her doctor giving her the test himself? He'd never done that before.

Letting Go

Ken noticed the look on Amy's face as she returned to the waiting room. He was on his feet and at her side. "What's the matter?" he asked. "What's going on Amy, are you ok?"

"I don't know, the doctor says it's nothing but I'm scared," she said. "The Doctor will call me on Thursday with the results of my second test. He said something about mixing up the test in the lab."

"If the Doctor says not to worry then we won't worry."

"Ken, what could be going on?"

"Nothing Amy. Now let's get home so you can get some rest."

Ken couldn't think of anything that could be wrong. He had a silent wish that they would tell her she was not pregnant, that she was late on her period due to stress. He knew that was a wasted wish because he had already noticed the changes in her body. She was definitely pregnant.

Ken wanted to see Brian; they hadn't spoken in a few days. He was wrapped up in trying to keep his marriage together. Just last week he was ready to walk away from it all. Now he had to stay and pretend the last few years with Brian were just him trying to find himself. Brian meant the world to him. They had stayed up many a night trying to figure out the best way to tell Amy he was gay. They had agreed that they would tell her together. Brian held the key to his heart. The adventures they had discovered together were hard to describe. They had shared so much as friends and lovers. He loved Brian and that was all he could say. He had promised Amy they would work things out for the sake of their kids, but once this baby is born she would have to leave and return to the states with the kids. He and Brian would finally have a life together. He wasn't happy with a black man raising his children, especially not Charles, but it wasn't worth staying in a marriage that was built on lies and deceit. He was not going to sacrifice his happiness for her!

Ken was on his way to see Brian, whom he had deeply missed. They had a lot to discuss. Ken needed to let Brian know that Amy would be coming with them to Japan for a while; at least until the baby was born. They would have to keep their love on the down low a little longer. Ken wasn't worried. Ken knew he would be worth the wait and he would show Brian that tonight.

He arrived at Brian's and let himself in as usual. Brian met him in the living room and they kissed as if they had been away from each other for months instead of a few days. "Man, I sure missed you," said Ken.

"Not half as bad as I've missed you! Ken, there are so many things I need to say to you! I wish I knew where to start."

"The beginning is always a good place to start Brian, try the beginning."

"I wanted to tell you this before we became intimate but it happened so fast I didn't think either one of us was ready or well prepared for what happened that morning two years ago."

"I'm just glad it happened Brian!"

"So am I Ken! I never told you about my past because it never seemed to be the right time. I'm originally from Maryland and my parents still live there."

"No, you never mentioned that."

"We had a falling out when I told them I was gay. They couldn't accept having a gay son. I tried to make them understand that I was still the same person; the only difference was that I liked boys instead of girls. My mom was ok with who I was. She loved me regardless; I was her son, her baby. She tried to help my father get past it but he just wasn't going to accept it. I moved away to keep from hurting him any more than I had already. That's when I moved to New York."

Ken watched Brian as he talked. He would have to let Brian know how he really felt about him; they had never said the L word to each other. He would tell Brian that he loved him tonight and he wanted to live the rest of his life with him.

"Ken, I met someone when I got there. He was older and full of life and was quite open about his sexual preference. I wasn't that open. I felt more or less like you did when you first came out," Brian said. "I felt ashamed of the feelings I was having for other guys," Brian explained to Ken. "This was wrong, I kept telling myself and I shouldn't be feeling like this. But that was what made me happy. Girls weren't the answer. I

Letting Go

couldn't find happiness in dating girls. All through high school I pretended to be something that I wasn't," Brian said.

Ken listened as Brian poured his heart out to him.

"Ken, the first real lover I had was a little older than me. He took care of me from the start. He had been on the streets and he knew that New York could be dangerous if you didn't know where you were going. We became lovers in the end. Ken, I didn't infect Shane, he was infected when we met. He never hid anything from me. I knew up front but he was so special that I stayed with him and when he died it took a part of me with him! I'm not going to lie; I cared deeply for Shane. I needed a new start after his death so I came back home to the Washington DC area to live."

"Brian, you're telling me that your last lover died of Aids!"

"Yes, Ken, that's what I'm saying."

"Why didn't you tell me before?" Ken asked. "Have you been tested? Did you ever have unprotected sex with him Brian?"

"Ken, listen to me. I was tested before I came here."

"What was the result Brian?"

"I don't know. I didn't have a chance to get the result. We never had unprotected sex Ken!" Brian tried to explain.

"Brian, you are not sure if you're infected or not, are you? You let me sleep with you knowing you may be infected; is that what you're trying to tell me Brian?" Ken was yelling at this point. "Brian, is there a chance that I may have the Aids virus?!"

"Ken, please let me explain everything! I need to finish telling you!"

Ken had to get out of there! He couldn't believe that Brian hadn't been honest with him. They had spent so many nights together as friends even before they were lovers. He had shared some of his deepest feelings with him. Ken needed someplace to think. He would have to figure this out on his own. He couldn't go home! He was not ready to face Amy just yet. Ken couldn't believe what was happening to him. He may be carrying the HIV virus! He needed to be tested right away! Amy! What if he's given it to Amy? How would he tell her that she may have been infected?

Ken began to cry. He knew he had messed up! There was a strong chance that he might test positive! He would go home and tell her now. They would have to decide what to do about their kids and the unborn baby, should she test positive. He did not want to take a chance on having a baby that would have the HIV virus. What will happen to my wife? Ken didn't know who to turn to. His best friend had let him down. He was on his own! Ken cried so hard his eyes were red and swollen. He could not go home looking like this because then he would have to explain why he had been crying. He had to stop at a drug store and pick up some eye drops.

"Brian should have told me!" Ken kept repeating to himself all the way home. He should have been given the option of whether he wanted to sleep with him or not. If Ken had known, he would never have been with Brian no matter what his feelings were. This was one mistake that he would never live down! He loved Brian more than anyone in this world. How did this happen? Brian should have told him! How would he live with this secret? It was already eating at his heart. How could he keep this a secret? It should have been his choice, not Brian's!

Brian had tried to tell Ken! Yes, he had had mixed feelings when it came to telling Ken, but Ken had a right to know and he took that right away. Brian didn't expect Ken to freak out on him! Brian wondered if maybe he should have waited and got his results back before telling Ken. Brian had to meet his boss at the office on Monday and tell him that he and Ken would have to cancel their trip to Japan. Brian had tried to get in touch with Ken at home but Amy said he was not back from the office. Brian thank her and said he would try back later.. Brian knew that was the alibi Ken used whenever he wanted to spend time at the house with him. There was no one at the office to answer the phone so he didn't have to worry about Amy checking on him. Brian noticed that Ken had thrown his keys on the floor near the front door. Brian knew Ken was not going to ever forgive him. At that point his heart went to pieces. What on earth had he done?! Brian, felt he had just destroyed the greatest love of his life. Brian was worried that he may have destroyed Ken also! He had to find him and fast!

Letting Go

When Ken arrived back at the house he was so worked up he didn't know exactly what to do next. He looked in on Amy. She was taking a nap. Ken studied her face. She was still the most beautiful woman he had has ever seen. Even after two kids she was stunning! She was barely showing. He would take good care of her. If he survived, he would never look at another man. Ken had tears in his eyes as he looked in on the girls who were already in bed. They were all he had left that was good in his life. They needed protection. He would make sure they were safe! Ken was thinking back about Amy's blood test. They both were trying to figure out what had gone wrong with the first test. The first test wasn't normal because the Doctor found the Aids virus and didn't want to frighten her with the result until he had retested her blood. Ken was positively sure she had the virus. He and his family would be the talk of the base.

Ken was standing in the middle of the kitchen when everything hit him like a brick! He and Amy were going to die. He broke down and fell to the floor, sobbing like a child.

Amy had been awakened by the phone. It was Brian looking for Ken again. She came down to see if he was home. Ken was sitting on the floor with his hands over his face. Amy wasn't sure what to do! "Ken, tell me, are you all right? Is it mom and dad? Did something happen at work? Ken! Please Ken, you're scaring me! What's going on Ken? Should I call the doctor?"

Ken managed to shake his head.

"What has happened, Ken?" All Amy could do was sit there on the floor and hold onto him while he cried. "Ken, Brian called looking for you. He's been trying to reach you all afternoon. Does this have something to do with him? Please tell me what it is Ken. I want to help!"

"No one can help me Amy!"

"Yes, we can work it out. I'm not seeing Charles, Ken, if that's what you're worried about. I made you a promise Ken. I haven't changed my mind. Is that it?"

The kids were awakened by the noise. "Mom, is dad ok?"

"Yes sweetheart, he's fine! Brittany, take your sister and go get back into bed. I'll be right there to tuck you both in. Ok?"

"Yes, mom! I hope you feel better daddy." The girls had not seen their father cry before!

Amy had to get control of the situation. She would call Brain. "Ken, I'm going to call Brian."

"No! I'm fine. I don't need anyone." Ken had stopped the tears long enough to decide he would tell Amy as soon as the girls were back to bed.

Amy went to tuck the girls back into bed. They would be alone now. She needed to find out what was going on with her husband. Amy returned to the kitchen where Ken was now sitting at the kitchen counter. "Are you all right dear? Is there something we should talk about now that the girls are in bed again?"

Brian wished he could take back the whole day. He should have gone and gotten tested first before bringing the subject up. Brian's mind was playing tricks on him also. He had never questioned the possibility of him having the Aids virus. He knew he didn't have the virus so there was no need for concern until now. What if he had tested positive? What would become of his relationship with Ken? Brian figured he had already lost him.

As soon as Ken left Brian tried calling the clinic where he had taken his Aids test two years earlier. The secretary answered the phone and informed him that she would have to research his files. She explained that their facility usually destroyed all results more than twelve months old. She took his name and phone number and promised to call him in a day or two. The clinic was open twenty-four hours a day. He knew because he had walked in one night at 3:00 in the morning to get his Aids test. It was the same night Shane had died!

Brian thought about going into town and getting another test. He needed answers right away; a couple of days might be too late. He called the clinic again, and this time he spoke to a nurse. He explained that it was a matter of life and death; that he needed to get his test result right away. Brian liked the sound of her voice. She had a kind voice and said she understood why this could be so important. The nurse explained that it might take some time because of the number of requests they had for test

Letting Go

results. She also explained that they were not allowed to give test results out over the phone. She could lose her job if she did.

Brian was not sure what to say next. He really didn't want her to lose her job, but he needed help. He explained that he had moved away before the results came in.

The nurse asked Brian to hold on. She would see what she could do. "Thank you!" Brian said. Brian wondered what was taking so long as he patiently waited for the nurse with the kind voice to come back on the line.

Brad Walker

Beth had not been the same since she spoke to Brad. She still woke up at night in a hot sweat! She had never experienced this kind of pleasure while she was asleep. Brad did things to Beth in her sleep that she would never be able to tell anyone. She couldn't even tell her best friend! She had never received that kind of excitement from any man before. He haunted her sleep at night and her mind during the day. She needed to learn more about this man that was driving her crazy. Jean would never let her live it down if she found out about the dreams.

Jean was feeling a little better these days. The scars that Charles left in her heart would be there for a long time. But Beth knew Jean. She knew that she had nothing on her hands but time. She would have to wait it out. She had asked Jean if she had heard from Charles. She was furious that he was calling all the time. She had refused to answer the phone on several of his calls.

"What am I to do?" Jean asked her one day. "He's been asking me for a second chance. I haven't given him an answer yet Beth." Jean told her how lonely she was and she told her to get a dog! She couldn't give her any advice on the subject of the heart. She had let Earl walk over her so many times she thought she was a doormat.

"The only joy I have is the knowledge that one day I will be financially able to leave him. When that happens it will be all about me and my girls. Until then, I'll play the role of the supportive wife. My goal is to beat him at his own game. I have God on my team! I'm sorry that I can't advise you Beth. Follow your heart. If you want Charles then by all means go back and start over. Just always remember that you were his second choice. Amy was his first!"

"Ok, now that you put it like that I feel foolish bringing it up! For someone who doesn't like giving advice, you sure have a lot to say!"

Letting Go

"That's the nature of the beast!"

"So Beth, are you going to call Brad?"

"No! I'm not calling him. Jean, he's not for me. He makes me nervous just by walking into a room. I can't call that man."

"Well, I suggest you get your body armor on because he will be back and I don't think he's the kind of guy women say no to. I remember the last time he held your hand a little longer than necessary. You were sweating like crazy."

"I'll be ready next time Jean, you watch!"

Jean was right!" He came back two days later looking for cap screws for his dress blue hat. There was the annual ball coming up. He had mentioned it the last time he was in the store. Jean and I had an open invitation to the ball, but neither of us had plans to attend. We were not the kind of women that go anyplace without the proper dress and we had no intention of going shopping.

"Let's go," I heard Jean say.

"Yeah! Why not?"

"Charles will be there and a bunch of our friends. I won't let people think that Charles has won. I say we go out and buy the most beautiful dress in DC."

"Jean, are you sure this is you talking and not that green monster that's going to show Charles what he lost?"

"Maybe a little of both! Who knows for sure?"

Charles was at the doctor's office first thing in the morning. His cold had lasted a lot longer than he had hoped. He was looking forward to going to the ball tonight. He had tried everything to get rid of his cold. It made him remember how Jean used to always take care of him whenever he was sick. He never had to get out of bed; she was always there with his medicine and love, pouring them both over him until he was better. Now here he sat alone with one of the worst colds he had ever had. He'd had it for almost two weeks now. He knew he was not eating properly and that he needed some rest if he was ever going to fight this cold. He had trouble sleeping. Every time he closed his eyes he would see Amy's beautiful face. Charles wondered if he would ever be the same again. Amy was everywhere. There were so many memories that he barely had a moment when she wasn't on his mind. He knew he had to move on. He had to let go of the memories; they were more dangerous than anything else. Sometimes the pain was so great he didn't even want to live! The sooner he accepted that she was out of his life forever the sooner he could start the healing process.

Charles had hoped Jean would take him back by now. He had asked her a week ago. He guessed she was still thinking about it. She would never be able to forgive him for the pain he put her through and the terrible things he had said to her. He had been totally mean and abusive and there were never any need to hurt her. She was more than willing to walk away if that was what he wanted. Charles got just what he had asked for. Now he was back with his tail tucked between his legs looking to come home.

He knew Jean was probably getting advice from Beth. She was the one Jean would pull her strength from. They would always be there for each other. Charles was glad that she had a friend like Beth. It was a great relief when he'd left her knowing that Beth would help pull her through this turmoil. Charles remembered he needed to call Jean and ask if she would go with him to the ball. It was a tradition with them that they all tried to attend together. He had to pick up his tux and get everything laid it out just in case he felt up to going. Charles' needed to see Jean. She would be a much-needed distraction to take his mind off his problems. Tonight he would forget Amy just long enough to work on his relationship with Jean. He wanted to know if she had made a decision about them. He would see old friends and catch up on old gossip.

He had to hurry if he was going to make it by the opening dance. He had to shave; he hadn't done that in a long time. After his shower and shave he felt refreshed and alive. He hadn't felt that good in a while, maybe the medicine was beginning to work. The doctor had given him plenty and told him to get plenty of rest. Charles was dressed and out the door in less than one hour. Charles looked, into the mirror as he passed through the foyer. He looked really good in his black tux. You couldn't even tell he had a broken heart, a broken marriage, and broken dreams. Charles would leave all those people and their issues behind him

Letting Go

tonight. Charles knew if he could start over tonight it would be a new beginning for him and Jean. He tried to find parking as close to the door as possible just in case it rained. He really didn't want to chance getting wet. With the cold he had he would surly die of pneumonia. There were so many limo's that you could barely park. Why were there so many limos? Once Charles found a parking space he checked his bowtie in the rear mirror and got out of the car. "This would be his night!" Charles thought.

Beth had agreed to go with Jean to the Ball. They would go alone. Everyone already knew that Earl was in Korea and that Charles had moved out. There was no reason for the two of them to feel uncomfortable about attending. Charles had called Jean and asked if he could escort her to the Ball. She explained to him that she already had a date and left it at that. Beth and Jean had hooked up to look for a gown for the Ball. Since Carol wasn't going this year she said she would watch the girls. Carol was in a wonderful relationship with Curtis. They had been together for several years. They were thinking of getting married soon. Carol and I met at the Post Exchange. She had fallen in love with Marie and Michele from the moment she saw them. The girls felt close to her also. Carol agreed to keep them while we looked for our gowns.

Jean and I headed to the mall to fine the perfect gown. Jean fell in love with a gown made of black chiffon with a flowing tail. It was beautiful! Jean felt that somehow wearing black signified she was mourning the loss of her husband. I on the other hand choose an off white button down the back with a matching cape - it was breath taking. The dress I chose had a tight fitted waist and slender neckline that enhanced my height. The cut of the gown gave me a model look and design. We picked our accessories for both gowns. Jean chose a black sandal with sapphires on the straps and around her ankles to show off her new designed toes. I chose a pair of Michael Kor strapless sandals with a matching purse.

Jean ordered limo service so that neither one of us had to drive. Jean wasn't big on driving and neither was I. Plus this kind of function called for a limo. We both had taken off work for the event. There was never any shortage of employees to fill in, which made my job so much easier. I had already given Jean a personal day off. We both had a lot to accomplish in a short time. Jean and I had gotten our nails, hair and feet done before going over to the MAC counter at Macy's for makeup. We would be as close to perfect as we could get.

Jean hadn't mentioned Charles once during the day so I steered clear of the subject. I was just happy to see my friend excited for a change. I hadn't seen that in a long time. She was enjoying the distraction and so was I. I watched as Jean's makeup was applied. She was very attractive. In all the time I've known her I had never seen her wear makeup before. She looked much younger than thirty-five. She should buy and wear makeup more often. Once my makeup was completed we left in separate cars. I headed home to take a bath and dress. The limo would be there shortly.

Carol and the girls were busy in the family room playing go fish. I went straight to work on getting ready. I couldn't keep my mind off Brad. Brad was getting under her skin and that made her uncomfortable. Seeing him and his wife tonight would most definitely put things into perspective. As I walked out of the bedroom the girls noticed the gown.

Marie said, "Mom, you look like a princess."

"Yes mom, a princess," Michele added.

"Thanks girls. I feel like a princess!"

Carol assured me that I would have every man's attention tonight. If she only knew, deep down inside I was craving only one man's attention. I realized I was missing the necklace my mother had given me as a wedding present when Earl and I got married so I ran back and got it. With the final touches on I was ready. Just as I was saying goodnight to the girls the limo pulled up. I felt free. I've been feeling that a lot lately. I haven't felt married in years! What has happened to me? Stay focused! You're still married. As I walked to the limo, I felt as if I was floating. This dress was magical! Jean and I were beautiful. We made a striking couple of single women, so to speak.

Jean walked ahead of me into the Ballroom. We had promised each other to have a good time and be out by midnight.

Letting Go

Then the spell we were under would wear off and we would both return to being ourselves. But for right now we were someone else. "Jean, your Lady J and I'm Lady B! Let have fun!" Beth said.

We took longer than most strolling into the Ball area, all eyes on us. We headed for the registration table to get our assigned seats. Jean and I were both excited to be there. We had not planned on standing out like sore thumbs, but we did and every eye in the room was on us. We had noticed a few other single females there, which made us feel a little better. I was hoping that Brad wasn't here yet and had not witnessed the charade Jean and I had put on in the interest of freedom.

Jean and I found our seats and ordered drinks. We noticed Brad was here. We hadn't seen his wife; she was probably freshening up. Jean had seen Brad at the bar. I wasn't sure if I wanted to see his wife. I knew to have a man like that she had to be something special. Jean was looking around the room as if she were looking for someone.

"Are you looking for someone, Jean?"

"No, not really, just checking out the beautiful gowns, that's all."

Beth knew her girl was lying. She was looking for Charles! I know my friend. Just then, who walks up? Darrell! He worked in the stockroom office on post. He had been trying to talk to me for the last few weeks.

Darrell spotted Beth as soon as she walked into the room but he wanted to make sure she didn't have a date before he made his move. Darrell noticed how stunning Beth was looking. She was perfect for him. He was staring so hard he never noticed Brad, who was on his way over. "Hello Jean," he said.

"Hi Darrell."

"Hello Beth. You're looking like a million plus dollars tonight!"

"Thank you, Darrell. Where's you're date?" Beth asked.

"I was hoping you would give me the honor and be my date," Darrell replied.

"Thanks Darrell, that's sweet! Once we're settled I'll look for you so we can dance," Beth said. "How does that sound, Darrell?"

"That's great!"

"Do you mind getting us another drink, Darrel, please? Coke for me and ice tea for Jean."

"So, tell me Beth, how will you get rid of Darrell tonight?"

"He's harmless Jean. It's Brad I'm worried about. Charles is on his way over here," Beth whispered into Jean's ear.

"Hello Ladies!"

"Hello Charles!"

"Jean you look absolutely gorgeous."

"Thank you, Charles!"

"You look good to Beth!"

"Why thank you, Charles." Beth mumbled under her breath, "You dip stick." She didn't need Charles' validation and neither did Jean. They knew they looked good. Let it go girl! Stay focused!

Charles was looking at Jean in a new light. She was breath taking. What on earth could he have been thinking of? Here's a woman that had worshipped him. She still loved him; he knew that. The love she had felt for him just didn't die overnight, at least he hoped it didn't. Charles knew he had to make his move tonight. He would ask her for her answer. He would beg if that was what it took. Charles had to let Jean know that he had made a mistake in leaving her and that they belonged together.

Darrell made his way back to the table with their drinks. He was introduced to Charles and proceeded to take a seat. "Brad would never come over to her table now," Beth thought. He would assume that Darrell was her date.

Brad was alone; he was always alone these days. His so-called wife was a wife in name only. She had mentioned the ball and had considered going but Brad had stopped her at once. She would not spoil things for him. She was a person that was never happy unless she was in the middle of drama. She would not ruin this night for him. He had the feeling Beth would be there with Jean. He wanted to see her again. They had made a connection and he wanted to pursue it further.

Letting Go

Brad had noticed Beth and Jean as they had strolled in so provocatively. He felt this was a show for him and any other man that cared to look. He was impressed, very impressed. He knew he would have to make excuses for his wife not being there. He had a couple of excuses ready. No one had to know that they were not in a relationship of husband and wife, that they weren't even friends. Brad had started over when he noticed someone else headed in their direction. Brad had never seen this guy before but he seemed to be all in Beth's face. Maybe it was her husband, Earl. He would give her space but he wanted to say hello!

Brad walked over to Beth and Jean's table and spoke. They were somewhat friends and he was curious about the guy that was sitting at their table. Brad was introduced to everyone. He did learn that neither man was Earl. Brad made an excuse, stating that his wife wasn't feeling well; she had stomach flu. He asked Beth for a dance later on and she agreed to dance with him. Beth hoped it was going to be a slow dance. Darrell was up on the floor the first dance. Beth had promised Darrell a dance as he was cashing in early.

Brad had to finish his rounds; he would be back shortly. Beth was more beautiful than he had imagined. Every since he had met her he hadn't thought of anyone else. He wasn't sure if she was interested in him or not, she didn't seem to be one way or the other. Brad knew that most women were always falling all over him whenever he was around, but Beth never seemed to give him a second look. He figured a woman that had her looks and abilities could have any man she wanted.

Beth was waiting on Brad to make his move. What was taking him so long? She'd had men in her face all night long. She refused to dance with Darrell anymore; he was getting on her nerves. Brad needed to rescue her from Darrell.

Brad waited until Beth was back at her table from the dance floor. "Excuse me ladies, again! It seems you're having a great time."

"Yes Brad," Jean said out of breath from dancing so hard. She had not sat down once since she started dancing. "I'm sorry your wife couldn't be here. I know she's the reason we haven't seen you on the dance floor tonight," Jean said.

"Actually, that's why I'm here. I want to ask Beth if she would like to dance."

"I would love to!" said Beth.

Darrell's eyes followed Beth all the way to the dance floor.

Jean had noticed a strange look on Charles' face while they danced. Then again when she had danced with Darrell. What's his problem? She could always out dance him. They often laughed about his dancing. Jean always told him he had two left feet.

Charles couldn't take his eyes off her. He headed to the table where Jean was talking to Darrell. Charles knew Darrell from the Exchange. He wasn't concerned about Brad after he saw him head to the dance floor with Beth. Charles thought he was such a looker he was glad he wasn't there for Jean. Beth saw the relief in his eyes when she and Brad headed to the dance floor. Charles had practiced what he wanted to say to Jean earlier. "Are you having fun Jean?"

"I sure am Charles!"

He had nodded to Beth and Brad as they strolled to the dance floor. Darrell had decided to wander off. Jean and Beth had taken turns dancing with him; it was time he moved on.

Brad whispered in a voice so soft and low that his breath made the hair on Beth's neck rise. "It's nice to finally have you to myself."

"It's good to see you also Mr. Walker!"

The music had dropped to a soft slower song that didn't require any movement. You know the kind of songs; the songs you just sway back and forth and hold on so tight that neither one of you can breathe; this was one of those songs. This was one of Beth's favorite songs. She could dance all night in this man's arms.

Jean noticed how handsome Charles looked tonight. She couldn't help but stare; it had been so long since she had seen him look so good. She still loved him! But was she in love with him? She would have to consult with Beth to see what the difference between the two was. She wanted to close her heart to

Letting Go

him and he kept trying to push his way back in. She would have to let him know that his key didn't fit her heart anymore. What would be his next move? Charles asked Jean to dance. They moved onto the dance floor walking hand-in-hand. Jean had to admit it felt good holding on to Charles. She loved the touch of his skin, the way he smelled, and that twinkle that came into his eyes when he smiled at her. Jean wasn't sure she could stand being this close to Charles. Her need for a man's touch was growing! It's much too soon! They moved in unison together. They were so close, yet the distance seemed to go on forever. No words were spoken, yet their bodies were saying what needed to be said.

Charles found his voice. He was suffering, being that close to Jean. "Jean I love you! I've never stopped loving you! I know I let you down and you may never be able to forgive me. All I'm asking is for a chance to make things right. There have been times when I think back on how I must have made you feel. I'm ashamed of myself for what I said and the things I've done. There is no way to justify my actions and I had to find someone to blame so I had to blame you. Jean, you were the perfect wife! The best wife any man could ever ask for, but I needed a way out and used your inability to give me kids as a reason to leave you. Jean, I'm so sorry!"

She felt tears on her shoulder. They were soft and warm. She knew he was crying. Jean knew her heart wouldn't survive another heartbreak! Yet, she knew she couldn't go on without trying at least. What should she do? Charles had scarred her pretty deep. She wondered if he had any idea of the pain he had put her through. She would never be able to trust him again!

As if reading her mind he said, "Darling I know you're trying to figure out if you will ever be able to trust me. I will never, ever leave you again Jean. I was so wrong! I want us to look into adoption right away, as soon as possible. I know that what I said all those years was a lie. If God gives me a second chance with you I won't deny us from having a family."

Jean couldn't believe what she was hearing! "What about Amy and the possibility of her child being yours?" she asked.

"That's all in the past. Amy and her husband will be leaving the end of this month for Japan. We have already said our goodbyes."

"What about your heart Charles? Has it said goodbye also? I can't be a substitute for Amy or anyone else. I won't let you hurt me again!"

"Please Jean, I will do anything. We can move away from the area if you want to. Just take me back!"

They continued to talk and dance. Jean had given this a lot of thought. She had moved on! She would be continuing as a single woman. Life wasn't that bad. Charles would never be able to live by her new rules if he was ever lucky enough to come back into her life.

The Kisses

Beth was dancing with the hottest man there tonight. There was so much heat in his touch that Beth was sure she had second-degree burns on her hands. They had walked over to a place in the corner of the dance floor that was shadowed by palm trees. This gave them added privacy, which Beth was sure they would need. She relaxed in his arms and they moved together in rhythm. Beth didn't dare try and speak for she knew her voice would give away the desire that was stirring inside of her. Brad chose not to speak at this time also; her closeness was having a similar affect on him. The music ended and Brad relinquished his hold on Beth. She stepped back away from his grip. "Thanks for the dance, Brad."

She was ready to turn in the direction of her table when Brad caught her hand and said, "Not so fast." Brad was trying to figure out why Beth was always running away from him.

She had no answers for him. She couldn't very well tell him the affect he had on her body, now could she? "I'm sorry Brad," she finally said, "I don't mean to be rude. It's just that you're married and I'm married and I don't think it's a good idea to dance so close together. People may start to talk."

"Is that what's really bothering you? The closeness?"

"I don't want anyone to get the wrong idea that we're disrespecting our spouses," she answered.

"Ok, then let's move over there where no one can see us." Brad led Beth to a more secluded corner of the room. "Does this make you feel better?" With that settled they both seemed to loosen up and enjoy the rest of the dance. They danced every dance until Beth was worn out. Her shoes had started hurting her feet and she needed fresh air. Brad went to get fresh drinks.

She knew there was nothing wrong in dancing and having fun with Brad. They had so much in common. They liked each other's company for one thing and he always seemed to make her laugh. She would have to keep her head clear of him because she could tell right away that he was dangerous. But that would be impossible; for he was in her every thought already. She had enjoyed the closeness of his body near hers while they danced. She wished tonight would last forever!

"Beth, there you are," said a voice that she had come to recognize so well!

"Yes! Brad, I needed to get some fresh air." He had reached her side as she turned around to face him. God, how do you describe this man? He has such an affect on my body it felt like I was being warmed from the sun inside out. I know that's crazy but that's how he makes me feel! This is very dangerous, the closeness we are experiencing at the moment. Beth knew she needed to get back inside fast before something happened between them. "Thanks, for the drink!"

"Beth, I've been thinking a lot about you. You've been in my dreams, night after night. I can't help myself! I'm running out of excuses to come over to your shop and see you. Please don't push me away!"

"Brad, this would be wrong. You have a wife and child at home! I have a husband and my girls! This would never work! This could only end in pain and believe me, I've experienced enough pain in my life to last me a lifetime already. My husband and I aren't on the best of terms; but while he's away in Korea I will have a chance to rediscover who I am and what I want from this so called marriage, if anything! There's no future in you for me Brad!"

Beth started to walk away and Brad blocked her path. She knew she would not be able to escape him that easily! She was in his blood! He would show her how to make this work. Before Beth knew what was happening Brad's lips were on hers. She was too weak to fight back; she had been wondering when he would finally kiss her. His lips were so firm, he held her so close she could barely breathe. Beth knew they were in danger; that what they were about to do would lead them down a road of self-destruction. Beth relaxed and enjoyed the kiss. She needed this man more than she realized. She had given in to her desire! She was sinking in the sea of love! Help me Father for you're the

Letting Go

only one that can save me now! I've been praying for a man, but I know he is not the one for me. He belongs to someone else! "Deliver me, for I'm weak and in need of your strength!" Beth prayed as Brad's kisses swallowed up her being. "Forgive me Lord!"

Charles Wants to Come Home

Jean wanted to wait on Beth, but Charles was ready to leave. She would send the limo back for Beth later. Charles had asked if he could spend the night. They needed to talk. They would lay all their cards on the table and see what turned up.

As they arrived home Jean wasn't sure she was ready. Things were moving far too fast for her. She wanted to slow down but Charles was determined to get an answer tonight. Jean walked into the living room and kicked off her shoes. How could she let Beth talk her into heels? She never wore heels and her feet are paying for it. Jean didn't have much time to linger on her feet. Charles was at her side asking her to have a seat so he could massage them. Jean jumped at the chance!

Charles had never massaged her feet before. Jean sat back on the couch and closed her eyes as Charles rubbed her feet with such tenderness. His touch sent a shiver of warmth through her entire body. Charles was ready to make a deal with the devil if he thought that would get him back in the house. Jean needed rest; her brain was on overload. Charles pulled her in his arms and kissed her. Jean couldn't ever remember his kisses being so tender. Tonight his kisses were different. She returned the kiss with such passion she surprised herself. She hadn't been prepared to feel what she was feeling tonight. She needed Charles to leave right now before things got out of hand! But, for some reason she had lost her voice. Desire had taken over her body and mind; she needed what he had to offer. Jean knew she had nothing to offer him in return.

Charles led Jean to the bedroom. They removed each other's clothes as if they were doing a TV commercial. Charles studied Jean's body as if he was seeing it for the first time. Jean had worn a very tight dress to the ball that didn't require any help from under garments so she had left them all in the drawer. Charles was caressing her thighs. Jean moaned with desire.

Letting Go

"Jean, are you sure you're ready?"

"I want you, Charles!"

"I want you too Jean. I just want you to be sure, that's all!"

"I'm more than sure Charles, I'm ready! Charles, I need you more than I've ever needed anyone." The heat ran through Jean's body and down her legs! She was more than ready; she was on fire!

Charles was breathless. He never noticed how passionate Jean was until now. She stood in front of him absolutely naked! She was beautiful! Why hadn't he seen this in her before? He started off by kissing the lobe of her ear; it was so erotic that Jean shivered. She would explode at any moment. Charles knew he was on the right track! He would pull out all the stops! He would make her his even if it was for only one night.

Jean was out of control. What on earth was she doing? Had she forgotten who this man was? What he had done to her? She was sleeping with the enemy!

Charles continued his kisses down her neck and onto her breast. He took his tongue and made circles around her nipple while he caressed the very essence of her being! There were no turning back; she was begging Charles for completion. Charles wasn't ready to give her what she wanted yet. He would take her to the next level. Charles moved his lips from her breast onto her belly button. He lingered there just long enough to hear her beg for more. His lips moved even slower to her womanhood. He wanted to complete her in a way that she would never forget. Charles knew the torment he was putting Jean through, but he had to let her know he meant business!

"Charles, please take me!" Jean cried.

"No, not just yet my love! I want to taste the juices of your field."

"No Charles! Please! You can't!"

It was too late. Charles was ravishing the crops of her field and Jean had to surrender for she had lost the fight. The pleasure was so great that Jean wasn't sure if she was dreaming. Then she felt Charles's lips on hers and she knew this was real. He had pushed her off the mountain into paradise. Charles entered her with such force she thought she would not be able to endure it but the pleasure took her away. She had never felt this much pleasure in her life! She tried matching Charles's moves but he was too much for her, so she laid back and enjoyed the ride. They held on to each other tighter than life itself as the rivers opened up and carried them away in passion.

They spent the night together. When Jean awoke she wasn't as sure as she was the night before about Charles coming back home. She would have to take it slow. One day at a time. But lying here in his arms felt like old times and she couldn't remember the last time Charles had made her feel so special. There were no words for the way she was feeling. She was seriously thinking about letting him come home.

Jean had felt bad about leaving Beth at the Ball, but she knew she was in good hands. Brad would be a perfect gentleman.

Beth was not sure of what had happened last night. One minute Brad and she were talking about not starting a relationship, and the next minute he was kissing her. She hadn't meant to return his kiss. The kiss was so tender, yet the need and longing was there and asking for permission for his body to invade hers, and her body had given permission without her approval. Beth's body was willing to take the pleasure that his was ready to give. The kiss had lasted longer than time allowed. Beth knew she was in danger. This was not going to be an easy guy to fight off. She had to get control of herself before she did something stupid. Beth broke away from Brad's grip and ran toward the door. She was ready to leave but she hadn't seen Jean and Charles for some time.

She had been left behind! Beth was calling a taxi, when Brad offered his services. "No thanks Brad! I can get home alright without your assistance!"

"I promise to keep my distance and no more surprise kisses. Please, Beth, let me take you home. You can trust me. I give you my word I won't try anything else."

"All right Brad."

Beth wasn't worried about Brad breaking his word, she was worried about her body. She knew it had let her down once and it would surely let her down again, especially after that kiss. His kiss had left her with promises of more to come. Beth was more embarrassed and ashamed than anything else. It would be so easy to lose her soul to this man. He was getting too close for comfort.

Brad dropped her off just as he had promised. He told her he would respect her wishes and not pursue her any longer; and just to show her he meant it he would like to invite her to lunch the next day. Beth agreed to meet him at the park for a short lunch.

Beth hadn't slept at all last night; she was awakened by dreams of Brad's kiss. Beth had promised to meet him for lunch today. She would tell him that she would not be able to see him anymore. She felt he would take advantage of her and no man was ever going to do that again.

Jean wasn't surprised that Beth was going to see Brad again, after all she hadn't really sworn off men, she had just taken a break. Jean was a little worried that Brad would hurt her. Jean knew Beth hadn't recovered from all the scars she received from Earl. Earl was a sad excuse for a husband. He had caused Beth so much pain she would never be able to go through that again without a breakdown.

Beth told Jean about her dreams and how real they seemed. In her dreams she and Brad had made love. "Jean, I have to tell you about my dreams. It was so explicit. Brad and I made love with such passion after the Ball. In my dreams he took me to the park at Hanes Point. We sat on one of the benches near the water overlooking the Potomac River. He started off kissing me the same way he had at the Ball. A teasing kiss. The kind that makes you hungry for more and believe me, I wanted more! I wanted everything he was offering! I felt his need as he rubbed against my thighs. I pressed my body hard up against his manhood so I could feel the size and see if he really wanted me. He was more than ready. Jean, this dream was so real I tell you! I was so sure this was happening that I let myself go completely. I wanted to feel everything! He then moved me on top of him and Jean it was on! We made love over and over again, right there on the bench. The park was empty so there was no need for us to worry about someone seeing us. He had lifted my dress over my head and I unbuckled his tux pants. I had never experienced that kind of loving. I never felt that even when I was awake with Earl. Earl was too busy loving everybody else. He didn't have time to show me any love or passion. Brad was everything I imagined he would be in bed. I awoke in a hot sweat. The things that guy had done to me weren't real."

"Jean, he had given me such pleasure! Now, do you understand why I can't see him anymore? This guy is messing with my dreams. Can you imagine what he would do to me if it were real? That's why I can't get involved with him. Jean, I believe he's got the power to destroy me! I would not be able to fight him and win! My body refuses to obey me when he's around. I have to cancel our date for lunch."

"No, Beth! Don't cancel your lunch date. If you do that he's going to think you're weak!"

"I am weak, Jean, especially when it comes to him."

"Beth, you have got to do this. Go to lunch and tell him that you're afraid of him."

"I can't do that, Jean! Why not tell him the truth?"

"I know the truth but Brad doesn't have to know."

She had to stay away from him! He called for her at the office but she had instructed Jean to say she wasn't in. Jean hated lying but I begged and she agreed to do it this once. Jean understood that my heart was too weak to take on Brad Walker at this time. Jean kept her word and she told Brad that I had left for the day. Brad called several times hoping I had returned.

I had no intention of ever seeing Brad again! I left work early so Jean wouldn't have to lie about me not being there - I hated asking her to lie for me but I was desperate! I had to clear my head! I drove to Hanes Point. I had to see the place where my dreams had taken me too the night before. I sat there thinking of Brad and how stupid this must seem. The truth is I was falling in love with the man. What was I going to do? How would I deal with these issues of the heart? I tried running and he caught me! What else is there?

After Beth had left the store Brad came by just to make sure she hadn't returned. He seemed worried and said he really needed to talk to her, but Jean had promised not to tell where she

Letting Go

went. She was feeling sorry for the both of them. She could see how much he cared for Beth and she knew Beth was falling in love with him. Why else was she trying to run and hide? What a mess they were in but Jean was sure they would work it out in the end.

Jean called Beth later that night to see if everything was ok and to make sure she had made it back from Hanes Point. "That place isn't safe at night for a single woman, excuse me, married woman," Jean told Beth. She also told her that Brad had stopped by the shop looking for her.

Beth assured her that she was fine and that she had done a lot of soul searching while she was at the park. "Jean, do you remember me telling you about Nina?"

"Yes Beth, I do!"

"I started thinking about our friendship overseas and how I was so needy when I met Greg. You remember Greg, don't you Jean? I told you about him."

"Beth, you told me so many stories!"

"Jean, Nina was the former supermodel for Playboy. She was married to Bill."

"Ok!"

"Jean, please listen carefully so maybe then you will see why I can't get involved with Brad."

"Ok Beth, please tell me once more why you can't get involved with Brad."

I loved telling Jean the story of how my friend Nina helped save me. "She turned me into a beautiful woman inside as well as outside. She showed me how beauty wasn't just skin deep, that beauty came from within. She was beautiful, yes, but she had something else. She had an inner beauty that would outshine any sunny day. People just wanted to be around her. She would show me how to fly even with clipped wings. She gave me the courage to stand up and be counted as an individual rather than just a wife."

Beth thought back to her first trip to Europe and how painful it was and how at some points she wanted to die. Earl had been at his worst in Europe. He would never change. "Jean, I had no friends at all, I was so alone!"

"Go on Beth!"

"I really needed someone to share my broken heart with if I was going to survive. I needed someone to talk too. I always felt isolated from the rest of the world when I lived in Europe. This kind of isolation would leave anyone felling sad, abandoned and unloved, especially if you had a husband like Earl. I guess he figured I was trapped. I made friends with people that I wouldn't ordinarily associate with."

"Then one day I met a person that would change my life forever. That person was Nina. She was wonderful! Nina had been a Playboy model for Hugh Hefner before marrying Bill. She still had the body and the looks. I was attractive but Earl had made me feel old and I was aging before my own eyes. We became instant friends. Nina treated me like her little sister. She showed me how to dress and how to use makeup to enhance my best features and to always dress to impress. I was learning how to appreciate myself for who I was and not what Earl had turned me into. Nina was married to Bill. Bill was a devoted husband. He was always underneath her so to speak! I often thought of him as more of a bodyguard than a husband. He knew he had to stay close to her because guys were standing in line to take his place!"

"Nina would always look for the rainbow in the clouds. Her marriage to Bill was going through turmoil so she needed a friend also. I remembered Nina telling me that one day Bill came home and asked Nina what she thought of having a foursome with another set of their friends. She didn't know what to think or say. She didn't want Bill to think that she wasn't hip but she hated the thought of sleeping with her friends. She asked me for advice. I didn't know what to say. I never knew people did that kind of stuff! I had read about it but that's all. It took me a minute to understand what she was asking. She asked me, would I do it?"

"Jean, you see Bill's friends thought just because she had modeled for Hugh that she was open to anything. She had been pre-judged! Do you follow me so far Jean?"

"Keep going Beth, I follow you!"

Letting Go

I said, "Nina, please don't do it! It will only cause you pain and heart ache! I told her I couldn't take a chance on seeing my husband make love to another woman. It's bad enough that I have to imagine it, but to see it would take me to a new level of pain. Someone would surely leave this green earth. I asked her if Bill had really thought about the affect this would have on their marriage. She said all he wanted was to try new things to keep their marriage exciting. I told her that would end her marriage."

"Later, Nina told me that she and Bill discussed the issue and they decided against it. I was glad because I really didn't want to lose my good friend. Nor did I want to see her in any more pain. I told her that having an open relationship with other couples would tear her and Bill apart. We continued to go out and have fun at the base clubs. The men there were always looking for something more than what they had at home. We were there for fun, nothing else seemed to interest us. We both had marriages that weren't worth the paper it was printed on. I was getting a lot of attention on my own now. Men were taking notice of me, thanks to Nina! I wasn't playing the role of the sweet and innocent housewife any longer."

"Jean, this is when I met Greg. He wasn't looking for anything but a pretty face. It was all because of my looks! That's what I'm worried about with Brad. Maybe he only sees my looks and not what's in my heart."

"Have you shown him what's in your heart, Beth?"

"No, Jean, I haven't!"

"What happened between you and Greg?"

"Well, while Nina and I were hanging out at the club partying and acting like single women Greg came into my life. Greg was soft spoken and over all a very nice guy. I enjoyed listening to him talk. I was at a very lonely place in my life. Needless to say we started talking more and more. We would meet on Friday nights at the club just to be in each other's company. Greg knew I wasn't looking for any long-term romance and neither was he. He was caught up with my looks! I wanted attention and he wanted sex! It was a fair exchange. We met whenever we got a chance. Earl was so occupied with doing his own thing that he never noticed that I was missing from the marriage. Greg stayed on top of things. He knew we were just there for the moment and when the moment was over we both would move on. Our fling lasted two months and was over just like that. No strings attached!"

"Nina wasn't having fun anymore. She was too busy trying to keep tabs on Bill. Bill was out of control and Nina didn't know how to deal with his infidelity. I told her she was talking to the one person that has been there, done that, and moved on, mentally speaking of course. She wanted her husband to settle down and leave the women alone. From the moment she told him no, that the foursome would be nothing more than an organized orgy; he had been different. I had tried to get Nina to go out but she would always say she was waiting for Bill to come home. He started staying away from home for days at a time. I told her that she would have to be the one to make changes in her life if that was what she wanted. She would have to take the first step. Nina left Bill the following week. She never looked back."

Beth hadn't thought about Nina in a long time. Their friendship was so long ago. "I don't think I can walk away from Brad as easily as I walked away from Greg. I never cared for Greg. I guess having feelings for Brad had brought up old memories that weren't that pleasant. Maybe this is my chance to be happy again and I'm just as afraid as Nina was when she left Bill." Beth wanted to leave Earl, but she didn't know exactly how to do it.

Nina had come to her and asked her how you leave someone who wants to stay married just for the sake of being married? She didn't love Bill anymore and she felt he didn't really love her. He was more in love with the way she looked.

"I will never get involved with another man while I'm still legally married to Earl. I know Earl is not much of a husband but we are still bound by the law."

"Beth, you need to take your time and learn to love yourself, you have scars deeper than anyone I've ever seen. Earl will leave you soon, you mark my words!"

"Thanks, Jean! That's what I'm hoping for!" I never told Jean that Earl was trying to sleep with one of our friends and I

Letting Go

still had to hang in there because I couldn't afford to leave him. Earl had so many lovers that whenever he would end one relationship he would come running back to me, trying to make things right between us, but I couldn't forgive him or forget what he was doing. My only concern was finding a way to support myself. This was going to be a new beginning. I had to break loose from this man! I tried to lose myself in my work. My only hope was that no one knew the shame I was feeling. I had asked Jean one day at work; "Does everyone in the office know what kind of husband I have?"

"Beth, where did that question come from?"

"Jean, I need to know! What do they say about Earl?"

"Well Beth, to be totally honest, we try not to discuss Earl. We all just hope you can get out in one piece. Everyone wants to see you happy, that's all."

Deep down, I felt that people knew my husband was no good; that he never even tried to hide the fact that he didn't love me. I was always able to look in his face and tell when he was cheating. I told Jean our marriage had gotten so bad that I was wishing and hoping that he would leave to take out trash and never come back.

"Beth, I know you're scared about Brad, but I've seen the way he looks at you and I truly believe he feels something for you."

"I know, Jean, but I refuse to get caught up in a married man. There's just no future!"

Beth was feeling scared about her feelings for Brad. She knew he was trouble from the moment she laid eyes on him. He was the only person she had ever been afraid of. He had the power to totally disarm the safeguards she had planted around her heart and that frightened her. She was lonely and needed someone, but she didn't want someone else's husband. She would have to pass on Brad Walker. The only question was, would he be willing to pass on her?

Charles was so excited! He knew it was just a matter of time before he and Jean were back together again. Charles had left Jean around noon. She had been on the phone with Beth most of the morning. Charles was happy Jean had friends like Beth. She had helped her a lot. Charles realized he hadn't thought about Amy in the last twenty-four hours. He was beginning to get his life back on track. Charles often asked himself how did he get so lost? He had gambled and thrown away his entire life.

There were loves, and there were great loves. Jean was a great love. He would never hurt her again. He had promised himself that he would never let her spend another night out of his arms. She had fallen asleep in his arms and Charles had remembered how good it felt having her close again. They were going to discuss adoptions later today and look into the process. He smiled at the idea of having kids and realized he did not have to sacrifice his wife to have them. He would have them both. He felt like such a fool to have given it all up for a woman he barely knew. He would start moving his things back in as soon as Jean gave him the ok. They had already wasted too much time apart.

Charles hadn't tried to call Amy or see her. He had given his word that he would let her go. He only wished the best for her. He thought he was in love with her, but right now he wasn't so sure. She had hurt him deeply when she had set him free. Charles wanted nothing else but his life to get back to normal. Jean held the key to his heart. He had given Amy a chance and it had failed terribly. He would never gamble on love again.

Brian's Test Result

Brian had waited for what seemed like a lifetime on the phone. He had to have those results ASAP! He would continue to hold until someone came back on the line. He would know tonight.

Finally, the soft voice came back on the line, "I'm sorry sir, it's just that we are so busy and all. I hope I didn't keep you waiting too long. I've got your test results right here. We don't usually do this on the phone, because of the Privacy Act, and I have no way of identifying who you are; it's just you seem so desperate."

"Yes Ma'am! You're correct. I'm very desperate. My whole life will change once I get those results."

"I'm sorry you had to go through this entire waiting process sir."

Brian closed his eyes and prayed like he never prayed before. He did not want to die, nor did he want to lose Ken.

"I'm sorry sir, did you hear me?"

Just as she gave Brian the results his phone beeped. He had another call from a telemarketing company. Brian fumbled with the phone. "Hold on Ma'am!" He got them off the line. "Ma'am! Ma'am! What were the results? I'm sorry, my phone was beeping!"

"They are negative, Mr. Davis. Sir, can you hear me?"

"Yes, Ma'am, I can hear you! You did say negative, didn't you?"

"Yes I did."

"Thank you Ma'am! Thank you! I love you! Thank you!"

"You're welcome sir!"

Brian couldn't wait to tell Ken! He said, "I will never, ever have unprotected sex again!" Brian wasn't sure who he was saying it too; he just knew he had to say it out loud.

Brian ran and jumped in his car, tears of joy streaming down his face! He had been given a second chance and he would not blow it. He had to find Ken right away. Ken had to know the good news, that he had tested negative. They could still be together and live out their dreams.

Ken had to pull himself together. He needed to get out of here, the walls were closing in on him. He explained to Amy that he would talk to her as soon as he got back. They had some important issues to discuss when he returned. Ken just had to think things out.

He drove to the Washington Memorial Bridge, parked the truck, got out and started walking around. He needed to clear his head. Ken knew he had made some mistakes. He had been with Brian for the last two years. He would have to deal with Brian later. How could Amy and his parents accept what he had done? He remembered the first time he had met Brian; he was such a man he had been jealous of him. There was no way for him to know he was gay. Ken went back to the first time they made love and his heart began to break all over again. That was the moment he knew for sure he was gay. He had accepted his fate and was ready to run away to Japan with the man he loved. He was so tired of living this way. He wanted to feel the way Brian made him feel all the time. Brian made him feel alive, special, and most of all, loved. Brian had completed his life! Ken was sure of one thing. Even if they never discussed their feelings he knew Brian loved him without a doubt. But all that had changed! There was this cloud hanging over his head that wouldn't go away. It was a constant reminder of what he had done. He knew Amy felt bad for cheating on him but at least she wasn't ashamed of what she had done.

Ken was ashamed of what he had done! Ken had betrayed his parents. He would never be able to hold his face up in church again. Once the word got out they would be the talk of the town. There was no way to prevent this from happening. Tomorrow Amy would get her test result back and discover she had tested positive for the Aids virus. How can I live with the guilt of what I've done? Ken's mind was racing. He did not want to live. What was there to live for? He had destroyed the mother of his children. Everyone was against gay men these days. They were blamed for everything including the Aids virus. Ken knew he

Letting Go

would never be able to live with Brian in the open. Ken would forgive Brian for what he had done to him. About his family he didn't know. Everything seemed to be making sense now. Brian loved him and tried to protect him, that was why he didn't tell him right away. Ken was sitting on the ground in the park under a tree. He had taken a note pad out of the truck. He had to write Brian and tell him just what he meant to him. Brian would blame himself for everything, but Ken wouldn't let that happen. Ken was in such a state that the only way out of this mess was to end his life! He would leave Amy a letter telling her that he loved her. She was a wonderful mother to his children and he tried to respect that. What he shared with Brian was bigger than the both of them.

Ken thought long and hard about the sin he had already committed with Brian. There was no sin greater than that. When he decided to leave this world it would be with his dignity and self-respect. He needed that! He would ask God for forgiveness for what he was about to do. Ken knew God was merciful and he had prayed that God would have mercy on his soul. He was sorry for what he had done. He knew taking his life wasn't the answer, but what was? There were so many people involved that would feel the pain of his actions he would never be able to face them. He wasn't worried about Amy; he knew God was watching over her and his kids! Ken started a letter to Brian:

My Dearest Love, Brian,

I know you would say I'm a coward for taking the easy way out for not waiting around for you to help me through this the same way you helped your last lover, but I'm not that strong. I think of you at night when I lay down to sleep and when I awaken first thing in the morning you're on my mind. I thank God for your friendship and love! I've always been able to be myself around you. You never judged me for being who I am and for that I will always love you. I know we made promises to each other and I'm sorry I won't be there to keep mine. I want you to know the last few months have been the happiest days of my life! Planning a future with you and living ones dreams should never be thought of as wasted time. If I could stay here on this earth without you I would cease to exist. I belong to you Brian, and I always will, even in death. My heart is complete because of what we shared in those short years as friends and lovers. I leave this earth a better person for knowing you. Thank you Brian, for letting me share in your world! I love you now and forever. You see I have never been good at saying goodbye.

Tears were running down Ken's face, he could barely see.

Please, you have to understand the life I've led all these years was a life I was living as half a man. Only after I met you Brian, was I complete. Brian, I know you didn't mean to hurt me and that you wanted us to be together forever. I guess it wasn't meant to be. I never told you that I loved you because I felt that would show a sign of weakness but I love you more than words can express. I should have told you! The happiest days of my life were with you! I loved Amy also but not the way I loved you. It's important that you know this. I don't want you to blame yourself for any of this. It's all about me and my weakness as a man! I will see you on the other side.
Love, Ken

He was crying so hard he had to put his hands to his mouth to muffle his cries.

Brian was rushing to get to Ken's house and tell him the good news. Even if Ken didn't want to be lovers they could be friends. He would accept anything Ken offered him at this point. He just wanted to be around him. That would be good enough for him he was hoping that one day Ken would forgive him and they could pick up where they left off. But right now he knew it was too soon to expect anything except anger from Ken.

Brian reached the house in record time. He practically ran to the door. He didn't see Ken's car but it could be parked around back. Ken would soon know the truth. Amy answered the door. It was getting late. She had just returned from dropping the kids off at her parents. Ken had promised that they would talk when he got back. She didn't want the kids to wake up while they were

Letting Go

talking. They needed time to fix whatever the problem was. Her parents would keep them a few days.

"Hello Brian. Is everything alright?"

"Yes Amy, it couldn't be better! Amy is Ken here?"

"No Brian, he said he would be right back. Brian, do you know what has happened to Ken? Something is terribly wrong. Please Brian, come on in if you want to wait on him. He said he would be right back."

"I'm sorry for barging in like this Amy. I just really need to speak to Ken right away! I have some information from the office that can't wait until tomorrow and I know he will be glad to hear it."

"I don't know Brian, he's upset about something and he wouldn't talk to me. I tried to get him to let me help but he said I wouldn't understand. At first, I thought it was because of my relationship with Charles but he said it wasn't. Brian, are you sure you have no idea of what's going on?"

"I'm sorry, Amy; I wish I could help you. Amy, Ken didn't say anything about what was bothering him?"

"No, he didn't. It scared me really bad. I thought he was worried because of my pregnancy and not knowing who the father is, but he said that wasn't it."

Brian was trying to think of where Ken might have gone. "Amy, he never said where he was going?"

"No Brian, he was so upset when he got back from the office. I'm not sure what happened. He just said he would talk to me when he got back. Whatever it is, it's causing him a lot of pain. I've never seen my husband so upset. He said he was going to get some fresh air. That doesn't even sound like Ken. I'm really worried Brian. I've tried calling him on his cell. Why don't you try and see if you can get him to answer? Maybe you can help him with whatever he's going through. He wouldn't confide in me! Maybe he will open up to you. Please try Brian."

Brian called Ken's cell and let the phone ring several times. He was just about to hang up when Ken's soft voice came on the line and said "Hello."

"Hey Ken, it's me, Brian. Where are you man? We need to talk. Can you meet me at the office in fifteen minutes? We need to go over some important papers before tomorrow's meeting."

"Sure Brian, I'll be there in fifteen minutes."

"Hey man, are you ok? Amy was a little worried about you."

"Tell her I'm fine and that I'll be home as soon as we finish at the office."

"He will be right home Amy! I promise I'll see if I can find out what's bothering him and make sure he's ok before I let him go."

"Thanks Brian, you're such a wonderful friend. Ken and I are so lucky to have you."

Brian was so happy no one would be in the office at this time of night. They would be able to talk. Ken sounded so sad. Brian wanted to yell into the phone that his test was negative but Amy was staring him straight in the face. It wasn't his job to tell her about him and her husband. He would leave that for Ken to do.

Brian drove to the office. It was only ten minutes from where they lived. He would get there and wait on Ken. Amy had mentioned something about orders for Japan. Had Ken told her he was going to Japan? Was he planning on taking her along with them? This was news to him. He would straighten things out when they got together.

Ken Breaks Down

Ken had no intention of leaving the spot where he had parked. He wanted this to be over soon before he lost his courage. He had written Brian's letter; now he would write one to Amy, the mother of his children. He was glad he had answered the phone. He had missed hearing Brian's voice! He had heard the desperation in his voice; he was worried about him! He knew Brian was going to be lost but right now he had to stop the pain. He would never be able to live with himself. Ken started Amy's letter.

My Dearest wife,
I've loved you from day one! You were the part of me that made living the life I had chosen to live bearable. I will always be thankful to you for that. I know if you're reading this my plan did not fail. I want you to know that what I've done has nothing to do with you. Please don't blame Brian for any of this. I lived a complete life with him for the last two years. I have never been happier than when I was with him. I want you to find Charles if it's not too late for you two. Make a life together and raise that baby and continue to raise my girls. I wasn't jealous of you and him, I was jealous of the fact that you were able to walk around unashamed of your life and I had to hide my love for Brian in a closet. So please live, love, and be happy. Please try and explain things to the girls in a manner they will understand. I will always love you Amy! Goodbye!
Ken
PS! Please talk to Brian about getting tested for the Aids virus.

Ken knew that Brian would try and find him and stop him if he was given the chance. He couldn't let that happen. His time here was running short. Ken had an old pistol his father had given him soon after he and Amy got married. He said it was for protection but after the girls were born he didn't want to keep a gun in the house so he kept it locked in the truck glove compartment. He had written his letters explaining to Amy and Brian why he had to end his life. The thought of living without Brian wasn't an option even if he didn't have the Aids virus. He would never agree to live without Brian in his life. The price was just too high. He had slept with Brian for the last two years. He had lived the life he was born to live. Ken had instructed Amy to be tested for the Aids virus. But he was pretty sure she would test positive. He was sorry for the pain he had caused everyone. Amy should also look into having the kids signed over to her parents if she should test positive. This is what the doctors were trying to tell her. They wanted a second test to be sure. Ken was so sure of this already he didn't need a doctor to tell him his result.

Ken knew he had failed her as a husband. He was ashamed of what he had done. Being gay was a way of life; it was the only time he had ever felt totally free. The only problem was that it would cost him his life. Ken thought back and all he could remember was that he never wanted to get married and he never wanted kids. He knew he was gay as a child. From the moment he was old enough to know the difference between the sexes he knew he was not going to be normal, that he would not like girls! He had special feelings for boys that he kept hid deep inside of him until he met Brian. Brian had brought him to life! Please, I pray that no one will think Brian made me gay. I was born this way and I will die this way. The only thing Brian did was help me face who I really am, and I thank him for that. Ken knew he was going to a better place where he wouldn't have to be ashamed of who he was. There would be no judgment. I will continue to love you Brian in death as I loved you in life. I hold no one responsible for what I'm about to do!

Ken took the gun out of the glove compartment and checked it to make sure it was loaded. He knew he only had one chance to get this right. He would not be given another. The area was deserted this time of night. His body would not be discovered until morning, or later when the park police made their rounds.

Letting Go

He was sorry. Ken said a soft prayer and placed the gun to his temple and said, "God forgive me!" Just as he was about to pull the trigger he heard someone coming his way. He would have to wait just a little longer before he could complete his mission. He waited until the sound faded into the distance.

Ken's body was draped over the dashboard on the passenger side of his truck. His mission was complete. He only needed one chance. Ken had left everyone he loved behind to mourn his passing.

Brian was at the office waiting on Ken. He had tried Ken's cell and there was no answer. He called Amy back at the house to see if he had stopped by the house first. Brain needed to talk to Ken ASAP. Brian knew he was upset but everything would be just fine once they talked. He wanted to make the pain go away. He realized he had hurt Ken by not telling him about his friend Shane, but there just never seemed to be a right time. Brian was starting to worry. Ken hadn't gone by the house. He had called there also. Brian remembered that Ken didn't have his keys to their place anymore he wouldn't be able to get in. Brian needed to head back home. Ken might drop by. Brian walked into his house and the memories hit him; Ken had spent so many nights at his place. He had practically moved in. He had as many clothes here as he did at home. Brian sat down to rest his heart and mind. He was on overload. He would wait up for Ken to call him back. He would make one final check with Amy.

He called her to see if Ken had showed up yet. Amy said she would call the minute he walked in.

"Brian!"

"Yes, Amy?"

"Do you think Ken has run off and left me because I cheated on him with a black man?"

"No, I don't, Amy. I think he may have gone somewhere and got drunk and was too wasted to drive home. He will be home as soon as he wakes up. You'll see."

"I hope you're right Brian. I'm scared. You didn't see him when he left here earlier today. He was so messed up he was crying and in a lot of pain. I couldn't seem to help him! It was as if his whole world had come crashing down around him! I asked him if it was Charles and he said no. I wish you could have been here. You would have known what to do."

Amy was crying now and Brian wished that he could have spared her this pain. "Amy, please stop crying. Ken is fine. It's not your fault he's gone; he just needed space. Everyone deals with things in their lives so differently. He may be one of those that get drunk and sleep it off." Brian knew he was lying but he needed to make her feel better. "But he knows you love him very much, and he loves you Amy. We all make mistakes sometimes. That's what makes us human and keeps us humble. Please get some rest and he will be home soon."

"I wish you were here Brian."

"I'll see you guys first thing in the morning. Amy, please call me when he comes in no matter what time of night it is. I just want to know he's ok! Will you please do that for me?"

"Yes, Brian, I'll call you."

The ringing in the background was getting louder and louder. Brian had no idea where the noise was coming from until he was fully awake and realized his phone was ringing. "Where have you been, Brian? I fell asleep. Amy? What's going on?"

"Ken didn't come home last night, Brian! I called the police station around 2:00 am and they said he would have to be missing for twenty-four hours before they get involved or put a missing report out on him. They did say they would keep an eye out for his truck. Brian, they called this morning. They said they found his truck! That's all they would tell me on the phone. I have to go down to the police station and identify the truck. Brian I'm really scared! Where is Ken, Brian, and why didn't he call if he was in jail?"

"Amy, I will pick you up in fifteen minutes or less."

"No Brian, I need to leave right now!"

"Where are the girls Amy?"

"They're at my parents. I called my dad and he's meeting me there also."

"Amy, stay put and I'll be right there!"

"Ok Brian! I'll wait for you but please hurry!"

Amy was frantic. Where had her husband been all night? Why didn't he call me?

Letting Go

Brian was speeding towards Amy's home. He would pick her up and they would go and bail Ken out of jail. Brian drove faster than he thought possible. He pulled up to Amy's home and she was sitting on the steps waiting.

"Brian, why hasn't Ken called me?"

"I don't know Amy, but we will have our questions answered shortly."

They drove the five miles to the sheriffs department and walked into the station. "We're here to bail out Mr. Anderson. I'm Brian Davis and this is Mr. Anderson's wife Amy. Can we please see him officer?"

Amy's father was just walking through the door. "Hi, sweetie," he said to Amy as he came up to her. "Where is he?"

"I don't know. They're going to get the Captain, apparently he's the one on the case."

The captain asked if he could speak to the family only, meaning Amy and her father. "No," Amy said. "Brian is a part of our family. What's going on sir? Where is my husband?"

"There's been an accident, or what looks like an accident, it's really too soon to tell."

"What do you mean accident?" Amy's father was asking the questions now. "Has he been hurt? Is he in the hospital? What hospital?"

"He's not in the hospital. Please, I will try and explain everything as clearly as I can. Please, let's have a seat in the waiting room."

Amy went into Brian's arms crying. "What has happened to Ken? Where is he, Brian? Why won't they tell us something?" Amy was not able to face this alone. She was glad her father and Brian were there. They took a seat. He motioned for the officer to leave the room. Amy was getting more agitated by the second. "What's going on? I want to know right now where my husband is!" She used the strongest voice she could muster.

"I'm sorry to tell you this ma'am, but your husband committed suicide last night around midnight."

Amy said, "No sir, you got the wrong man. My husband would never do something like that!"

"Ma'am, he left you a letter and one for someone named Brian. He left a note explaining why he has done the things he did."

"I don't believe you. I want to see my husband right now. Brian, tell this man that Ken would never hurt himself."

Brian was taken aback. He tried to maintain his composure. Brian's mind was racing! "Sir, what makes you think it is Ken Anderson?"

"The note states it, plus the registration was in the vehicle."

"What happened officer?"

"He shot his brains out in the front seat of his SUV. We are still searching for the gun. Someone may have picked it up. Probably some kids, I'm sure it will turn up."

"Why would he do that Brian?"

"Dad, you know Ken would never kill himself."

"Amy, please try and calm down honey. You're pregnant; think of the baby!"

"But daddy, Ken's gone!"

"I know baby! I know!"

Brian was in shock!

"Brian, why would Ken kill himself? What made him do it?"

The officers handed them each a letter. Amy was crying too hard to read hers so her father took it. Amy reached for it. She wanted to read it herself. "Can you handle this sweetheart?"

"Yes, daddy, I have to know what was so bad that my husband had to kill himself." She noticed it was Ken's handwriting and she began to sob uncontrollably. She would have to take it easy, for the sake of the baby. She tried to read the letter between tears and she made out the first sentence.

"My Dearest wife! I loved you from the moment we met you were the part of me that made living the life I had chosen to live bearable. I will always be thankful to you. Amy, please remember that!"

"Brian, what is he talking about?" It wasn't making any sense to her. She knew he loved her. Amy read the rest and she looked at Brian who was busy reading the last words he would ever get from Ken. "Brian, what does Ken mean about me calling my doctor?" Her father was standing next to his daughter

Letting Go

to give her support. He noticed that she looked as if she could pass out at any moment. "What does Ken mean by Aids? What do you have to do with this Brian? Why is he asking me to get tested? Did Ken have Aids Brian?"

"No Amy, he didn't have Aids."

"I received a call from Dr. Gray before I left to come here today. My tests are fine! The doctor was concerned that my sugar level was high because my other test had gotten contaminated in the lab. That's what he was trying to tell us. He didn't want to make a big deal out of it because he had hired a new lab technician and he didn't want to draw to much attention to her. Why did Ken think he had Aids Brian? Please tell me what's going on. Why is Ken asking me for forgiveness? What has he done that he needed forgiveness? Why is he telling me not to blame you Brian?"

"Honey, this can all wait until later!"

"No, dad, I need answers now!" Amy continued to read the letter. "It says you and Ken have been lovers for the last two years! Is that true, Brian? That you saved him! How could you save him and he's dead now? How Brian? Please tell me!" She was delirious now with pain. Her father wanted her to sit but she was in Brian's face looking for answers that she felt only he had. "Brian, please explain to me what has been going on between you and my husband."

"Amy, I know this will be hard to understand but Ken and I weren't just best friends. We have been lovers for the last two years."

Amy slapped him before she knew it. Her father held her back. "Brian, how could you?"

"Ken discovered who he was, that he had been living a lie all these years."

Amy let the letter fall to the floor. She wiped the tears from her eyes. Brian picked up the letter and gave it to her father.

"Why has Ken done this? He could have talked to me! I would have understood!" She wasn't asking anyone to answer; she just had to put the question out there.

"Ken was worried that he had given you the virus. That was his main reason for not wanting to live. I can only blame myself for that Amy."

Amy asked Brian, "Were you in love with my husband?"

He hung his head to hide the tears he had been holding back from the moment he found out Ken was gone. He nodded his head to Amy that, yes, they were in love. Brian was crying for the second lost love of his life. How much more was a man supposed to bear? Brian held his head up. "Yes, Amy, we were going to tell you after our last trip to New York, right after Valentines Day, but you told him you were pregnant and everything changed. He didn't want you to know about us until we had left the States. He stilled loved you, that was no secret. I'm sorry Amy, Ken and I didn't want to hurt anyone. We never meant for you to find out."

Amy kept her head down. She couldn't believe what she had read and heard. Her husband was dead. What would become of her and her kids? Amy asked Brian to explain again exactly why Ken decided to kill himself; she had to be missing something. It just seemed too stupid to think a smart man like her husband would kill himself without the facts. Brian went into the spiel about Ken thinking he had the aids virus and had passed it on to her. Amy had been standing close to Brian for she was having a hard time focusing on what he was saying. "Why didn't you and Ken use protection Brian?"

"It was just that once Amy!"

"Once is all it takes! What on earth were you two thinking about! Look what you've done Brian!"

"Amy, please calm down. I tried to tell him that my test came back negative but it was too late. I never had a chance to talk to him except those few minutes when he answered his cell and said he was going to meet me at the office. He had no intentions of meeting me!"

"You think, Brian! Brian how could you be so careless with other people lives?"

"I'm so sorry Amy. If I had a chance to do things all over again I would do them differently. This wasn't supposed to happen. Ken and I were going to move away together to Japan!

We had accepted a job there and would leave the end of this month."

"I invite you into our lives and family and this is the thanks I get! You take my husband away from me and his kids. I will never forgive you for this Brian for what you have done is unforgivable. Brian, from this moment on you're as dead as my husband! Stay away from my family and me!"

Brian knew it would be hard for Amy to understand that he truly loved Ken and that Ken was his future. She thought the pain of her loss was much greater than his, but if she only knew how much he loved him then she would understand his pain also. Brian would never be able to understand Ken's reasoning for his action.

Amy had to call Ken's parents and let them know that their only child was dead. How could she make them understand how useless his death was and that he took his own life? Amy knew she would never be able to tell them the whole story. She would have to tell them that he had just been depressed. They would have to live with that. Only she and Brian and her father would ever know the truth.

When Amy left the police department she was driven to the morgue where she had to identify Ken's body. She wasn't able to do this alone; her father would have to make the ID. Her father was glad she had asked him to come with her. She was going through a lot of pain and there was nothing he could do but be there for her support. She had explained all the missing pieces of the puzzle to him on the drive to the morgue. It was up to him to tell her mother. She never wanted to discuss it again.

Amy had no clue as to the condition of Ken's body. All she knew was he had shot himself in the head. The details were not clear. The policeman had said he blew his brains out. What does that really mean? Is his head missing? Her father was only concerned with the health of his daughter. He did not want her to go in there and see Ken. He knew this was taking a toll on her and that she would soon break down. He needed to get her home to her mother before the reality of it all hit her! Her mother would know what to do. Her father did not want Amy to see the body but Amy refused to let him go alone. She needed to see for herself! The officer was ready to take them in. Amy stood outside the morgue door thinking of how fast her life had changed. One minute she was discussing moving to Japan and the next she's identifying her husband's body. Amy walked over to the table where Ken's body laid draped with a sheet. My how small he seemed; she never realized he was that thin.

The morgue attendant gave them plenty of space to move around to the end of the table. The officer was waiting for Amy to say the words. She almost lost her balance once but her father was there holding onto her arm. She was glad she had called him. She needed him to help her through this. The policeman lifted the sheet and Amy saw Ken's framed profile. She was facing him on his right side which was the side that was still intact. She wanted to see his face. She had to face him once more to ask him why? Why did he do this to them? Amy's father tried to pull her away, but she refused to leave. "No, dad, I have to see what he has done to himself."

"Amy, this is crazy! It's Ken. We need to leave now sweetie! He's gone to a better place!"

"No dad. I have to see all of him!" She asked the mortician to move the sheet back so she could see his entire face. The mortician looked to her father as if asking for permission to move the sheet. Her father motioned for him to do so. Amy stood there with her hands to her mouth; the tears had started falling the moment she walked into the room. Amy let out a loud scream that rocked her father's soul. She was crying harder than she thought possible! She was yelling, "Ken, please get up! You can't leave me! What about the baby? Please Ken, get up! What am I to going to do without you?"

The tears were running down her father's face. Why did this have to happen to his baby? Her dad led her out the door. He would have to get her home fast and call the doctor. Amy cried all the way home; she was limp from weakness. Her father had called her mother and told her that Ken was dead.

She was having a hard time with the kids, they had been asking for their mother and father all morning. What would Amy tell her kids? Her mother was trying not to show the tears from

Letting Go

her crying when Amy and her father pulled up. Amy ran into her mother's arms and collapsed.

Amy's father gave his wife as much information as he had. There were still a lot of unanswered questions but there would be plenty of time for answers later. He only wanted to help his daughter get through this tragedy. The doctor came by the house and gave Amy a sedative that was mild enough for her condition. He said she needed a lot of rest and not to wake her and let the sedative wear off. Amy slept through most of the day. When she awakened the sun was going down. Her mother was at her side. "Mom, he's gone and I'm alone. He left me, mom, with the kids!"

"I know baby, but you will be just fine. You have us and we will never leave you."

Amy closed her eyes and let the tears fall. She was still very weak. She needed to see her kids. She would have to pull her strength from them.

Amy explained as little as possible to the kids. They were just old enough to understand that when you die you go to heaven and you're never sad again. This is how Amy explained it to the girls. She said daddy had to go away for a long time. He's in heaven right now, he was a little sad but now he's happy because he's with God. She kissed them both on the forehead as their grandfather took them away and answered the many questions they had about their daddy. Amy was so happy to have her family so close. She would have been lost without them. She needed to make some decisions about the funeral and Ken's truck. She never wanted to see it again! Right now all she wanted to do was sleep. Amy's mom told her that her father had called Ken's parents and they would make the arrangements for the funeral. "Thanks mom! Tell dad I love him!" With that Amy reached over and kissed her mother on the cheeks and said, "I love you too mom!"

Her mother knew this was the one thing she would never be able to protect her baby from. Death was something we faced head on and most of the time it was unexpected. But her daughter would fight and win because she had too much to live for. "We love you too, sweetie," her mother replied.

With that Amy rested her head in her mother's lap and fell sound asleep.

The Funeral

Amy fell into a bad dream and needed to wakeup; someone was trying to hurt Ken! She was screaming for them to stop! Her mother had to shake her to wake her.

"Sweetheart, you were dreaming."

Amy wasn't sure what was happening. "I was dreaming that Ken was alive and someone was beating him and I was screaming for them to stop."

"I know, honey. You were having a nightmare."

Amy needed to get out and get some fresh air. Ken was haunting her. She would go by her house for a change of clothing for her and the girls. She had slept in the guest room with her mother. She dreaded walking through the doors of her home and facing Ken's ghost. She had showered and was ready to leave. She asked her mother if the kids could spend a few more days with them. She would be back tonight. She wasn't ready to get back into her bed just yet. She needed time to adjust to being alone. Amy had started to replace hurt with anger. Ken had left her "holding the bag" so to speak; he went off and killed himself so he wouldn't have to face being gay.

Why did he stay married to her for so long? Why didn't he let her go? There was no reasoning behind what he had done! She would not let this destroy her life; she had to think of the girls and her unborn child. At that very moment Amy thought of Charles. She would have to call him and tell him before he reads about it or sees it on the news.

The phone rang and Charles knew it would be Jean; they had such a wonderful time last night that he was sure they would be back together soon. It was just a matter of time. He had made a bad mistake but he would fix everything. He would let nothing and no one stand in his way.

Charles answered the phone with a smile, "Hello, my love!"

"Hello, Charles."

"Oh. Hello Amy, I thought you were someone else. How are you?"

"I'm fine, how are you? I just wanted to tell you about Ken before you read about it or saw it on the news."

"Tell me what?"

"Ken killed himself last night!"

Charles was in disbelief. "I'm so sorry, Amy!" He really didn't know what to say. "How are you and the girls holding up?"

"We're doing the best we can."

"What happened, Amy?"

"He just wasn't happy."

"Was it about our affair and your being pregnant with what could be my child that led him to do such a horrible thing?"

"No, Charles, it didn't have anything to do with us. Ken was suffering from depression. He hadn't confided in anyone. He was all alone Charles. He couldn't even talk to me about his life."

Charles felt really bad for her, but what could he do? He would not be able to help her. She would have to go through this alone. "Please Amy, call me if there's anything I can do, and please don't hesitate. I'll be there for you and the girls as a friend if you need me."

"Thanks Charles, I'll keep that in mind." Amy hadn't thought about Charles in a while. She had made Ken a promise and she had stuck to her promise. She would have to do this alone.

Charles wasn't sure if he should tell Jean about Amy's husband's death. Jean would be worried that they may start talking again. After all, she's no longer married but Charles would keep his distance. Amy needed time to heal and he wanted his wife back. He would do the right thing and stay away from Amy. Charles decided to call Jean later in the day. They were scheduled to have dinner together. He was so excited he remembered how Jean had looked at the Ball. She wasn't the woman I married. She was sexy and desirable and had plenty of confidence. Charles didn't recognize the new Jean.

Letting Go

Jean was in the middle of dressing when the phone rang. It was Charles. "What's on the menu for tonight?" he asked, smiling into the phone.

"Not me," Jean replied with a short laugh. "I was hoping you would call, what's going on?"

"Not much."

"I was just going through a few things, trying to find something to wear tonight. Where are we going tonight Charles?"

"That's a secret, you'll just have to wait and see."

She loved playing these kinds of games it reminded her of the Charles she had married. Jean still wasn't sure if she would ever trust him again. She would not rush things. She had too much at stake here.

Just before Charles was scheduled to arrive Jean called Beth to see if she had heard from Brad. Beth said they had a date. She was considering calling it off but she didn't have a way of reaching him. She was hoping that Brad would forget to call. Beth had decided that they would not go any further than they had the other night. She would call it off after tonight. She had made herself a promise. "Where are you guys going?"

"Charles won't say; it's a surprise!"

"What will you be wearing?"

"I have no clue."

"Well if you need help just let me know, I'll come over and give you a hand."

"Thanks, Beth, but I've got this well under control."

Jean had to stay focused. Charles had hurt her really bad. She has to remember he couldn't be trusted! What about his possible baby? What would he do if it's his baby? There were a lot of ifs in her life and Jean didn't like not knowing. She would have to get some answers first before she committed to anything.

Charles was ready to get back with Jean; he had planned to discuss adoption tonight. He knew just how much kids meant to her. He would do what ever it took to get her back but was he sure he wanted Jean? Yes! He was sure! Charles' mind wandered back to Amy. He had seen Ken on the news. A man was found dead in his truck. They said the cause was an apparent suicide.

"Follow-up on the late night news!" He was not sure what worried him most of all. Was it the baby that Amy was carrying or was it Amy being alone? He had to stay focused on Jean. Amy was out of his life now. He would not hurt Jean again; he had made her a promise.

Amy had to get things together for the funeral. She called Ken's parents about the funeral arrangements. She had several black suits that Ken looked really good in. She would bring one by the house for Ken to be buried in. The kids would need dresses. She would have to find a black maternity dress for herself. She had begun to show. She missed Ken so much. He had left so many things incomplete; their marriage for instance. She had been ready to walk away from all of it but what would she do now? He was gone! How would she piece everything back together and go on?

Ken's funeral was set for Saturday at 2:00 pm. She would meet Ken's family at their home and ride in the limo with the family. Her parents would be close by; that would give Amy the added strength she needed to get through the day. The funeral was one of the saddest days of her life. She had noticed Brian once or twice. He had been crying. She never understood why he turned to Brian. Ken had found something in Brian that he couldn't get from her and that was completeness. Brian gave of himself and never asked for anything in return whereas she was needy and gave him as little as possible of herself.

Ken wrote in his letter that I shouldn't blame anyone, especially Brian; that Brian completed him. That these last few years were the happiest he's ever been! That he had never been happier than when he was with Brian. Amy had noticed the change in Ken but she figured it was his new assignments. She had no way of knowing he was in love. She was in love herself. She wasn't wasting any time worrying about Ken. Now it all made sense! It was because of Brian. He had changed her husband's life and made him happy. She felt sorry for Brian because he had no one to help him through this. He had told them that he hadn't spoken to his parents in years; some misunderstanding they had. She had her parents and the girls. Brian was totally alone.

Letting Go

Brian saw the pain that he was responsible for in Amy's eyes. He was sorry for that only. He was not sorry for loving Ken! He missed him so much! This was his chance to say goodbye. They never stood a chance. They were doomed before they even met. Brian realized he never told Ken just how much he meant to him. That he was the reason he got up in the morning and that he gave him the strength to take his next breath. One day they would be together again but until then, rest my love, your work here is complete. Brian laid a white rose which showed signs of purity on Ken's casket. He touched two fingers to his lips and placed them on Ken's coffin. He then turned and walked away. He would one day let Amy read the letter Ken wrote to him before his death. But for now they both needed to grieve their loss.

Amy knew she would have to pick up the pieces and move on. She would start by moving out of the company home she had shared with Ken. She would need help with that. Amy called Charles to see if he knew of any homes that were available near the school and that were affordable. They still worked in the same office, but Charles had requested a transfer to another office outside the branch. He told Amy that he couldn't think of any place at this time, but he would look into it for her and call her later if he came up with anything. Charles explained to Amy that he was trying to work things out with Jean and he didn't think it was a good idea for her to be calling him. Amy offered her congratulations to Charles and wished him the best. She apologized for calling but he had said that if she needed anything to please feel free to call. She wished him the best and said goodbye.

Charles knew he had handled that poorly but he wasn't expecting her to be on the line. He had gotten confused after hearing her voice. She still had the power to bring him to his knees. Charles would have to get his phone number changed. He couldn't have Amy calling him whenever she felt like it. She had made her choice long before Ken died. She would have to live with the choice she made. Charles knew he would have to concentrate hard on Jean. He had plans for dinner with Jean. He liked taking her to special places.

She was wearing a red halter dress that looked stunning on her; it showed off her slender shoulders that he had never noticed before.

He admired her. Even with all the hard times she never was nasty or tried to hurt him. She was truly a lady to have in your life and he was glad he had her in his.

They drove over to Alexandria to the Skyline Tower. It was one of her favorite places. Jean had been there once before with Charles. They had danced for hours and had gone upstairs and made passionate love before returning home the next day. Would that be Charles's plans for them tonight? She could only wish. She had enjoyed making love to Charles these last few weeks.

She had never felt such passion. Jean knew it was her new attitude that was behind her new life. She had refused to let Charles destroy her. Charles ordered all her favorite foods and she ate with much energy. She was ready to enjoy the night whatever it turned out to be. Tonight it would be all about her and Charles. She would not let memories destroy any of it. She finished her meal in record time and was ready to dance. Charles must have read her mind. He led her to the dance floor where they danced for hours. Charles had Jean in his arms again; he couldn't remember the last time he had so much fun. They laughed, talked and made plans for the next few weeks. They would fly to Orlando and settle the property they were selling. But tonight they would go upstairs and relive moments that had been lost to them so long ago.

Charles was so tender. Jean had forgotten how beautiful his body truly was. She felt desire building up in her as she watched him undress. She realized she still loved him, but was it enough to build a life on. She would have to wait and see if she could tell the difference between being in love and love. There had to be a difference. She would have to do it soon. Charles was waiting on an answer and he wasn't the kind of man you keep waiting. Charles wanted to come home, but Jean wasn't sure she was ready yet. She would have to wait and see. They made love until they both passed out. Jean wasn't aware of the passion she was capable of until these last few weeks. Again, she surprise herself and Charles.

Letting Go

Beth was waiting to hear from Brad, he hadn't called. She needed to cancel their date. There was no way she could face him again.

Brad was trying to think of a way to leave the house without a fight. Ellen would always cause a scene whenever he wanted to go out. He would leave her a note while she was in the bathroom. He would leave her a note. He had to see Beth. He would not wait another day! He knew how Beth felt about him being married; she would try and stay clear of him. He never told her that he was married in name only. He knew he had to be careful because he didn't want his wife to suspect he had an outside interest. She was not an easy person to be married to. Brad called from his car around five to see if they could start a little earlier.

Beth answered the phone on the second ring. "Hi, Brad! I'm glad you called I need to cancel our date tonight."

"Too late Beth, I'm already in the area and was hoping to pick you up a little early."

Brad was downstairs in the parking lot. Carol had already picked the girls up. Beth wanted to cancel but how could she? She held the phone away from her ear as though Brad could hear what she was thinking. She would have to go and end this tonight. Beth placed her ear back to the receiver and told Brad she would be right down.

Beth wasn't sure she could calm her nerves down long enough to handle sitting in the same car as Brad but she had no choice. The plans had changed. She was supposed to meet him at the movies. They never talked about him picking her up. She wasn't that worried about Brad, but she had heard stories about his wife. She lived in housing and didn't want people to start rumors that weren't true yet. She knew how people talked! Beth tried to concentrate on what Brad was saying and hoped he couldn't hear how loud her heart was beating.

They drove to the downtown movie theater. Brad really didn't want to share her but they would have plenty of time to be alone. Brad was sure they would have a special relationship that would last a very long time. He didn't want to move too fast and scare her off.

"Brad, how's your wife feeling these days?"

"She's much better, thank you." Brad wanted to tell Beth the truth about his marriage but there was time.

Beth knew this guy was dangerous. People were saying he had a way with the ladies. Beth didn't need anyone to tell her that; she could see that for herself. She would end this friendship tonight. After the movie Brad drove over to park where you can see the planes land and take-off. Neither one of them could relax; they both seemed on the edge. Beth started the conversation talking about her marriage and how it had failed and most of all how Earl had treated her. She didn't want Brad to think she was going to try and use him to even the score. Brad explained to Beth that they had so much in common. He too is in a failed marriage. They both had been hurt at a very young age by love. Beth had a hard time believing anyone could hurt him. Brad explained that his marriage wasn't really a marriage that his life with his wife was unbearable. He had planned on leaving her before his son was born. Then one day out of the blue she walked in and announced that she was pregnant.

"I was sure I wasn't the father because we had not been together in months." Brad explained that they had a paternity test and it proved he was the father so he continued to do what any good man would. He stayed with her for the sake of his son. Every time he threatened to leave she would use their son as a weapon against him. He couldn't let her do that to his son.

Beth saw how much Brad cared for his son. She realized he was a good man. There weren't too of many of them left. Beth gave Brad enough details about Earl without telling the whole story. That would take a lifetime. They only had tonight. Beth made him understand that she was a serious person. "Brad, do you think your wife will ever want a divorce," Beth asked.

"To be honest Beth, no! I feel she would live in separate bedrooms for the rest of her life if I choose to live on like that."

"You know Brad, that's really sad. I lived so many years with Earl in heartache that I promised myself that one day I would walk away and I will. Brad, I don't do one-night-stands and I don't have casual sex anymore. That was the old me. I'm

Letting Go

not looking for anything or anyone to complete me. I discovered that I had to complete myself to be truly happy."

Brad was glad to hear that. He wanted more from her also. He wasn't sure what he wanted but he knew he wanted her to be a part of it. Brad explained to Beth that he was always careful because his wife could be dangerous if given a chance. They had long decided that they would stay married only for the sake of their son.

"Brad you are not sleeping with your wife?" Beth had asked the question before she knew it.

"No Beth, we haven't slept together in the last year! We are married in name only! We have a child and he didn't get a chance to pick parents that loved each other. He had to have ones that despise each other. That's really not his fault. I have to do my part Beth!"

"Yes you do Brad."

Beth had a hard time imagining Brad staying married to a woman that he didn't love. She wanted to know more about Brad Walker but was it worth her time? He wasn't committed to his wife, yet he would never leave her. There was no future in this guy. At least she would go in with her eyes open.

Later that night Beth looked at Brad really hard. He was past handsome, his looks was regal. He had the look of a man that knew what he wanted and how to get it. He would not give up without a fight she thought. On the way back to the car Brad tried to hold Beth's hand. She refused to let him.

"Beth it's only your hand."

"I know Brad but today you want my hand and tomorrow you'll want my heart." She wouldn't let him know he already had it! She had to appear strong.

Brad stopped Beth. "I want to get to know you better Beth."

"I'm sorry Brad but you scare me. You're the first man that I've ever met that scares me. I've learned quite a bit about you tonight. From what I've learned I have every reason to be scared. Your wife is dangerous and you're not in love with her, which makes her even more dangerous; not to mention you're trapped. That pretty much sizes it up Brad. Did I miss anything?"

"No Beth, you covered everything."

"Brad, there is no future for us."

He pulled her into his arms and kissed her. She knew she was sinking fast! It took everything she had to pull away from him. "Brad, please, we can't do this. Please take me home."

Brad reluctantly let her go, walked to the car and opened the door. "This is not over Beth, not even close!"

She knew that was a promise. She had tried to say goodbye and good luck, she would never see him again. That was easier said than done. He knew where she worked and lived. He would make it hard for her. She knew she would have to fight to stay out of his bed. Beth didn't know if she was that strong but she would stand her ground.

Brad drove home with the taste of her lips on his. She was what he wanted; that he was sure of.

Beth, thought about Jean and was wondering if she was seeing Charles every chance she got and was she having some of the same problems she was having with Brad. Beth was still saying no to Brad. It was getting harder and harder everyday. Something had to give! She hadn't seen much of Jean since Charles had started romancing her again. They were moving full speed. Charles had left his past behind him, he would move on in Jean's direction. He would wait for her to decide what her next move would be.

Love at First Sight

Jean and Beth were scheduled to work late tonight for their semi-annual inventory. They had been preparing all week. They both needed a break so they headed to the officers club for happy hour. Jean also needed a break from Charles and Beth just wanted to get out. Once in the club the music took them both away. Jean closed her eyes and enjoyed the song. Tonight's music was right on point. "I Got Love on My Mind" was playing in the distance. She hadn't noticed the two newcomers that just walked in looking for directions. Jean's eyes were closed and she had wrapped herself in the music. They came over and sat down at the bar next to Jean. They were asking the bartender for directions to the best place to get something to eat on post this time of night.

Jean hadn't heard them come up. Beth turned around and was about to tell them of her favorite place to eat when Jean opened her eyes. The two introduced themselves as Jack and Chris. "We're looking for a good place to eat after hours around this place." Beth said the best place to eat this time of night was Denny's. "It's about two miles from the main gate on your left. You can't miss it."

Jean wasn't aware that she was staring at Jack. She was acting as if she had never seen a man before.

"Jean. Jean." Beth had to call her twice before she could get her attention.

"I'm sorry. What were you saying Beth?" Jean was unable to turn her head! She could not believe her eyes. Jean had never felt such chemistry before for a man. She was drawn to him like a magnet. Jack had to be in his early forties. He wasn't the kind of guy Jean would ever think of twice. She was into the more settled type. She would leave the pretty boys to Beth. They couldn't be trusted! Neither could the settled ones for that matter! There was something about Jack that Jean couldn't shake.

Beth wasn't sure what was going on. She had never seen this side of Jean. Was this new Jean the one that had evolved from being left by Charles? She liked it. She could see his interest in Jean, but Jean was going to take Charles back wasn't she? She shouldn't be looking at another man. Beth was sure she was misreading Jean's body language.

Charles hadn't heard from Jean but he knew she had to work late tonight. He was hoping she would have called and asked him to come over. He was hoping she would make a decision about them soon. He needed to make some decisions about Amy and his baby. He was sure it was over for him, but he needed to find out about the baby and what part he would play in his life. He felt responsible somehow for Ken's death even when Amy said it wasn't about them. He felt she was keeping something from him.

Charles would have to ask Amy for the truth. He deserved that much. He was still very sorry for her and her loss but she made the decision to stay with him. He had given up everything for her; what else could he have done? Charles called Amy to find out how everything was going. They hadn't spoken in over a month. He knew she was having a hard time. The word around the office was that her husband had been having an affair. I guess they got the rumor mixed up. It was she who had been having an affair.

Amy seemed ok, her voice had lifted some. She explained to Charles as much as she could about Ken's death without saying too much. He was looking for answers and she didn't have any for him. He wanted to know if she was staying in the area and she assured him she would stay. Her last words were about the baby. She told him she was sure the baby was his and she wanted him in her child's life.

"Charles," Amy said, "I've been given a second chance at happiness and God doesn't make any mistakes. Ken was who he was and what he did was foolish but that was his choice. He never gave us a chance!" Now she was available not by choice. Someone else had made the choice for her. "Charles, I never

Letting Go

stopped loving you. I remember telling you before leaving that you would always be in my heart. I've loved only two men in my life! One I lost to his stupidity! Charles, I know you think you want your wife back, but that's because I wasn't available. Now I'm here having your child. This was meant to be and Charles you're worth fighting for."

After Charles hung up the phone he wasn't sure what happened or what went wrong. One minute Amy was talking about Ken's death and the next she's planning a future with him. He really needed to see Jean. His mind needed clearing. How would he tell Jean that Amy wants him back and that she will pull out all the stops to get him? Charles wanted Jean didn't he? But what if Jean didn't want him? She's not rushing and he didn't want to rush her but he needed answers and he needed to see her. Charles was surprised and frightened by his feelings for Jean. Had he always cared this deeply for her or had her changing changed him also? All he knew was that he wanted to spend the rest of his life with her. He would stop by the club on his way home for a drink before going in. Charles would touch base with Jean before leaving the club, just in case she wanted him to stop by on his way home.

Jean had all her home calls forwarded to her cell just in case Charles called. Beth and she had decided to take Chris and Jack up on their offer for breakfast. They were so nice! Beth was missing Brad. He hadn't called in a few days; isn't this what she wanted? Maybe he was tired of being turned down. She needed a man in her life. Chris was married and I was happy that he showed no interest in me. We talked about our jobs and family. Jack and Jean talked as if they had known each other forever. They kept finishing each others sentences. The meal was good and so was the company but something was missing. My mind kept returning to Brad. Was I falling for this guy? That can't be the case. How can I fight him off the next time he comes calling if I'm falling for him? I can't say I'm not interested when my body says otherwise.

We didn't get in until late that night. There were several messages, but none from Brad. Why hadn't he called? This is crazy! Get control of yourself! Should I call his cell? No that would be foolish; he would be with his family. She would be patient and wait for his call.

Jean and Jack made plans to see each other again. Jack was a real estate tycoon who specialized in foreign land deals. Chris was into the stock market. They had been friends since middle school. Jean was fascinated with Jack. After dinner we said our goodnights and started home. Jean and I drove back together to the bar where we had left her car. "So, Jean, what do you think of Jack?"

"It's strange but it seems like we've known each other all our lives even though we have never laid eyes on each other until tonight. Have you ever felt like you knew someone in another life Beth?"

"No I haven't! What's happening to you girl?"

"I don't know Beth! It's love at first sight! I love him and I don't even know his last name Beth. What is happening to me Beth? I didn't want to leave him tonight!"

"What? What about Charles, Jean?"

"What about Charles? He left me for another woman. He just didn't leave me, he tried to destroy me in the process and you're worried about Charles. He told me basically that Amy was his soul mate. He said they had been looking for each other their whole lives."

"I'm sorry, Jean, it's just that you two have been spending a lot of time together. I thought that you two were headed back together."

"Beth, I need to be honest with you, you're my best friend and I feel I can tell you anything."

"Yes, you can Jean!"

"When Charles left me I thought my life was over. I had no one to turn to but you. I wanted to die! Mrs. Charles Brown was all I ever wanted to be my whole life, nothing more. Beth, now that's sad. I lived for Charles. He was my all in all and when he left I thought I would lose myself."

"I can't believe this, you sound like me. That was the way I felt every time Earl cheated on me!"

"Beth, I had to reach deep down inside me and find myself. I prayed to God and promised Him that I would place no man

Letting Go

before Him ever again. Charles was my life, now God is my life. I belong to no man. I will always be thankful that I found out now what kind of man Charles was instead of later."

Beth felt the tears run down her face. Jean had never discussed her pain. Beth knew it had to have been hard but she hid it so well.

"My life is what I make of it. No man will ever have a chance to take my kindness for weakness again."

Beth couldn't believe what she was hearing. This was a totally different woman, one to be reckoned with! Beth was learning more about her friend each day. She liked the new Jean much better. She always felt Charles wasn't good enough for her. Beth felt sorry for Charles. He had destroyed his marriage for a woman that never truly loved him. Jean was lost to Charles forever. She was sure of that!

Beth felt the pain that Charles would feel once Jean told him that they would never be man and wife again. She had remembered the many times her heart had failed her. She would cry for him, she would walk in his shoes, and let the pain settle there. Beth was hoping he was strong enough to pick up the pieces and move on. He would have to let go of Jean the way she let him go. We all have to let go once in a while. Jean had suffered from the inside; she would never let anyone see her true pain. She kept her heart in a cast now. Jack had penetrated Jean's cast! Charles was her last true mistake!

Jean was her friend and whatever her decision was she would support her and not question it. This was her life. She had to make her decisions, good or bad, they would be hers. She would be the one to live with them. Beth loved her friend and would always be there for her. Jean said goodnight and hugged her before saying goodnight and heading home.

Jean checked her cell phone for calls that may have been forwarded from the system. It was designed to transfer the calls to her cell. It never worked right for her. She would have to get a better service.

Charles had called several times. He wanted to get together tonight. Jean needed to think of a way to let him know they would not be getting back together. That their divorce had been set in motion the week he left. It would be final the end of May. She would have to tell him soon, very soon.

Jean had fallen head over heels with Jack the moment she laid eyes on him. How was that possible? She wasn't thinking properly. She couldn't be in love with a man she had met less than six hours ago, but she was and she was sure he had felt something very strong for her. Jean was beginning to question herself. She thought just maybe she was insane. Insane or not she was in love. The feeling she felt was nothing she had ever felt before. She had watched him all night. They sat and talked while eating. He was what she wanted and needed. They had felt like they were old friends. He's the one! She had no doubt in her mind. Her heart would not fail her again. This was true love. Her palms were sweating just thinking of him. Her body was aching with desire that Charles had never made her feel. She knew she couldn't live without him!

Jean called Charles and asked if they could meet early tomorrow for breakfast. He agreed there were things he needed to say to her also. He would tell her everything; they would have no more secrets. Jean made another call to Beth. She wanted to make sure she had gone straight home.

"Yes, Jean, I went straight home. I was thinking about going to the park where Brad and I had gone the other night but I changed my mind. I miss him Jean!"

"Beth, you have to wait on love sometimes and this is one of them! Beth if he's the one he will come back to you with no strings attached! Just be patient and pray!"

"Jean is it ok to pray for a man that's already committed to someone?"

"If he's where God wants him to be, your praying won't break that union, but if he's not and he's the one meant for you, God will bring him to you. Just remember that!"

"Thanks, Jean."
"You're welcome!"
"Jean, I love you."
"I love you too Beth. Goodnight!"

Charles met Jean at IHOP for a long breakfast. She hated going into the city but Charles wanted to make sure she was

Letting Go

relaxed. Charles met her at the door and kissed her and took her back to their table. He had insisted on a table in the back. They would have some privacy. They had a lot to talk about. Jean looked lovely Charles thought. Jean noticed that Charles looked as if he needed rest. "Charles is everything ok? You look tired."

"I'm fine, how about you?"

"I'm fine Charles."

They made small talk while the waiter took their orders. They waited until the meal was over before they started talking about the real reason they were there. Charles cleared his throat. He wanted to confess his love again. He began to tell her he wasn't in his right mind when he left her. He was looking for something that he thought was missing out of his life. He made a mistake and he wanted to come home. He wanted to cancel the divorce and start over again tonight.

Jean was speechless; she had to tell him it was over. She wouldn't play games with him. She still cared for him, but she would never be able to trust him again. It was very important that Charles understood the why behind her decision. She would not mention her feeling for Jack, that would add hurt on top of hurt and she didn't want to hurt him any more than necessary. She was hoping they could still be friends.

"Charles," Jean said slowly, "I know you want things to be like they used to be, but I'm not the same woman you left. I've changed Charles. You leaving me opened my eyes. There's another world out there, a world where people learn and respect and live honestly. I've been living in your world Charles. I have a chance to live in the real world now. I know what we had wasn't what marriage was all about. Marriage should be built on trust! I loved you so much Charles, there was nothing in this world I wouldn't have done for you. When we said our vows I took them very seriously. When you told me you would take care of me forever I believed you. Then you come home one night and rip me apart. You made me feel like you never loved me, that our whole marriage was a mistake! How could anyone live that down? You killed me that day Charles. You might as well have taken a knife and cut my heart out! If I didn't have prayer; I wouldn't have made it! I'm telling you this to let you know the pain I went through. Even when you came to tell me that Amy wasn't leaving her husband and you and she weren't going to make it. Charles, I had to deal with your pain on top of mine. I was wondering, how much am I supposed to take? I felt sorry for you because you had lost your dream and I know what it's like to lose your dreams. I'm sorry Charles, but I wont be able to be with you. I was hoping that I could let dead dogs lie but I won't be able to. Our future will be spent apart from each other. I will always be your friend but nothing else. We will cut our ties once the divorce is final. I wish you the best of everything. I hope you find happiness and true love."

Charles felt the life leave his body. He was transposed into a daze, his eyes filled with water. He would not drop a tear. This was his fault; he had no one to blame but himself. Where is it written that you should be given a second chance when you make a mistake? Some mistakes are just too big to be forgiven! This was one of them! Why was he being punished for his infidelity?

The tears were running down his face now and Jean had tears in her eyes. Hadn't she cried enough for this man already? "I wish things were different Charles, but women love hard and we love with our hearts," Jean said. They both were crying and Charles was glad he had picked a table in the back of the restaurant. He didn't want anyone to see the pain and tears in his eyes. He told Jean he would miss her and that she was a wonderful woman, and the best thing that ever happened to him. He wished he had learned that long ago. Then his marriage wouldn't be ending.

Jean had stopped crying and she wiped the last of her tears away. This chapter of her life was over. This was the second time she had to "let him go." She must now start a new chapter. Charles was a strong man who wore his feelings on his sleeve. He would be alright. Jean was sure he would bounce back like a ball.

Before Charles left he told her about Amy's husband killing himself and that he had felt somewhat responsible for what had happened. He wished he had never met Amy. "Charles, just think of it like this," Jean said, "There's a fifty percent chance

Letting Go

you're going to be a father. God doesn't make mistakes Charles. If it hadn't of been Amy, it would have been someone else. You and I weren't soul mates. We both still have time to find them and for that I thank you."

Charles was grateful to Jean. She could have been nasty and bitter about the whole thing. She had grace and pride and she blamed herself the whole time, never the other woman. That's the kind of person she was. "I will miss you, Jean!"

They hugged and said goodbye.

She held the final tears until she reached the privacy of her car. This would be a total abandonment of her love for Charles. Charles would be missed only momentarily. The pain he caused in the last two or three months of their marriage was more than enough.

Goodbye Charles!

Jean was surprised at how good she felt when she awakened the next morning. She had put her life in order. She would always remember that love doesn't love anyone and that a woman loves twice as hard as any man.

She would meet Jack tonight. This would be their first real date. She needed to call Beth for advice. She didn't want to come across too eager but she was in love and she didn't care who knew it. She had found the man of her dreams. It's amazing how you search all your life, you even get into a senseless marriage and then one day you wake up divorced and realize you never lived; you were going through life asleep. "Well I'm awake and ready for the ride of my life." She laughed at how silly she sounded.

She wasn't going to let anything or anyone stop her. She was headed to the chapel.

Beth and Brad Make Love

Jean called Beth. "Can you please meet me at Macy's? I need a new dress for tonight. I have a date with Jack! We're going to the Opera in New York."
"The Opera? Where?"
"Yes in New York!"
"You have to be kidding me!"
"No, Beth, I'm not! Jack has his own plane. So, I need a special dress for the occasion! So what are you doing tonight, Beth?"
"Oh nothing. The girls and I are going to watch scary movies with some of their friends. So I'll be chilling unless you want me to fly with you guys to New York?"
"That's ok. I've got this one well under control."
"I bet!"
"Beth, have you heard from Brad?"
"No nothing! That's fine. The guy does have a wife to occupy his time. Plus I'm not trying to go there with him. You and I both know there's no future in a married man. He can never give you what you really need when you need it and as often as you need it. I wonder how Earl keeps his ladies happy? He couldn't give them any major holidays like Christmas and Thanksgiving. They can all have Valentines Day!"
"I know that's right!" They both laughed.
"I know he's not giving them any money because he doesn't have any. Jean, Brad really doesn't have any time for me. That's why I'm not getting anything started, especially if I can't get a one hundred percent profit off my investment. Plus they say Brad's wife is dangerous. I can't expose the girls to a crazy woman like that. I'm staying clear. So, let's change the subject. I'll meet you at Macys in ten minutes."
"What color gown are you wearing tonight? I would like to see you in a rose gown. No black or whites. Black is a sign of

Letting Go

mourning and white is a sign of purity, you're neither one. Let's look at the rose color to bring out the highlights in your hair."

Jean was so excited she had to pinch herself to see if she was dreaming. She had met Mr. Right! She would not hold back tonight! Jack would get lucky tonight! Jean had already surrendered to him and they hadn't even kissed. "What man makes a woman give herself to him before he even asks?" Jean said.

"I hope you're not expecting an answer to that question. Is that a rhetorical question?"

"You just ask it and let it hang out there."

"Because, I'm not the one to ask. I've given myself to Brad so many times in my dreams that it's shameless."

"Beth, this isn't a dream. I'm serious, and this isn't just any man, he's the answer to my prayers. He's every woman's dream, and every ex-husband and ex-boyfriends worst nightmare," Jean said.

Beth was excited for Jean. She had chosen a rose gown that brought her to life; she had truly blossomed. She was in love; there was no doubt about it. Whenever Jack's name was mentioned she blushed. She would be dessert tonight!

She had the perfect outfit! Beth felt a little envious of Jean. She knew Jean had never felt anything like this in her whole life. Beth wished Jean the best tonight.

Jean would reach for the sky tonight and fly past it. She would climb the highest mountain, swim the widest sea, and reach for stars that were unreachable; and step into a time machine and enjoy every moment where each ounce of pleasure was more pleasurable than the last. Where the joy she felt would be everlasting for today and tomorrow were entwined. The beginning had no end and the end had no beginning. I just wished that I would one day feel that kind of love.

Beth wanted to hear from Brad; but deep down inside she knew it was wrong. She was lonely and needed a man's attention but she didn't want just any man, she wanted Brad. But he had baggage and she wouldn't be able to fit it into her closet at the moment.

The moment she returned home and was opening the door, the phone started ringing. It was Brad. He told her that he would be right over. Beth tried to tell him that was not a good idea with the nosey neighbor and all; they would be watched. Brad didn't care, he was on his way over. He wouldn't take no for and answer. This would be settled tonight. Beth hurried and showered and straightened up the living room. She would not let Brad leave the living room. They would not become lovers tonight, as bad as she longed for his touch. She would have to be strong and hold on.

Beth was putting on the last of her makeup when she heard the knock on the door. The girls would be back shortly with Carol. They had gone to pick up movies for tonight. Tonight was their weekly popcorn and movie night! What would she tell them about Brad? Beth had to think fast. She would have to play it by ear.

Brad didn't knock hard on the door for fear of the neighbor who would be checking out who was coming and going from Beth's home. They all knew her husband was in Korea. Beth opened the door and quickly pulled Brad inside. Before she could break away his mouth was on hers. "I've been missing you like crazy!"

Beth pulled away as fast as she could, but not before giving him a sample of her need for him also. "Brad, I don't think this is a good idea. This is where I live. People will talk! Suppose your wife followed you here tonight! What then?"

Brad wasn't worried about that because he had called back to the house and she was still there. "She didn't follow me. Beth, relax! I needed to see you Beth. I've tried not to think of you but every minute of my life is filled with you! When I'm sleeping I'm dreaming of you! Now here we are! Can you please tell me how I'm supposed to live like that?"

Brad started walking toward her and Beth's heart was beating out of her chest. "What should I do Lord? This man is so fine, and I haven't been with a man in almost a year! How do I stop my body from responding?"

"Beth, I just wanted to see you and hold you. I know the kids will be back soon."

Letting Go

She was wondering what was taking so long. She called Carol's cell to see where they were. "Where are you guys?"

Carol had the days mixed up. She had taken the girls to her apartment and they were settled in watching movies. "Aren't you supposed to be coming here Beth?"

"I'm sorry, Carol! I had my days confused. I thought we were meeting here tonight. I'll be over in a little while. I have to take care of a few things first." Beth looked at Brad and smiled.

"Ok, Beth. We will see you later, and Beth..."

"Yes, Carol?"

"The girls asked if they could stay the night. I told them I would have to ask you."

"That's fine Carol, they can stay. I'll see you later." Beth hung up the phone and explained to Brad that she had the nights mixed up. They were meeting at Carol's place to watch movies. "I think you should leave, Brad."

"I will leave after I do one thing." Brad took Beth and kissed her lips slowly. He held on to her lower lip a littler longer than necessary and Beth felt her knees begin to give way. She hadn't realized her response had been that of a lion who hadn't eaten in several weeks. His fingers had begun to massage her middle back and were beginning to move down her back to her lower waist. Beth realized what was happening and pulled clear.

"Brad! We can't do this," Beth said in a voice latent with passion.

Brad wasn't listening. He pulled her back into position. He placed his arms around her waist so that she would not run away from him. He lifted her chin to face him. "Beth," he said in a voice heavy with passion, "I won't force you to make love to me. I need you and I want you but it has to be your decision."

Beth couldn't look away. She was locked in a trance. She moved even closer until her breast was resting close to his chest. "Brad, I care deeply for you but I'm scared of what may happen between us. I'm not good at hiding my feelings and you're the kind of man that a woman wants to be seen with. I'm not sure I can play the secret lover game!" Brad was so close Beth could feel his heart beat!

"I won't hurt you, I promise. My marriage is basically over. I've been saying that for a long time now. I'm working on a way out."

"Brad I can't be a part of your plans to leave your wife. I don't want to get between you and what's going on."

"You're not going to be in the middle, Beth! This has been going on for sometime now."

Beth felt a little better. Maybe they could be friends until he was divorced.

"Beth, please don't send me away. I've wanted you from the moment I saw you!"

Brad was so close she could barely breathe. He started to kiss her again and Beth felt tingles run up her spine. Brad had locked his arms around her waist. They kissed with such passion she needed him in the worst way!

Brad felt as if he would not be able to last she was so beautiful. He reached under her blouse and touched the tip of her nipple. She let out a sigh of pleasure. He replaced his finger with his tongue and got the reaction he was hoping for.

Beth opened her legs so he could move in closer! She felt his desire and knew they would have to stop soon or they would not be able to turn back. Beth was having a hard time standing. Brad had unbuttoned her shirt and bra. He placed tiny kisses on her neck and chest. She needed him! Brad was taking her skirt loose. She motioned for him to move over to the couch and have a seat. Beth let Brad remove her skirt and underwear. She stood naked in front of him. She closed her eyes to hide the desire that had taken over her body. Beth took his belt loose and let his pants drop to the floor. His manhood was protruding out of his briefs. She ran her fingers over the object of her interest and heard him moan under her touch. She placed it in her hands and massaged it until she thought they both would explode at any moment! She was losing control. She needed to feel him inside her. She hadn't been with a man in over a year! It had been that long since she was with Earl and even then he never took the time to truly love her. It was always about him. Brad was different; he wanted to please her. They moved onto the floor where Brad laid her on her stomach with ease. He entered her

Letting Go

with such grace she begged for relief. He knew they both were only moments away from total delivery! The last stroke of passion sent them both into complete eruption! She had done this so many times in her dreams and in the end she would awaken with such emptiness. Tonight her dream had come true! She would complete her journey! Tonight she had experienced true ecstasy! She wanted more! "Brad, do you think we could do it again?"

"Sure, Beth! I was hoping you would ask for more!"

Beth couldn't believe it. She never understood what her friends meant when they said they had multi-orgasms. She was sure they all had lied! She didn't know it was possible until now. She would have to call them and apologize. They laid in each other arms and slept. She had gone too far to turn back. She cared deeply for this man. She had given him the power to destroy her or would he be her savior? Only time would tell. She knew she would have to take only what he was willing to give and never ask for more. She had no right to this man for he belonged to someone else and so did she.

Brad had awakened around eleven. He had to get home. Ellen would be asking questions, she always asked questions. He was angry for thinking of her at this time. He didn't want to leave Beth, but he had to. There would be more of these nights, he was sure of that! But right now he would have to go home where there was sure to be a scene. There was always a scene! He would have to ask her again for a divorce. She would eventually have to "let him go!" He just wasn't sure how to do it. Ellen had lied and told him she was an orphan and he had felt sorry for her when they got married. He later found out her parents and family was living in New Jersey. She had moved here to attend college. He was lied to from the beginning of their relationship. She was not going to let him go without a fight. They had discussed separation before and she had gotten so angry that she took their son and threatened to take him away where he would never see him again. He would have to be careful with her. She was dangerous and so were her friends.

When Brad returned home Ellen was sitting on the porch with fire in her eyes! There was no way to avoid her. He would have to go through the motions every time he left the house, regardless of how long he stayed. "Where have you been, Brad?"

"Out, Ellen. I told you I was going out before I left!"

"Where did you go?"

Brad hated lying but he wanted to live another day and this was not the way to deal with her. "Ellen, we have not been together as man and wife for over a year. Why are you acting as if I'm in your bed every night?"

"Because you are still my husband!"

"Yes! I am on paper only!" Brad wasn't prepared to get into this now but she was pushing his buttons. "Ellen, I've asked you so many times for a divorce and you've held my son over my head every time. Now let me tell you this woman! I'm sick and tired of not being able to go out and come home without twenty questions! I never question you or care when you go out! On Monday morning I'm going down to my lawyer's office and re-file the divorce papers again, and I want you to know that we will have joint custody of our son. Do I make myself clear?" Brad hated losing his temper but there was just no letting up!

"Brad, I'm sorry. I know we can work this out!"

"Ellen, please go back to your room! I have to get up early tomorrow and take Jamie to the park, and I promised him we would go to breakfast at IHOP. Plus, I need to wash my car before I leave." Brad escaped into his bedroom. He showered and went straight to bed. He would relive each moment he shared with Beth tonight. Their lovemaking had taken him to new heights. He was in love with her but was it too early for her? She was scared of him for some reason. She would need time to adjust to his situation with Ellen.

Brad was so deep in thought that he hadn't noticed Ellen coming into his bedroom. She proceeded to get into bed. "Brad, I need you!"

"Ellen, can you please leave my bed? There won't be another accidental pregnancy. You set me up and got pregnant with Jamie, who I truly love, but it will not happen again!"

"Brad, please, I need to feel your strong arms around me!"

"No, Ellen, this marriage is over and has been for some time now!"

Letting Go

Ellen couldn't understand the coldness in his voice. She knew he didn't love her; she'd known that for two years now but he'd never talked to her the way he did tonight. Something had changed. He was different some how. Ellen pulled the covers off Brad and threw them on the floor! Ellen yelled, as she left the room, "Who is she Brad? I know there's someone! You better tell me now because I will find out sooner or later, I always do!"

Brad knew that she was right! She always seemed to find out. She would go as far as following him. He would have to protect Beth and her girls. Beth would never be able to deal with Ellen. He would let Beth know tomorrow that they would have to be very careful. He would not think of that tonight, though. He wanted to dream of her and the possible life they could have together.

Beth was so tired she called Carol and said she had a headache and needed to skip the movie night. Beth had never been made love to like that before in her life by anyone! Sleep would never grace her with its presence tonight. She would lay awake and hold on to the memories of Brad's loving! How would she handle her feelings for him? Or better yet, what if he had no feelings for her? How would she deal with that? Would he feel guilt in the morning or shame that he had found love in her arms? Would he still want to be a part of her life? Beth needed advice! Is he for real? Is he the one? There's just one small detail - he has a wife! Beth refused to take him away from his family at any cost; she would be no better than the women who she had always despised for coming between a man and his wife. She would not be a home wrecker! She needed to speak to Jean. Jean would help her sort this mess out and make the right decision.

Beth called Jean early. She knew Jean would have plans again tonight. Beth wanted to tell Jean about her night with Brad but she felt a little uncomfortable with his being married. It took some of the excitement out of it for her so she didn't mention it. But if Jean brought it up she wouldn't lie to her, she would confess! Jean wasn't really listening. She was rambling on about being in love with Jack. Jean finally met the man she would spend the rest of her life with. Beth was so happy for her friend, She deserved it.

"Well, Jean, please tell me what happened with Charles."

"Well, Charles wanted to get back together, you know."

"Yes!"

"I told him it would never work and that I would never be able to trust him and in the end he understood that we were headed in different directions. I wished him the best of everything. I hope he can find Amy and she can fill the void she helped make in his life. Charles told me more than one time that she was his soul mate. I wished him farewell."

"How did Charles take it?"

Jean would never tell her friend that he cried like a baby. "He took it like a man!"

Amy Lets Ken Go

Charles drove home thinking of his next move. He was a free man now that Jean had released him from his vows. He would wait for Amy. She said she would need six months. He wasn't sure why Jean wished him luck when all he really needed was her, she was his luck. He would let her go. It seemed he's been doing a lot of letting go lately. He would try to build a life with Amy now. It would take everything he had to make it work but he would be happy with her. Interracial couples were common nowadays and blended in just fine. He had chosen her based on love, not on the color of her skin.

Amy was headed to the doctor today; she hadn't been feeling well lately. The nightmare of Ken's death was still haunting her dreams. She would have to let him go. Was she that bad of a wife that she had turned her husband gay? She was not the reason Ken was gay; he was born gay. She had to stop blaming herself for his death. He had chosen Brian as the man to love for the rest of his life. Not her! That had caused her more pain than his killing himself. She would never be able to say that to anyone. She knew she didn't pull the trigger but she still somehow felt responsible for what happened. She needed to see Charles. She missed him so much! She would tell him everything in time. He had finally accepted the fact that they were meant to be together. Amy was happy he had called. She was sure that he called to tell her he wanted her back. She would be waiting. She made the kids a snack and called Charles back.

He was feeling better already! He wouldn't tell Amy that Jean had let him go. He would leave it alone. They would start planning for the future, for the birth of their child. They talked about the baby, her not sleeping, and the time they would be apart. Charles wanted to see her now but she had to think of her kids and what her parents would say. She would have to wait another three and a half months.

She didn't owe Ken anything, but she would give him that much respect. Charles knew not to push. They would have a future together in the end. He would have to wait. Charles met Amy after her appointment. She told him everything was fine with her and the baby and that she would deliver in five months. Charles was so excited he was going to be a father. He had waited his whole life to become a father and now it would happen in five months.

He and Amy discussed names for the baby and what they hoped to have and of course where they would live. Charles was concerned about Amy's parents accepting him. He didn't want Amy to have any pressure from either set of parents about his being black. He wanted them to know that they were involved before Ken died. Charles knew they would blame him for Ken's death. He would have to tell his parents soon that he would be marring Amy. They would need to know everything. He never lied to his parents and he wasn't about to start. The time he spent with Amy was precious; he needed to be with her. She was beautiful pregnant. He had called back and asked if he could come over once the kids were in bed.

They would have to be careful not to make too much noise. He would have to be gone by the time the kids awakened in the morning. Amy asked Charles if they could meet outside of the house. It was still too soon for him to be coming to the house. She needed to tell her parents first. They were so excited about telling their family they would wed in a few months. Charles was worried about Amy's parents for two reasons; first was they would say he had caused her marriage to end, and second that he was the reason Ken killed himself. Charles knew this could happen. He had asked Amy to explain Ken's state of mind to her parents. If he was going to make his relationship with Amy work he would need her parent's acceptance.

It was time she told Charles the truth about Ken's death. In a sweet voice one could barely hear she said, "Charles there's something I need to tell you about Ken's death. I didn't tell you all of what happened."

Charles gave her his full attention. He stopped washing dishes and sat across the table from her. "What more was there?

Letting Go

He was depressed and he killed himself, how many ways are there to say it?"

"There's more! Charles, Ken was gay! Charles, he was in love with one of our closest friends. They had been lovers for the last two years. His name is Brian and he worked with Ken. They were usually paired up to work together on major projects and they got sent out of town a lot on business trips. Charles, I wanted to tell you before now."

Charles was speechless. He kept shaking his head no. "You got to be kidding me! He was gay and on the down low! I've heard about that but I never believed that kind of stuff happened!"

"Yes, it does, and it happened to me!"

"I'm sorry Amy, you should have told me!"

"I know Charles, but I was too embarrassed to tell anyone. The only people that know are my parents and of course Brian. Ken was planning on leaving me and moving to Japan with Brian. Then I told him I had been sleeping with a black man not knowing he was sleeping with one also. That must have been a joke for him. We both found love in the arms of black men," Amy said. "He kept pressing me until I said I was pregnant and that you could be the father. There was no way he was going to let me leave him and be happy with you. All along he was having sex with Brian. He had planned on leaving me after Valentines Day."

"Why didn't he tell you?"

"I don't know! I think he was afraid I would judge him or tell his parents. He figured if they found out they would disown him, which they probably would have. His family is from the old school and they're Catholic. So he kept his little secret to himself until he thought he had infected me with the Aids virus."

"What?"

"Yes! That's why he killed himself. He thought he had picked it up from Brian because they had unprotected sex."

"Why, did he think that Amy?"

"Brian's last lover died of Aids. Brian didn't have a chance to tell Ken he was clean."

"So, Ken would rather kill himself than face you and his parents with that news." Charles was in disbelief. He couldn't imagine what was going on in Ken's head. "Amy, how did he hide his being gay all these years? Why hide it! You never had a clue that this was going on."

"No, Charles, I was in the dark until I went to the police station with Brian and read his letter. I'm sorry I didn't tell you earlier. I just couldn't believe it myself. I'm still having nightmares after seeing his body in the morgue!"

"What on earth made you go there?"

"My father tried to stop me but I had to see him. I couldn't believe he had done something so stupid. Charles, he left me a letter. Can you believe that? I was in bed next to him every night for the last ten years and he was gay. All he could do was leave a stupid letter saying he was sorry for being gay. How does he expect us to deal with what he's done? What about my girls? What kind of life will they have if they ever find that out?"

"There's no way they will find out. Your parents will never tell them and I don't think you will have to worry about Brian telling anyone," Charles said.

"Brian received a letter from Ken also."

"Did you read it?"

"No, I was too torn up to read it. I could barely read the one he left me."

"What about Brian? This must be hard for him since they were so close and for so long. Have you spoken to him since this happened? You did say he was also your friend as well as Ken's."

"I told him never to call or come to my house again!"

"You know, Amy, Brian didn't make or turn your husband gay. He was born with those feelings. Brian just showed him how to release them. I really feel sorry for Ken. He must have been terribly unhappy," Charles said. "Why didn't he let you go so he and Brian could have had some kind of life together? I'm very sorry, Amy." Charles took her in his arms for the first time since she started telling the story. His heart went out to her. She would have a hard time living with Ken's death, plus his sexual

Letting Go

preference had left her with doubts of her own sexuality as a woman.

"Charles, I knew I would have never been able to compete with a man," she was saying to Charles as tears ran down her face. "I would have been happy to "let go" Charles!"

"I know, sweetheart, you weren't given the chance!" Charles was glad she had come over. She needed him. She had suffered the loss of more than a husband. When Ken killed himself he killed a part of her self-esteem! It was hard for her to understand how a man could pick another man over her. She had questions that only one person could answer. She would have to see him face to face, Charles thought. Brian would have the answers she needed!

Charles was still holing her tight; he needed to make sure she knew she was safe with him and that he would never hurt her.

Amy loved the feel of Charles arms around her! He was so strong and loving! This man would become her husband in less than four months, just before the baby is born. Charles had insisted that they wed before the birth of his child. She had wanted to wait just in case. Amy would have to tell her parents in the morning about Charles. Her dad would understand but her mother wouldn't be so easy going. They had made love for the first time since Ken's death. She had wanted to wait but she needed Charles and she could tell he needed her. Amy didn't ask what had happened to Jean. She really didn't care. She was just glad they were on the right track again. She would never make that mistake again.

On the drive back from taken Amy's home he was in a new state of mind. He had a lot to think about. He was a lucky guy or was God watching out for him. He had been riding on the back of the devil's wagon for so long. It was time he jumped ship! He would have to change some of his bad habits. He knew he needed Jesus more in his life. Jean had always talked about God. He just never took the time to listen until he had lost everything. He knew he had been given a second chance with Amy. Charles said a little prayer. "Our father, God in heaven, if I wake up in the morning and you've taken everything away from me that I hold dearest to my heart I will not even question your action again! You gave me a new life and a new beginning. When I fell down you picked me back up and stood me on my feet. I want to thank you Lord for loving me enough to allow me to prove worthy of your grace. AMEN!"

It sometimes scared him that he could love two women at the same time. He loved Jean for her loyalty and devotion and he loved Amy for her spirit and the fact that she had given him life and possibly his first chance at fatherhood. He would make up for lost time. Time they had spent apart. There would be changes in his life. He wouldn't make the same mistakes he made with Jean. He was thankful Jean had "let him go!" Jean had promised that they would remain friends and he was happy for that. He didn't have many friends and having Jean as a friend was very important to him. He would call her to make sure she had adjusted to being single.

Amy Tells Her Parents About Charles

Amy paid a visit to her parents. She had dropped the kids off at school. She needed to tell them about Charles and her unborn child. Amy knew her father would have questions different from her mother's and she was ready to answer them all.

Amy started telling them first of all that she and Ken loved each other very much at first. Then something happened and they drifted apart. In the end, they hadn't shown any emotion toward each other. Amy also mentioned that they had stopped sleeping together as man and wife and that they usually made love only once or twice a month. At the end they hadn't been together in months. She said, "We both knew we weren't attracted to each other anymore. That's when I met Charles. He's a black co-worker that worked in an adjoining office. We had started talking one day and found out we had a lot in common, plus we enjoyed each other's company a lot more than we should have. Before we knew it, we were involved. We fell in love. We hadn't planned it, it just happened! There is a good chance this is Charles's baby I'm carrying."

Her mom had been standing but she had to sit down! "Amy, how could you run around on your husband? He was so good to you and the kids. If you didn't love him why didn't you get counseling? They would have helped both of you!"

"Mom, please, it wasn't that easy! Can I finish mom? Charles is not the reason Ken and I weren't getting along! We had stopped being man and wife long before I met Charles."

"Charles and I didn't plan on falling in love, it just happened! I stayed with Ken even after I told him about Charles. He wanted us to try and make our marriage work so I stayed but Charles had already left his wife and got a place for us to live. I should have left when I started to. That was my mistake. Maybe he would still be alive. Mom, Dad, I'm sorry that I disappointed you two, but life is too short to be unhappy in these days and times! I wanted to tell you both but I didn't want you to blame Charles and me for what happened to Ken. Ken was having an affair and was planning on leaving me! He was sleeping with Brian!"

"Brian! Our friend Brian?"

"Yes, the one and the same!"

Amy's parents knew Brian well! We had all taken trips and picnics together. Amy's mother was speechless! She had turned pale! She looked at Amy in shock. "How could this happen?" her mom asked. What made him gay? Was he always gay?"

"Mom, I'm sorry. I can't answer any of those questions. The only person that can do that is gone! I wish he would have told me," Amy said. "I would have tried to help him!" Amy's tears fell. She felt pain every time she thought of his dying alone. "Ken was a good father and I was grateful for the time he had with his kids." Her father was at her side. "I'm sorry," was all Amy knew to say. Her mother was trying to make logic out of everything.

"Ken was a good man, and he will be missed," her father said.

Her mother took her in her arms and Amy released all that she had held back since Ken's death. She would finally put him to rest. This was the final chapter. Her mom held her tight. She loved her daughter very much and would support her in any way she could. She told her parents she had to let Ken go, yet he still seemed to haunt her dreams. When she closed her eyes at night he was there. "Will he ever let me go, mom? I have to try and move on!"

"It will take time sweetheart, to deal with any loss but to deal with it in this manner is even harder," her mom said. "You just have to pray on it!"

Amy was glad she had mentioned that Charles was black. She was hoping it didn't matter as long as he loved her, and was willing to accept her and her kids without any conditions. She was thankful to him for his love and devotion.

Letting Go

Amy drove back home and decided that she would have to tell Ken's parents that she would wed soon. She felt she needed to give them that much respect.

Charles was waiting on her when she returned. "Well, how did it go?"

"It wasn't as bad as I thought it would be. My mom took it hard; she really loved Ken. It will take some time for her to deal with and understand Ken's sexual preference."

"I was more interested in me," Charles said in an apologetic voice.

"My mom was trying to understand why I stepped outside of my marriage for affection. She was a little disappointed in me for doing that. She'll get over it in time."

"Amy, when I look in your eyes I see the pain that Ken left there. He left so many unanswered questions that you will never let him go!"

"I have let him go, Charles."

"No, Amy, you haven't! You keep saying it but you still have questions that need answers. When Ken died his answers died with him. There's only one person that can answer your questions and that's Brian! You need to call him and get the answers you need so we all can "Let Ken Go!""

"I can't call Brian! I was so mean to him the last time we spoke."

"You were confused and wanted to blame someone for Ken's senseless death. You were blaming the wrong person. Ken was hiding behind you all those years. Brian just showed him how to be himself."

"You are right, Charles, it wasn't Brian's fault! Brian was the one he loved in the end, not me! He couldn't take my leaving and running off with you. He had to give up his only true love and come back to me. That's why he killed himself. He didn't want to leave Brian! Here I am thinking it's all about him thinking he had given me the Aids virus. It never was about the virus, it was about Brian all along! He didn't want to live without Brian!"

"Amy, you're jumping to conclusions, you are reading too much into Ken's death."

"In the letter he wrote how much Brian had meant to him and that I shouldn't blame him. That the last two years were the happiest years of his life. I have to call Brian! Brian was there when I wasn't. How could I have blamed him for making my husband happy! Charles I have to make things right. Brian has to know that Ken loved him with every fiber of his being. That's why he killed himself, he didn't want to go on without him!"

"Amy, slow down and think about this before you make the call. Brian has suffered also if he loved Ken half as much as you said he did. He's suffered enough. Telling him that Ken killed himself because he couldn't be with him, that may make matters worse."

"No, Charles, it won't. Right now Brian is thinking Ken killed himself because he thought he was infected. So I blamed Brian for everything. I need to apologize to him Charles. Please, Charles, will you go with me?"

"Are you sure you want to do this love?"

"Yes, I have to help him and by doing this I will help myself also."

Amy called Brian. He was surprised to hear from her. They hadn't spoken since Ken's death. "Hello, Amy!" Brian wondered why she was calling him now. It had been four months now and he still had times when his pain was hard to deal with. It was his punishment for loving! He wondered if he would ever find a true, lasting love. Brian knew Ken was his soul mate and there would be no other. They had talked and laughed about getting married one day! He would have enjoyed being married to Ken. He had such a free spirit. He didn't know when it had happened to him but Ken completed him. When they were together there was nothing they couldn't manage. They would have taken on the world!

Brian had made a collage of all the places he and Ken had gone and framed it for his bedroom. He missed Ken with the passion he had loved him with. He touched a picture of Ken's face and remembered the feel of his skin. They were great together! They had taken advantage of every chance they had to be in each other's company. Brian knew he would never feel that complete with anyone ever again. It still was a mystery as to why

Letting Go

Amy wanted to see him. She would be coming to the home that he and Ken had shared.

Amy and Charles arrived at Brian's place. She had spent so many hours at this house celebrating birthdays, family outings and cookouts. It was hard thinking of it now as her husband's love nest! "Ken practically lived here with Brian on most occasions. This was the girl's and my second home also. We often teased and laughed about the amount of time Ken spent here with Brian. Now it all makes sense," Amy said to Charles.

Amy introduced Charles to Brian. Charles felt like a left shoe. He would let Amy have her say. He couldn't understand why she was putting herself through all this. She needed closure, he guessed, and he was there for support.

Amy didn't know where to start so she just said, "I came to tell you that Ken loved you very much and I'm sorry for the way I treated you. I was just so hurt and surprised, that's all. Then my pride got in the way. I couldn't face the fact that my husband had chosen you over me. That hurt even though I was doing the same thing he was doing, but somehow I felt more betrayed. When Ken took his life I couldn't understand the meaning behind it. I kept looking for someone to blame and you were the perfect target. I believed Ken used the Aids factor as a way of escaping me. He wanted to be with you and he saw no way out after I told him about the baby. He wanted to do the right thing by me so the answer to his prayer was death! That was the only way he saw he could get out and still be free."

"Amy, where on earth did you get this information from?" Brian asked.

"It's true Brian. I figured it out myself. Ken had been so happy these last few years. It never occurred to me that he had met someone and fell in love, but now it all finally makes sense. It was you all along! How long do you think he would have stayed married to me if he couldn't see you? Not long! He wanted to be with you Brian! He wanted to share your life. You were the driving power behind him. He was living a complete life and he never felt that way with me. The few times we made love in the last two years there always seemed to be something missing. I'm being honest Brian! I want to thank you for giving

Ken his last two years of true happiness. I'm sorry for the way I treated you!"

She was standing up in front of him now. He opened his arms up to accept a hug from a woman that he felt he would never see again.

Brian was relieved that he was not the total reason Ken had taken his life. He would have to try and put his life back together. He had let so many things go. Ken would have wanted him to live for the both of them. Brian thanked Amy for coming and kissed her cheek goodbye. He thought of her as a brave woman. She had put her feelings aside and come to terms with what her deceased husband might have been going through. Brian was happy that she cared enough to set him free also.

Amy wasn't sure if what she had done made sense, but she had to release Brian from the death hold that Ken had hanging over the two of them. It wasn't his fault, why should he pay anymore than he had already? Ken's refusal to face his destiny his whole life was what killed him. On the way home Amy was relieved that things had been settled.

Charles looked over at her profile and saw that her face looked as if she were smiling. He said, "You look even more beautiful pregnant!"

"I want you to say those same words three months from now when every bit of me is two times its normal size!"

"I will," Charles laughed.

"Thanks, Charles!"

"Why are you thanking me, love?"

"For being here with me. You are truly a wonderful person Charles."

"I felt this was something you had to do even if I didn't agree at first. I'm happy you went to see him, he's free now! When Ken committed suicide, he killed more than just himself. Brian will be able to pick up and go on now. It sometimes amazes me to experience some of life's pain. One minute you're living at the top of your peak and the next you're digging up out of the barrel. Love can bring you so much joy! Then turn around and that same love can plunge you so deep into darkness. You think all hope is lost! I think that might have been what

Letting Go

happened to Ken." Charles knew how Ken must have felt when he had to leave Brian because that's how he felt when Amy first left him.

"You are right, Charles, that's probably what happened."

They continued the rest of the drive in silence. Charles was going to love this woman with everything he had. He was glad to see a different look in her eyes. The look of hope and possibilities were there now. He would do everything in his power to keep it there. Charles' mind kept wondering about Brian. What kind of guy was he that Ken had fallen so in love with him? He seemed like a really nice guy. Charles was happy that all this was behind him and Amy. They would be planning a wedding in a few months. He needed to touch base with Jean and find out when the divorce papers would be ready for his signature.

The Engagement

Jean was running around looking for her favorite shoes when the phone rang. Jack was calling to see what was taking her so long, she thought. She answered the phone in one breath, "I'm on my way darling."

"Hello, Jean!"

"Hi Charles. I'm sorry. I thought you were Jack. I'm running late for my date!"

"So Jean, who is Jack?"

"Just a friend! Charles, how are things going with you? Is everyone doing ok?"

"They are fine, thanks for asking. How's Beth?"

"She's fine! Charles I'm really in a hurry. Could I please call you back tomorrow? I'm off from work!"

"So what about four o'clock in the afternoon? Would that be good for you?"

"Thanks, Charles! Goodbye!" Jean hated to be short with Charles but she was running late.

The limo was down stairs waiting on her. From the moment she had laid eyes on Jack neither one of them had looked back. They were to be married in secret in two weeks, only Beth knew of her plans. She was living the dream of most women. Her prince was too good to be true! He was unreal! They were going to meet his family tonight. They would announce that they would marry. They just wouldn't say when. Jean had to stop eating out so much; she had noticed her clothes fitting a little tight around the waist - she would have to cut back on sweets. It had been four months since she and Jack started seeing each other. They would celebrate their four-month anniversary tonight after dinner. They had gotten engaged the second week after they had met! They wanted the same things in life Once they were married they would fly to the Bahamas for two weeks.

Letting Go

Then they would fly to California and meet one of Jack's executive officers in his company. Jean was never as thankful to Charles as she was at this moment. He was the reason for her happiness, her newfound love. It's awesome sometimes to see the rainbow when there are so many clouds, but Jean's cloudy days were behind her. She was ready for the new life that Jack has promised her. They would adopt a few kids. Jack was more excited that Jean was about the adoption. They both wanted lots of kids!

Jean couldn't wait to tell Beth everything. She had waited on Jack. God sent him just like she knew he would! He didn't just send her a man he sent her a real man! Sent me a man of substance and stability! She got weak in her knees just thinking about it. Jean ran to the limo, she was at least one hour late, but she would be worth the wait. She was meeting Jack at his condo. They would ride to Jack's family vacation home in Potomac, Maryland. They were meeting his parents and his sister for dinner.

Jack met the limo in the driveway. Jean didn't have a chance to say she was sorry for being late. Jack rushed to the car and had her in his arms before the driver could pull off.

"I've missed you, lady!"

"I missed you," was all Jean could mutter. He was taking her breath away with his kisses! This man belonged to her! How strange that seemed. She had never even cleaned or cooked for him. All she had to do was love him and that's all he would ever ask. Jean said a soft prayer to God, "Thank you Lord for this man. I've been waiting for him all my life." She was happier than she had ever been in her entire life! Jack made an apology for their late arrival. Jack's parents were in their early sixties, Jean estimated. Jean was quiet most of the night. Jack had promised to stay close and she had held his hand under the dinner table whenever she had a chance. It was so important that they like her; she didn't know why but it was.

Jean tried to make small talk with his sister Lisa. She had also inherited the family good looks. She was younger than Jack. Jack's parents told stories of his upbringing. The air was light and perfumed. They had arranged for dinner to be served on the patio. The weather was beautiful for this time of year. Jean needed a little fresh air because the perfume that was in the air was making her sick to the stomach. She excused herself to check her makeup. She started to get up from the table and had to sit back down because she was a little dizzy. She held on to the table to steady herself.

Jack jumped to his feet, filled with concern. "Are you alright love?"

"Yes, I just got up a little too fast. I'm ok sweetheart!"

"Are you sure?"

"Yes, I'm fine!"

"Would you like me to walk you to the bathroom?"

"No Jack. I'm fine now. Stop fussing over me, you're embarrassing me."

"Jean," Lisa said, "I need to check my makeup. Come on, Jean, let's go!"

"Thanks Lisa."

Jean wasn't sure what had happened, she would have to slow down. Jack had her on a rollercoaster and she didn't want to get off. Jean made it to the bathroom and back. She wasn't going to tell Jack that she had almost passed out while walking to the bathroom. Thank God, Lisa had gone with her. She would call her doctor and have a check up before the week was out. Lisa was very sweet; she never mentioned what had happened to Jack.

They talked a little about how Jack and Jean met. How they were drawn to each other like magnets! Jean was going on and on about how happy they were and she didn't realize she was babbling until Lisa said, "Jean, believe me, you're all he's talked about for months. My parents were beginning to think you weren't real. Jack has never brought any of his lady friends home before. We were surprised when he called and said he was bringing a friend home for us to meet."

"Jack has made me so happy these last few months! He needs to slow down and let me catch my breath," Jean said.

"That won't happen any time soon," Jack cut in. They were headed back to the living room. Jack had waited on Jean at the end of the hall. "Are you all right sweetheart?"

Letting Go

"I'm fine, Jack, stop your fussing over me!"

Lisa looked at Jean and winked. Jean liked Lisa and his parents. Jean was still feeling a little dizzy when she walked into the living room. She had to get control of herself!

Jack got drinks for the big announcement. Jean was standing next to Lisa when he started his announcement. "Excuse me, could I have every one's attention?"

Jean felt her knees turn to butter. It was happening, this wasn't a dream. She was actually awake and this man was telling his family that he was in love with her and that he wanted to live the rest of his life with me! Tears were running down Jean's face. Jean felt she would explode at any moment. This man had declared his love for her! She felt her heart skip she was so moved. If she were to die this very minute she would have had the opportunity to experience true love! The kind of love that comes from loving yourself so that someone else can love you!

Jack announced that they would be married. Jean was crying now and Jack's mom had tears in her eyes for when she looked in Jean's face she saw the love that she had for her son and knew that this woman will never hurt him. He had found her, and they were in love from the moment they met. Jack's mother walked over to Jean and said, "I know you will be good for my son. I see it in your face. You both have my blessing! Sometimes it takes only a glance to know you have found that special person. Cherish each other and never take prayer out of your home!" She hugged Jean and her son.

Jack went over to shake his father's hand and hugged him. "Congratulation's Jack. You found a keeper!"

"I know, dad! Thanks!" Jack went to Jean and placed his hand on her cheeks and raised her lips to his. The kiss was a definite yes! "I love you," he whispered in her ear.

Jack had already proposed to Jean but he needed to do it correctly so he got down on one knee, took Jean's hand and asked the question. "Will you marry me?" He then pulled out a three carat Tiffany engagement ring and placed it on her finger! He had made it official!

She pulled him up to face her and tiptoed to reach the tears in his eyes. She kissed them away and said, "Yes!"

They would wed in two weeks. Jack was hoping to marry as soon as her divorce was final. Jean wanted two weeks and he gave his word two weeks was all he was willing to wait to make her his wife. He insisted she quit work after they were married. He would spend each and everyday day thanking God for sending her to him! She deserved so much more than the last man had given her. He would protect and keep her safe. "Thank you, Lord, for intrusting your angel to me. I will do the right thing!"

Jean had felt him drift away. "What were you thinking about, Jack?"

"I just wanted to thank God for sending you to me and Jean, remind me to thank Charles later." They laughed and said goodnight.

Jean had told Jack that she would think about quitting her job. There was no problem with quitting; she could do that right now. but what would she do about not seeing Beth everyday?

Jean had the whole day free. She only had two weeks before her big day! She received a message from Jack saying that he had to go out of town on another business trip but he would only be gone a few days. She felt a sharp pain of loneliness come over her. She had never experienced love so deeply before. She would have to suffer through two days without him!

Jean wanted to touch base with Beth. She hoped things would work out for her also. "Is everything ok Beth?"

"Yes, I'm great! I'm losing my mind and my best friend at the same time."

"I don't know how much of this I can take, you're not losing me!"

"Yes I am, Jean! Jack is going to take you away from here. Jack is not going to let you work or do anything. How much more special can life be?"

"You are right, Beth! That is special!"

"So how was meet-the-parent's night?"

"It was heavenly. His parents are wonderful people and he also has a sister. She's very sweet Beth. I need to run by my doctor's office and have a few tests made. I've been a little under the weather lately. Can we meet after work?"

Letting Go

"Sure, what time? Around five would be good."
"I'll see you then. Hey Beth?"
"Yes, Jean?"
"You are never going to lose me. Remember "Sister's for Life!"
"Sure Jean!"

Beth wasn't just missing Jean she was missing Brad also, they hadn't spent much time together these days. Brad seemed to be spending more time worrying about his wife than anything else. Beth was feeling abandoned. She had made some bad choices in the past. Was Brad going to be on that list? How would she survive his leaving? He would have to give her up. There could never be room for what she wanted.

She had written to her husband and asked him to come home, they needed to discuss their marriage or lack of a marriage. Earl had promised to be here before the month was out.

She never made plans to be with Brad, he usually just showed up unannounced. The kids would always be out when he showed up. They had never met him and that was how it was going to stay. I needed more from Brad, but I promised not to push him from the beginning and I will keep my promise. I'll walk away before I push him and take time from his family.

Brad had stopped by the store a few times last week to check to see if she was ok. Beth was lonely! She had made the mistake of telling him that she needed him! He made a big issue out of the conversation saying he was lonely for her also but they were in a no-win situation. It would take time. She would have to be patient.

Earl Comes Home

Beth had to find closure in her life before she went any further with Brad. She needed to see her husband. He had left more than six months ago and now they really needed to talk! He would send a few dollars home every now and then, nothing to really bank on. The kids were growing so fast they needed a father figure in their life. They needed their father!

Earl came in from Korea on a rainy Saturday afternoon. He was due in at noon. The girls were so excited they could hardly wait. Since Marie was the oldest she had asked more question about when her father would be home. Michele had been very small when he left and didn't have a lot of memories of him. I wanted all that to change! I was hoping that when Earl came home he would be ready to settle down and raise his kids.

Earl arrived later than planned. He had no desire to come back to the States and live. His marriage was over but he couldn't tell Beth that just yet. He would have to move them into a home first. Once they were settled he would leave for his next duty station. He would give her the other information later. Beth picked Earl up at the airport.

"Earl what do you want to do about this marriage?" Beth was trying to find out where Earl's head was these days.

"Beth I've told you before, you guys mean the world to me."

"Then why aren't you here with us? Why are you moving to Kentucky?"

"I have to finish my tour. Then I'll move home to be with you guys! It's a short tour."

"Have you ever thought about taking me and the girls with you? They need their father, Earl. Michele doesn't even know you."

Letting Go

"I'm sorry, Beth, I'll come home more often now that I'm going to be stationed in Kentucky. I bought the house we looked at in Maryland for you and the girls to move into."

"I don't want to move to Maryland Earl. I want to stay where I am. Why can't we stay in housing?"

"Because I'm stationed stateside now and you will have to move out before I leave for Kentucky next week."

"Why don't you take a few weeks off Earl and help us gets settled?"

"I can't, I need to get back to the base and check in. I'll be back in a month or two."

Beth prepared the kids for the move. Two weeks had passed and she was still unpacking. Earl came home unexpectedly. "Why didn't you call us and tell us you were coming?"

"I didn't want you to be worried if I didn't make it. Beth, I need to speak to you in the family room."

"Girls, go upstairs and play while I speak to your father." She thought maybe Earl had changed his mind and decided to move back home.

"Beth, I'm not coming back here to live. The reason you can't come with me to Kentucky is that I'm moving there with my new family. I met her when I was stationed in Korea and we've been living together for the last six months. The reason my tour was cut short is she's pregnant and we're having twin boys. Beth, she's Korean and her culture is pretty strict about unwed mothers. I couldn't leave her there in her country. I have to do the right thing and marry her. We are trying to get married before the boys get here. I brought the divorce papers here with me, all you have to do is sign and it's official we are divorced."

"Earl, am I hearing you correctly? You want to do the right thing! What about the right thing about us Earl, the family you already have? Who's going to do the right thing and take care of us!"

The girls heard their mother raise her voice and came down the stairs. "Dad, what's the matter with mommy? Why are you two arguing?"

"Your dad is leaving. Take Michele and go back upstairs and play. I will call you before he leaves to say goodbye. Please

Marie, I need you to go now. Daddy and I are still talking about his new job."

"But mom, dad just got here!"

"I know, sweetheart. But he has to leave for a new job that starts tomorrow. He will be back soon; now go back upstairs! I'll be up in a minute and get you guys before he leaves. I promise."

When the girls were out of the room Beth had only one question for Earl. "Why move us way over here to Maryland and then leave us? Why didn't you move us closer to our friends? Earl, please tell me what are we supposed to do?"

"You're going to be fine Beth, you're a strong woman!"

"Is she white, Earl?"

"Beth, she's not white, she's Korean!"

"I knew it would be close! What, you couldn't find a white one?"

"Let's forget about the race for a minute! She's the one I chose! So let it go! I'm truly sorry for not giving you more notice but we knew this marriage was over long before it started."

"You're right there Earl! It was over the day it started!"

"I just took the decision out of your hands and started the ball rolling Beth. I'll be leaving the area in the morning. I have a motel in Virginia for tonight." He pulled the divorce papers out of his coat pocket and handed them to her. "Sign here, Beth, and you're a free woman!"

"Just like that Earl? You can come in here and move your family way across the state and throw divorce papers in my face and walk out to live happier ever after. I'm not signing your divorce papers until I've had a chance to look them over and see what's in it for the kids. Will they be getting support from you, Earl, or is that being taken away also?"

"You don't need child support. You're a top manager in your company, you can take care of yourself and the girls."

"You are going to sit there and tell me that you are not going to support your kids? You won't get off that easy, buddy! One day your past is going to catch up to you and you will pay. What goes around comes around, it's called "Karma. It may not be today or tomorrow but one day when you least expect it your

Letting Go

past will catch up to you and you will pay full price plus interest!" Beth signed the papers and asked him to leave her home. "I never want to lay eyes on your lazy behind again!"

She went upstairs and asked the girls to come down and say goodbye to their father because he had to leave tonight. Marie ran past Beth faster than light, she didn't want her dad to leave. She loved him so much. What will her babies do without their father? He would become someone else's daddy now. Marie ran into his chest full force! She was crying for her daddy not to leave. "Please don't go daddy! Please don't leave Michele and Me. I'll do better in school dad! Please don't leave us!"

"I'm sorry baby, I have to leave. I'll send for you and Michele once I'm settled. You can visit this summer, how about that? I'll call you everyday, I promise."

"Mommy, please make daddy stay! Everyone else has a daddy, why can't I have one mommy? Why does daddy have to leave?"

"He has to go to work sweetheart."

"He can stay here and work like you mommy. You're supposed to love us and stay with us forever. Isn't that what marriage is all about daddy?" She was smarter than her nine years gave her credit for. "How can you just leave daddy?"

"I'm sorry Marie, I have to leave now."

Earl realized he would have to explain this to her in a way that she would understand. He knew she had heard the whole story about the other family. Marie was sitting at the top of the stairs listening; she made sure Michele didn't make any noise so that she could hear what her mom and dad had been fighting about earlier. She heard him say he had another family. He was leaving them. He loved someone else. She had to stop him. Daddies aren't supposed to leave their family.

Earl took another approach. "Marie sometimes people have to let go of the past in order to reach for the future. When things go bad it's not good to hold onto them. The pain can only make you sad and unhappy. I have to let your mother go and she will find a new life for herself."

"That's good Daddy, but what about us? Are we going to have to find another Daddy also?"

This was breaking Beth's heart! The tears were falling down her face and Michele was wiping them with her tiny hands saying, "Don't cry mommy; I won't leave you."

"I know baby!"

Marie wasn't finished. "So daddy, what you're saying is that when a marriage gets too hard and a little pain sets in you run and leave that family and start a fresh one where there is no pain. Is that what you're doing Daddy?" The tears were streaming down her face but she said her piece and held tight to her beliefs. She got up and took her sister out of her mother's arms and said, "Goodbye, Daddy, please don't call us, we're letting you go also. We will find us another Daddy that won't walk out on us when times get hard." Marie took her sister's hand and they both ran upstairs.

Beth started up the stairs after the girls, then turned back to look at Earl. "You're one poor excuse for a father and a husband. I hope you have found what you've been looking for all these years! Now get the hell out of my house!"

Beth went up the stairs behind her daughters. Marie laid on her bed and cried. "I hate him, Mommy! I hate him for the pain he's caused us! I will never marry Mommy!"

"You will marry and be happy one day and you don't hate your Father. You're just angry and you will get over it. He's not a bad man, he's just a little confused. He loves you girls and he's not leaving you and Michele, he will still be your Father. No one will ever take that away from you. It's just that now you will have to share him with his other kids." Beth was sorry her baby had to go through that. She wished she could have spared her. Marie was still crying and telling her, "Don't worry, Mommy it will be ok; we're going to get a new Daddy. God will take care of us."

Beth was happy to have such a mature young lady. When did she grow up? She stayed with the girls until they both had fallen off to sleep. She would wake them for dinner later. These were some of the best years of their life and Earl had missed most of them. Beth felt sorry for him. She had signed the papers making it official. He had always been free from the moment they wed; he never gave up any of his old loves. This just made

Letting Go

it official. She was thankful and relieved that it was over. She would now need to concentrate on building a life for her girls. They would be her center.

Later that night Beth prayed to God, "Please send me a man worth having; a man with substance." She had prayed that prayer before but this time would be different. She didn't need another Earl, she needed someone like Brad, but he was someone else's bridge and she would never take their bridge away.

The Wedding

Beth slept with the relief of freedom! She knew there was nothing left to hold on to. She was strong and didn't need a crutch. From now on she would put all her faith in God, her savior. She knew that "man" would always find a way to disappoint you, but "God" would never let you down.

Beth's first call was going to be to Jean until she realized today was her wedding day. She and the girls would be picked-up in two hours by the limo. They would spend the weekend at Jean's new ranch while they planned the wedding events. Beth hung up the phone. She wouldn't put a damper on her friend's big day. She would celebrate Jean's happiness this weekend with her and Jack. The girls were almost ready. Marie had tried to pick out the best outfit for Michele, but Michele wasn't happy. She wanted to pick it out herself.

Michele was the spitting image of her father. Why did she have to look like him? Marie was a carbon copy of her aunt. Marie was sweet and upbeat. We kept each other going on our worst days. She would always look for the rainbow. I called her my little angel. "Hurry up girls, the limo will be here soon."

Brad would be at the reception. Jean had invited him and he had accepted without hesitation. She would keep her distance. The limo was on time. Marie was the first person out the door dragging her sister behind her. The ranch was beautiful this time of year! Jean was so lucky they had purchased a home overlooking the Potomac Lake in Maryland. It was breathtaking. The girls loved the horses and all the farm animals. Jack took really good care of the girls. Beth thought of how wonderful it would be to see him taking care of his own kids one day. Jean looked wonderful. They had flown in from a short business trip; she had refused to let Jack go without her.

Jean had gone to the doctors as planned the day after she almost passed out. She wasn't worried about her test. She was

Letting Go

happier than she had ever been in her whole life. There was nothing wrong with her that loving Jack couldn't cure. She just had to get her doctor to confirm it. Jean was rushing around preparing for the wedding and almost missed her appointment. Tomorrow was her big day. Jean ran into the doctor's office fifteen minutes late. "Excuse me, miss, I had a four fifteen appointment. I'm sorry. Traffic was crazy today. My name is Jean Richards."

"I'll let the doctor know you're here."

Jean was wondering why she had to come into the office. She normally gave her the result on the phone and sent the prescription to the pharmacy ahead of her. Dr. Gamble had been her doctor for over ten years. They weren't just doctor and patient; they were friends. She had sent Dr. Gamble an invitation to her reception. "I'm sorry I'm late, Judy!"

"I'm not surprised. Are you ready for your big day tomorrow?"

"Almost, my nerves have been acting up lately. Other than that I'm fine, never been happier in my entire life. Will I see you and Dan on Saturday?"

"Of course, we wouldn't miss it for anything."

Jean went over and took a seat. Dr. Gamble started her examination. "Judy, what's seems to be the problem?"

"You're pregnant!"

"That's impossible! I've been very careful. Jack and I have always used protection, plus you told me that there was a chance I couldn't get pregnant."

"I also told you that it was risky. Jean, if I said chance then that means you still could and you did! I want to run a few more tests just to make sure your baby is positioned properly. When did you have your last cycle?"

"I think it was about three months ago! I've been so excited lately that I thought it was my body adjusting to all the new changes. How far along do you think I am Judy?"

"I would say about three months if you gave me the correct dates."

"I thought Jack was the reason I was late, we've been everywhere together."

"Jean, Jack is the reason you are late. He's going to be a father! When are you going to tell Jack?"

"I'll tell him on our wedding night, maybe at the reception."

"Jean, before you tell him let me run a few more tests. Do you have time today?"

"Well I'm here; I might as well get it over with. Judy are you sure the test was mine?"

"Yes, Jean, it's yours! You're going to be a mother! Congratulation dear." Judy gave her a hug. Tears were running down Jean's face; she didn't know what to say. "I'm going to be mother! I'm pregnant! Jack is going to be a father!"

"Jean, if you don't stop that crying right now I'm going to have to call Jack."

Jean wiped at her eyes with a tissue and gave her friend another hug. "Thanks for the best wedding present anyone could ever receive!"

"You're welcome, but don't forget to thank Jack later."

This explained the dizziness and throwing up that she thought was food poisoning. "Judy, when will you have the test results back?"

"I will rush them through the lab today and call you as soon as I can. I'll have the lab call me at home with your results as soon as they get them."

"Thanks for everything Judy."

When Jean was seated in the limo she closed her eyes and prayed. "Thank you Lord for this gift, I will cherish it and love it. I will teach him to have faith in you and to love you as I do. Lord you have given me so much in such a short time. I will forever live in your grace. AMEN!" Jean would tell Beth about the baby. She was sure Beth would take one look at her and guess her secret.

Jean was waiting by the phone when Beth walked in. "What's up girl? Are you ready for tomorrow?"

"Yes, I've been waiting on this day and that man for what has seemed like a lifetime."

"Do you have everything you need; something old, something new, something borrowed and something blue? I'll be something blue for you! Just kidding, here's something blue. It's

Letting Go

and angel for an angel. Someone gave it to me at my wedding and now I'm passing it on to you. She watched over me and now it's her turn to watch over you! What's the matter Jean? You aren't going to start crying are you?"

"Beth, I know I can tell you anything can't I?"

"You know you can, girl."

"Where's Jack?"

"He's with the girls down at the stables."

"I'm pregnant!"

"What?" Beth hugged her friend and kissed her on the cheek. "Congratulations! That's wonderful, does Jack know?"

"Not yet! I'm waiting for Dr. Gamble to call me with my test results. Beth, I was told that I would never be able to have kids but God has blessed me with Jack's child. He will be so happy. Beth, I'm afraid to think of it as ours yet; what if there's something wrong with the way it's positioned? What if it's in my tubes? How will I live if I lose this child? I won't tell Jack until I know it's ok. I'm not going to put him through that." The phone rang. Jean had it in her hands before the ring ended.

"Hi Judy. Yes, ok, I'll call you when I get back. I'll see you on Saturday. Thanks for calling." She hung up the phone and just stood there.

"What did she say, Jean?"

"The baby is fine! I'm fine; everything is fine!" Jean started crying again. "Beth, what have I done to deserve such happiness? I never question God; everything will be revealed in time. I have a man that truly loves me and now I'm about to present him with God's greatest gift, a child!"

"Ok, Jean, when do we tell Jack; the good news?"

"What good news?" Jack asked as he and the girls entered the room. Beth and Jean were so busy crying and talking they missed the door chime signaling someone entering the house.

"Beth wanted to tell you that we have to keep the girls for a week here at the ranch once school is out for the holidays."

"Is that why you're crying?"

"Yes! I'm just so happy they're coming."

"That is good news, right girls?"

"Thanks, Aunt Jean and Uncle Jack, I can't wait for the holidays."

"Thanks, me to!" yelled Michele.

"Mom, do you think we could have a horse some day?" asked Marie.

"Yes, baby girl, I think that's possible," Jack answered.

Beth looked at Jack and smiled. "You have no clue as to what you've done!" Beth knew Jack loved the girls and would spoil them rotten if she let him. He was always trying to teach them new games. He was teaching both girls how to ride. He was the father figure that had been missing from their lives. Jean admired the way Jack cared for his soon to be nieces. She was glowing from ear to ear. She would make a wonderful mother and wife. Beth loved her friend dearly; they were closer than any sisters! She could always count on her.

Beth had left the girls outside playing with the dogs. They enjoyed being here around all the animals. Michele had asked if she could have a dog. Beth thought she would have to get her one soon. Beth knew she was lucky to have them. They were life's little treasures. There was so much peace and serenity here at the farm.

She hadn't heard from Earl. He should be settling into his new life. He wanted to marry the lady. She must be pretty special; he had never wanted to marry any of his girlfriends in the past. Maybe now he would settle down and be a real husband and father. She hoped anyway. "Good-luck and good-bye Earl," Beth thought to herself.

Brad arrived at the ranch around four. He was flying to Las Vegas with the wedding party. Jack and Jean had asked him to be one of the witnesses for the wedding. Beth was shocked; she knew he would be at the reception but had no idea he was flying with them to Vegas. She found Jean in the bedroom changing. "Brad tells me he's coming to Vegas. Jean why didn't you tell me Brad was going with us?"

"I knew you would have something against it."

"You're darn right I have something against it, Brad's married!"

"So are you, and we're taking you."

Letting Go

Beth was hot! "How and why Jean?"

"Beth, I asked Jack to call Brad yesterday and invite him to Vegas. He was coming to the reception anyway."

"There are more people at the reception. I could avoid him all night. I won't be able to avoid Brad on the plane and once we get there will I Jean?"

"Stop running, Beth! Brad is not going to go any further than you let him."

"Jean, Brad isn't the problem the problem is me. I can't seem to think and use good judgment when I'm around him. Where is Chris, the best man? Won't he be there?"

"No! His wife had a family emergency and they couldn't make it tonight. They will try and make the reception tomorrow."

"Jean, how could you do this? You know I'm not in the best of mind?"

"I had too. Marie sneaked and called me yesterday. She heard you crying! She said her dad had asked her mommy for a divorce and that he was leaving to live in Kentucky with his new family."

"The little snitch!"

"She asked me not to say anything Beth! Why didn't you tell me Earl had divorced you?" Jean asked. "She's really upset with her father. Beth, you cannot let Marie know I've told you and that I've broken her confidence. She said she never wanted to see him again. I told Marie that grown ups don't always make the right decisions that they make mistakes also. We just have to forgive them and move on."

"Thanks, Jean! I should have seen it coming," Beth said. "She was so hard on him yesterday. I didn't have the strength to fight back; nor did I want to. I've spent my whole marriage fighting for what; a man that would eventually walk out anyway. This was my chance to "Let go" so I did. I signed his divorce papers and he left! Jean, my life was already hard, why make it harder by trying to hold on to something that wasn't mine from the beginning? Earl had been looking for something else his whole life. I was never what he really wanted I was just the best of the four. Hey, this is your big day! That's enough talk about me. Let's go get you married! I love you, Jean!"

"I love you too, Beth."

They would change in the hotel where the chapel was located in Vegas. Jean was so excited! "How many brides get to fly to Vegas to get married and fly back the same day for her reception?"

"Not many," Beth told her. "You're living my dream life Jean!"

"Do you have everything you need, Beth?"

"Yes, Jean, I have everything. The girls will stay with Isabella until we get back in the morning. They are already settled. Jean, stop worrying, everything is taken care of. All you need to do is marry the most eligible, rich bachelor on earth."

"Thanks, Beth!"

Beth was speechless at what Jean was wearing, her dress was so simple yet she looked priceless. She was beautiful! Beth remembered what people said about brides; there would never ever be an ugly bride. Jean was beautiful inside and outside. She looked as if she were floating into the church on Brad's arm. Beth had never really paid that much attention to Jack's looks before. He was handsome with a great smile. He wore his hair cut close with medium side burns. He was perfect for Jean. They would have beautiful children. Jean had made a fine catch, not to mention the money! Jean would not be returning to work. Beth had dreaded the thought of going back to manage the store alone. It would never be the same now that Jean was gone.

Beth had been many miles away when Brad caught her eye as he escorted Jean into the chapel. Brad had noticed Beth the moment she entered the church. She would make a beautiful bride and would be envied by the women who witnessed her beauty. She had grace and dignity! She was more woman than he would know what to do with, yet she was all he wanted! He loved her and needed to tell her that. He was willing to take whatever she had to offer him and would wait as long as it took, even if it took a lifetime. She would be worth the wait. Brad knew she had avoided him on the plane.

Letting Go

Beth could feel Brad's eyes burning into her skin! She would hide the affects of his stare and stare him down. Brad had to turn away as he handed Jean over to Jack. He went over and stood next to Beth. He was standing so close Beth could smell his cologne, it was playing tricks on her mind. She was sure she was losing the battle of staying focused. She would lose consciousness at any moment. She had to regain control. She hated this guy for the affect he had on her and she hated Jack for bringing him along.

Jack and Brad acted as if they had been friends all their lives. It bothered Beth that people just wanted to share his space, male and female. Brad had a special charm that drew people and made them feel they always had his full attention; no matter what was going on in the room. Jack had mentioned to Jean that he liked Brad and wanted to see more of him. Once the ceremony was over, Jack escorted his wife out of the chapel and Beth was escorted by Brad. Jack invited Brad and Beth to come by before going to their rooms to change. Jean had a glow that only an expectant mother would have. Brad poured four glasses of apple cider for the toast and passed them around. Beth had explained to the clerk at the door to please switch the wine for cider in Jack's hotel room. She had sealed the deal with a twenty dollar tip. They toasted to the new couple and headed to their rooms to change.

Brad walked Beth back to her room. "Beth, I know things are a little confusing right now, but I want you to know that there is no place in this world that I would rather be than here with you. From the moment we met you touched my heart. I love you." He brushed his lips across hers and walked one door down to his room.

Beth stood there for what seem like eternity. She could think of only him! She waited until Brad closed the door to his room. She turned to walk into her room and realized she had always done the right thing but tonight she would follow her heart. She closed her door and went down the hall to Brad's room. She knocked on Brad's door. He opened it and she walked in. Beth threw herself into his arms. She gave him everything she had been saving. There would be no more waiting, she wanted him to make love to her again. They weren't expected downstairs for another hour and that would be plenty of time. She placed her arms around his neck and tiptoed to reach his lips. She kissed him with urgency. "Brad, I need you to make love to me now!"

"I'm sorry Beth! It's not the right time."

"What do you mean, it's not the right time?"

"I want to be free when I give myself to you again. I'm working with my lawyer on my divorce. I can't put you in the middle of all this! Things could get ugly in a few weeks. I would rather you and the girls not be involved."

"Brad, I'm already involved. Why didn't you think about this before you started pursuing me? Is this some kind of game to you? You get a girl to fall in love with you then you turn her away the minute you find out she loves you?" Tears were running down Beth's face. She was finding it hard handling Brad's rejection.

Brad wanted to take her in his arms and make love to her but he couldn't, he had made promises that he needed to keep. "Beth, please try and understand that I care for you also. I want us to be a family one day but I can't start acting as if I'm not committed to another and so are you. You have a husband to deal with and I have a wife."

"Yes."

"We can jump into bed now and I could take you to places that you have only dreamed about, but when it's over we both have to get up, get dressed and act as if it never happened. I won't do that to you. You deserve so much more. Beth, I want to give you everything you deserve when the time comes."

Beth knew what he was saying was true. She did deserve so much more. Wasn't this the same thing Earl had been doing to her all those years. "I'm sorry, Brad, it's just I've never been turned down before. I would love a life with you but I see that will never happen. I hope we can still be friends."

"Beth, didn't you hear me? I love you woman! I will make things right and we will be together in the end. Please have a little faith in love."

Letting Go

"Brad, love has always let me down! Why should this time be any different?"

"Because I love you and I don't make promises I can't keep."

"Good-bye, Brad! Thanks for everything."

Brad knew she would need some time to see the big picture. He was hoping he wasn't making a mistake.

Beth had waited for the newly weds to come downstairs to the hotel lobby. She needed to get back and end the weekend before she made a bigger fool out of herself. Jean, Jack, and Brad all came down together. They would all fly back tonight for the reception which was scheduled to start at six. Then Jean and Jack would fly off to the Bahamas for the honeymoon.

Beth envied her friend Jean. Jean saw what she wanted and made every effort to make it happen. Prayer does change things. Beth was a true believer of that. She would never give up her dreams of meeting "Mr. Right". He was out there somewhere looking for her, Beth was sure of it. She would be patient and wait. When everyone got back to the ranch, guests had already started assembling. Isabella informed Jean that some of the guests had been there since this morning. Beth had called Isabella from the plane to check on the girls. They would all stop by the Main House and freshen up before going down to the reception area at the back of the farm. They had several hours before it was to start. There were so many people in the house, most of them Beth had never seen before. She located the girls. They were having a great time. Isabella assured Beth that they were little angels. Beth had arranged for Isabella to stay until the affair was over so she could see the girls to bed. That would free her up to help Jean and enjoy the reception.

Jack and Jean were announced as they proceeded into the reception area to be congratulated. Jack shook hands and received hugs from his parents and family. Jean was happy to see all her and Jack's family having fun together. Her mother loved Jack from the moment she met him. She had told Jean that he was going to fill all her dreams and so far he was right on track. Jean's mother knew how bad Charles had hurt her daughter.

Brad came and sat next to Beth. They hadn't spoken since she left his room. They were too close; their knees were touching under the table. Beth had to readjust her seat. They both felt it. "Excuse me," they both said in unison. The tension was so thick between them.

After dinner Brad stood and made a toast. "I would like to take this time to wish two very special people all the joy that's mortally possible. May you have the best of everything! To Jack and Jean! May God bless this union!"

"Thank you, Brad! Jean motioned for Beth to join her. They went to the center of the stage.

Jean said, "I have a toast to make to my new husband."

Jack looked at his new bride with such pride. He had chosen a winner in everyway, he thought.

"Jack," Jean said as tears started to build in her eyes, "I promised myself that I wasn't going to cry. Jack, you have given me my life back. Who ever said that prayer doesn't work needs to see me later!" Jack was standing. He headed in the direction of his wife. He stopped at the end of the stage. "Jack, I've never given anyone what I'm going to give to you." Beth reached in her purse and pulled a small pair of booties out. They had chosen yellow because they didn't know what sex the baby would be. "Jack, you are going to be a father in about six months!"

He had already started moving again but when he saw the booties he was speechless! They held each other and cried in the middle of the stage. She was carrying their first child. Jack yelled out, "I'm going to be a Father! Mom, dad we're going to have a baby!"

"We heard, son! Congratulations!"

Beth hugged Jack and Jean. Beth moved back down the stairs to where Brad was standing. He saw happiness and sadness both in her eyes and it broke his heart. She was filled with such loneliness. He had the power to take the loneliness away but it would be only a temporary fix. She would wake up in the morning with the same lonely feeling. He wanted to fix the problem forever. That would be his goal.

Beth tried to smile at Brad as she returned from the stage, but something was lost, the smile never made it to her lips. She

Letting Go

wasn't a good friend at the moment because she wished she were Jean. Beth was jealous and feeling sorry for herself. The first dance call was made for the new couple. They danced to Jean's favorite song "Can't Get Enough of Your Love" by Barry White. Jean was holding on to her husband as if he were the last man on Earth. Beth could relate to her actions.

Brad found Beth standing out on the porch. She had been thinking of the day she married Earl, it was so different; she had relived almost the whole event. They ran off to the justice of the peace. With strangers as witnesses. She had been blessed with the company of the courts. Theirs was a quick "I DO" and off they went back to work on the following Monday. Their lives had started off sad. Earl didn't have any money and they lived from paycheck to paycheck. They were doomed from the beginning.

"Beth," Brad called to her from behind. She quickly wiped her eyes and tried to smile. "Would you please come in and dance with me? They are playing our song."

Beth had to laugh because she knew they didn't have a song. "Sure Brad, I'll dance with you." He guided her to the dance floor holding her body just a little too close. The song was soft and mellow. Beth couldn't help herself; she had fallen in love with this man before she even knew his name. Beth was ready to walk away; she would do it in style. She would do it later; right now she only wanted to enjoy the dance. They danced for two more songs. She then danced with Jack and Brad danced with Jean.

Jean asked Brad to do her a favor. "Whatever I can Jean."

"Beth's husband divorced her yesterday. He has now moved her to Maryland and he has moved to Kentucky to be with his new family. She's in so much pain, Brad. It runs deeper than anyone of us know. Beth has already been through a lot. She couldn't survive another heartbreak Brad," Jean said. "She's been feeling a little sorry for herself today. I guess it's the wedding and the baby and everything. She not missing him, she was happy he made the first move. She's just not sure where to go from here. She is in a delicate spot right now she has feelings for you, but she will try and hide them because of your situation.

She's been there. She knows there's no winner when this kind of game is played. I just don't want to see her hurt again, Brad," Jean said. She deserves more than cheep hotels and a hit or miss, "every-once-in-a-while romance." She can do badly all by herself. She doesn't need help with that."

"Jean, you may find this hard to believe; but I'm in love with Beth. I want to take care of her and the girls but I'm not in a position at this time to give her what she needs. I'll need time. I've asked Beth to give me time and I will do the right thing."

"She does not want you to leave your family for her Brad; that would go against everything she has ever believed in," Jean said. "It has to be your decision and yours only."

"Jean, this is my sole promise to you. Whatever I decide to do about my marriage is going to be my decision. I'll never hurt Beth, Jean. I've never envied anyone in my whole life until I met you and Jack, you have everything you ever wanted and you're perfect for each other. That's what I want for Beth and me. Beth deserves that kind of happiness and I'm the one to make it happen."

"Thanks Brad for watching out for her. She's a good woman! I don't know if she told you this, but she loves you. It will be hard for her to tell me she loves you and I'm her best friend," Jean said.

Jack came over to steal his wife away. "Brad, can we exchange our visions of beauty? You take mine and I'll take yours."

Jack handed Beth's hand over to Brad. Beth was mentally tired. They had made plans for her and the girls to stay the night at the ranch. She had said goodnight to Jean's parents a while back, they had to fly out early in the morning. Jack's parents were heading for the door. They were waiting on Jean and Jack to head out for the airport before they left. Beth had helped Jean change clothes for her trip. They had a long goodbye. Beth said to Jean, "At least you can't come back knocked-up."

"You got that right!"

They both fell on the bed laughing!

Letting Go

"To late, Jack got a little ahead of himself." Beth had been serious all day. She would be all right. "Jean, please take care of yourself and my niece or nephew."

"I will, Beth." Jean patted her stomach. "This is a miracle baby from God!"

They hugged and headed to the limo. Jack was waiting at the top of the steps and everyone threw birdseeds and blew bubbles as they walked out to the car. They both turned and waved goodbye. Brad made his way to Beth's side. Beth would spend the night wishing it was her driving away in that limo! How selfish!

Brad touched her arm and bought her back to the present. "Why don't we see the rest of the guests off?"

"Aren't you leaving tonight Brad?"

"No, Jack asked me to stay over and make sure you and the girls get home safe in the morning."

"We're fine Brad, we wouldn't want to put you out. What about your wife? Isn't she waiting on you at home?"

"No, she is in New Jersey visiting family."

"Does she know where you are this weekend?"

"She knows I'm at a friend's wedding. That's all she knows. Do you feel better knowing she's in New Jersey?"

"Yes, I do, Brad! I'm only concerned that she doesn't get the wrong idea about our relationship!"

"That's what I need to talk to you about later, Beth. Let's clear the house first. Then we can sit out here on the porch and talk."

They greeted friends and family as they made their final departure. Beth looked in on the girls before returning to the porch. They were sound asleep. The caterer was the last to pack up. Jack had left instructions for the tent to be removed on Monday. Beth sat in silence. She was mentally and physically exhausted. She had taken a week off from work to move. Beth felt as if she had been on a roller coaster ride all week. Why couldn't she get off in Pleasantville? One quickie marriage and one quickie divorce. What was next? "So Brad, what's on your mind?"

She had sat on the love seat without thinking. Brad was standing near the edge of the porch. He came over to sit next to her. "Beth, I need to say something to you and I want you to just listen until I finish. Please, can you do that? First I want you to know that I will never hurt you. I will do everything in my power to always keep you from harm's way. My wife and I are divorcing; this has nothing to do with you! We haven't slept together in years! I know this does not concern you. I just wanted you to know that. She tricked me into marrying her by getting pregnant. She first claimed she was on the pill and then two months later she turns up pregnant claiming I was the father! I took a blood test which proved I was the father. I had to do the right thing by my child and marry his mother. I met her when I was at a low point in my life. I've paid for that weak moment every since. I love my son very much, that's why I've stayed as long as I have. I wanted him to have something I didn't have. I wanted to give him a stable home. I had a very hard life growing up without my father and I wanted to spare him that type of growing up."

"Brad, people always stay married for the wrong reason. Marriage should be about what we witnessed tonight, not the children. Yes they are important, but they shouldn't be what the marriage is built on; it should be built on love, trust, and honesty! That's what was missing from my marriage. We never had trust. I didn't trust my ex as far as I could see him." She realized she had said ex!

"Beth, you said ex!"

"Yes, Brad I said ex. I signed the divorce papers yesterday. I'm a free woman. Brad it only took one day."

Brad would never let on that Jean had already told him about the divorce. He did not want her to know that Jean had broken her word and confided in him about her personal life.

"Earl should be married by the end of the week."

"You don't sound bitter."

"Why should I be? I'm relieved! I have lived a lie for so long. I was waiting until I was financially stable before I left him. He just beat me to the punch. I'm starting over with new instruction and direction."

Letting Go

Brad didn't know what to say to her. He had told her that he was headed in the same direction. Brad didn't want Beth to feel responsible for his marriage ending. He would do it for all the right reasons. Brad was holding her hand in his. "You know, Beth, I've been doing things in this marriage that I'm not proud of. I'm not blaming anyone but myself for the mistakes I made. I have a chance now to make things right and that's what I have to do." Brad stood and pulled Beth to her feet. He placed both of her hands in his and placed them over his heart. "I want you to feel my heart and know that this is where I keep you! Each and everyday! I can only hope that we can follow in Jean's and Jack's footsteps. I have to leave now before I break a promise to someone that I've come to respect as a friend."

He knew she wanted him in her life. But this was not the time. She would have to be patient. He had issues to work through. She said goodnight and they both headed off to bed.

Beth wasn't sure of what Brad's next move would be. She only hoped he would make it soon. They had spent their entire married life married to the wrong people. Beth knew she would have to wait for the tables to turn.

Brad left her confused but he couldn't stand being that close to her and not have her! He had to leave this ranch tonight! He knew he couldn't sleep under the same roof with her and not have her in his bed. He would need more will power than he had at the moment. Brad waited until everyone was in bed before calling for a taxi to take him back to his car. He would avoid Beth at all cost until he had something more than just broken promises to offer her. The time would come when his heart was free and he could accept her and the kids as his family. But for now he must let her go and pray that one day she would come back.

Brad decided to start his day off by calling his lawyer to check on his separation papers. They would need processing as soon as possible. He hadn't told Ellen that he was leaving. This was definitely going to get ugly. He knew he would never be able to leave her without a fight. He had never thought of his marriage as a charade before but that was what it was and they both knew it. He would end it for good.

Charles Gets the News

Jean and Jack arrived at their hotel in the Bahamas. It was more than she could have imagined. They walked the beaches until late at night. The sand was a perfect place to make love. They were more than just man and wife, she was his soul mate and they would share everything together. Jack was overjoyed about the baby.

"Why didn't you tell me about the baby, Jean? When did you find out?"

"Yesterday, right before we left for the airport."

"How could you have kept that a secret?"

"Well, I knew I would be giving you the best present in the world if I could tell you you're going to be a father on your wedding day."

"How did this happen? I thought you couldn't have kids?"

"That's what I thought also, and after we got engaged the first week I stopped using protection. Dr. Gamble said the baby and I are fine. The baby is in a good position and we should have a normal pregnancy."

"We will! I'm not leaving you alone when we get back. I have one short trip to Alaska with Chris but I want you to come with me. I have to make sure you're taking care of yourself and our baby."

"No Jack, I'll be fine. Please don't start worrying about me. I want you to go to Alaska with Chris and then hurry back home to us. This will give me a chance to set up the house for Thanksgiving! I haven't really had a chance to do much. I need to do a little decorating. I'll call Beth over and let her help me. She is having a tough time lately."

"That sounds good!"

Jean knew she had a complete package. She would call Charles and tell him she was married an expecting their first child.

Letting Go

On the return home she made her first call to check on Beth and the girls. Beth was down and out because she hadn't heard from Brad or seen him since the reception. Jean heard the pain in her voice. "I'm sorry Beth, you just need to be patient and keep the faith. If it's meant to be, it will be. Just remember that those are your words."

"Thanks Jean and welcome home. I've missed you!"

"Me to! We will talk later!"

Jean called Charles. She knew he was living with Amy now so she dialed his cell. They would be married in a week. "Hello, Charles, how's life been treating you?"

"Wonderful!"

"I've got some great news! I've gotten married again Charles!"

Charles fell speechless! "You're married?! When did this happen and to whom?"

"It's been two weeks now and his name is Jack Morris. You don't know him; he's from California. I'm also expecting our first child! Charles can you believe it? I'm going to have a baby!"

"Yes Jean, that's wonderful news. I came by the store a few times."

"Beth didn't mention it. She just said you were out of town. I thought it was business."

"I asked Beth not to mention it. I wanted to tell you myself, Charles."

"I'm really happy for you, Jean. So when is the baby due?"

"In four and half months. I'm so excited! I can't believe it. How's Amy, Charles?"

"The baby is due in two weeks!"

"I guess you are pretty anxious to see if it's yours?"

"Yes, I am, but either way it won't matter I'll love it regardless. Amy is such a wonderful person! We will be married on Friday!"

"Congratulations, Charles. I hope you're as happy as I am."

"Amy didn't want a big wedding, you know, because of what happened with Ken."

"I can understand that. You can always do it later."

183

"I'm very happy for you and Jack, he's a lucky man!"

"No, Charles! Luck didn't have anything to do with this. He was a blessing from God and so is our baby. Charles, I want to thank you and Jack asked me to thank you also."

"For what?!"

"For Letting me go Charles! If you had never let me go then I would have never known what true love felt like. Charles, I'm not trying to be mean. I just wanted you to know. I know Amy is your soul mate. I remember you telling me she was. So what you've done is a wonderful thing. You helped two people find what most search their whole life for. You found Amy and I found Jack. Thank you again!"

Charles hung up the phone with a puzzled look on his face. Jean sounded so different and so full of life. He felt a twinge of jealousy. He had given her freedom. He had no right to be feeling anything but joy. His soon-to-be wife was going to give him a baby in less than two weeks. Charles was looking forward to fatherhood and a new marriage. Jean wasn't the only one happy. He made the right choice in leaving her! She wasn't the woman for him after all. Amy was what he needed! They both wanted the same things, a career and family. Jean only talked about adoption and kids and keeping house. Yes! He had made the right decision in leaving her. He should have left earlier!

Amy had been listening to Charles on the phone. "Who was that, Charles?"

"Hi, sweetheart. I didn't hear you come in. That was Jean. She was calling to say she had gotten married and is expecting a child."

"Why that's fantastic! Who did she marry?"

"Some guy name Jack Morris."

"Did you say Jack Morris?"

"Yes! Do you know him, Amy?"

"Charles, Jack Morris is one of the Morris' and Morris Real Estate tycoons. They have one of the largest real estate firms in California. She has married a millionaire. Well if she landed him she's one lucky woman!"

"No, Amy, she's a blessed woman!"

Letting Go

"I guess you're right, Charles. She is truly blessed! He's worth over five hundred million dollars. Of course he has partners so I guess you could say he is worth millions."

Charles was hoping Amy would shut up about Jean and her million dollar man. He had heard enough. Charles was speechless. "Why didn't she say something?"

"Maybe she didn't want to make you feel bad, Charles, because you did leave her. Now she's one of the richest women in America!"

Charles had heard all he wanted to hear! "How do you know so much about this guy Amy?"

"Charles, his picture has been on almost every fortune magazine for the last two months; something about the property value in Alaska is sky rocketing due to the oil prices and his company had made a big investment in land over there. I can't remember all the details but it's big! Well, Charles, are you alright? Your ex-wife will never have to work, that's for sure!" Amy was excited that Jean had gotten married. She had never considered Jean a threat, after all Charles left her. She was just glad she was off the market.

Amy was thrilled that Jean was married! She would wed Charles on Friday. She wasn't sure if Charles was getting cold feet, but he had seemed different lately, like he wasn't sure he wanted her as his wife. Now with Jean married and happy he wouldn't be looking at her as a possibility. Amy needed to be reassured that Charles stilled loved her. Maybe he was in love with the idea of being in love. She needed to know before she said "I DO." Amy had started feeling a little weak at the end of the week. She wanted Charles to hurry home; they needed to leave soon to be at the courthouse at 2:00. Today was her wedding day, but she wasn't felling the part! Her parents had the girls and would keep them for the next week. That would give her and Charles a week to celebrate their marriage. The baby was due in one week.

Charles drove up. He had been trying to find the perfect present for his bride. He wanted her to feel as special as she was. He wasn't sure, but every since Amy had mentioned Jean's husband, he had felt nothing but jealousy. He wanted what Jack had but he knew that would never happen. He would show Amy that he had chosen her! He would never let her know that in the end, Jean had rejected him. He would give Amy everything possible, and make sure she would never want for anything.

Charles walked into the room with the most beautiful bouquet of roses. It matched her dress perfectly. She was delighted.

"Are you ready?"

"I'm as ready as I'll ever be Charles! Let's go before the baby decides he wants to be here first."

They were married in less than thirty minutes. Amy's excitement threw her right into labor! "Charles, my water just broke."

"You're kidding!"

"No, Charles! We need to get to the hospital right now!"

Charles turned the truck around and headed to the hospital. He called Amy and his parents on the way. "The baby is coming" was all he had time to say. "Meet us at the hospital."

Amy was in labor for less than five hours before giving birth to a healthy baby boy. They had chosen the name Anthony. Charles was in the delivery room with her when the baby was born. Those were the proudest moments of his life! Charles was the first to hold his son. He was perfect. He had all the features of his mother and father.

The baby wasn't Charles's. Charles noticed that right away. He felt as if he was run over by a car. Amy read Charles's face and she knew the baby was Ken's. There was no need for words. The moment they had all wished for was now over. Ken was Anthony's father and nothing would change that. The baby would be raised as Charles's son. Charles would love him as his own. There would be minor changes made to the birth certificate. Amy was angry that Ken was her child's father! She hated him even more! He was dead and still ruining her life. Why couldn't Charles be her baby's daddy? She couldn't hold back the tears. She knew how much this baby meant to Charles. Amy was unable to comfort her husband. Words would not be enough. She told him, "We will have many more kids and your blood will run through all their veins!"

Letting Go

He smiled, and kissed her forehead. "I know sweetheart."

Charles assured her he would love Anthony as if he was his own. Amy was released from the hospital three days later. Charles had his family complete. He made sure Amy was comfortable. He then sent the girls outside to play and headed out to the kitchen to make dinner. He wasn't very domestic around the house; Jean had taken care of all those things. He loved having a family. Charles had only one wish and that was that one day he would have a child of his own. But for now he would have to settle for someone else's "Child."

Charles called Jean and told her he was a father. He explained that the baby was Ken's. "Jean, even from the grave he's in control of my family. Jean when will he let go of his hold? I can't fight a dead man."

"You won't have to Charles, you're the one that's breathing. Take control of your son. Tell Amy you want to adopt him as yours. I'm sorry he's not your blood Charles, but he can still be your son." Jean knew how much this must be hurting Charles. He had gambled everything on this baby and lost.

The Missing

Jean called Beth to ask if she and the girls would like to come out to the ranch for Thanksgiving. Jack should be home by then and the entire family would celebrate Thanksgiving dinner at the ranch. "Please Beth! I haven't seen my husband in six weeks so at least I'll have you. I'm lonely Beth. If you come I'll make you're favorite desert." Beth agreed to come on out, and bring the girls.

Jean was waiting to hear something from Jack, he was over due. She had invited Jack's family and her family for their first real holiday together. Everyone had agreed to come and Jean cooked the entire meal. She cooked for two days while waiting on Jack's call. He called last night and said he would be home first thing this morning. Jean was so excited she had made all Jack's favorite dishes and had purchased him a coming home present. It was getting late and there was still no word from Jack. Jean had started serving dinner when the phone rang. Beth was the closest to the phone and picked it up. Jean wasn't really paying attention to what was going on, she was making sure everyone was eating. "Beth, is that Jack? Find out how far out he is. Tell him he's very late." Jean had called the plane and his cell phone and there were no answer. She figured he had already landed. Her parents had tried to hide their concern; they didn't want to upset her.

Jack had left the airport later than anticipated. The weather wasn't cooperating, it had started snowing again. But Chris was a very good pilot and they both wanted to get home for Thanksgiving. He had tried to call Jean but the lines were all down. He would call once they landed. Chris had no problem once the ice had melted off the wings. So they started home. There were several other individuals flying back with them. This trip had lasted three weeks longer than scheduled. Jack missed

Letting Go

his wife and knew she would be worried sick. They had spoken only briefly on the phone.

He had assured her he would not miss their first Thanksgiving dinner. They were flying over the Alaska mountain front when the engine lights came on. Usually this wouldn't be a major concern for Chris, he would just shut the one down and fly off the other three. But tonight the weather was causing other problems with the ice reforming on the engine wings. Jack took his seat immediately. He would help Chris if he needed it but his co-pilot and he were doing a great job keeping the plane in the air. The plane shifted into a whirlwind and Chris was loosing control. They were going to hit a major storm. Jack had been warned that there was a storm on the horizon. He was hoping they would pass in front of it.

The plane was being forced down! Chris had lost another engine to ice. Chris informed everyone to get into a crash position. They were going down fast! He wasn't sure of their position. He radioed a mayday that they were going down in the middle of the mountains. Chris had attempted to radio his location but got no response, hopefully they were on radar. Jack was wondering if they would survive the crash. Even if they survived the crash the temperature was twenty degrees below zero. They would never last until someone found them. Jack prayed as the plane crashed landed. There was no way they would survive long in this temperature. They would need to find shelter! Chris had noticed a building as they were going down about two miles back before the crash. He mentioned to Jack that he and his co-pilot would go and find help.

Jack knew they could not stay here, that they all would have to go together. "There's safety in numbers," Jack told Chris. They looked around the plane for extra clothing to use as a shield from the freezing wind there were no extra clothing. They would have to go and leave the crew and hurry back as fast as they could. Chris led Jack in the direction of the building they had spotted from the plane. The building was located in a clearing in the middle of nowhere. There were lights surrounding the building and grounds. It seems to be some kind of medical center, Jack thought.

Chris and Jack had taken about twenty steps toward what looked like a main door when a huge iron door swung open! A man stood at least seven feet tall in the door. "My God he's tall!" said Chris. He was holding a gun!

"What can I do for you gentlemen?" the man asked.

"Our plane crashed about two miles from here. We were wondering if we could use your phone to call for help," Jack asked. Sir, do you have any kind of vehicle we could borrow to get to the nearest Ranger Station?"

"Our phones are out because of the storm. Where are you guys from?"

"We're here from Washington DC."

"You fellows are a long way from home, aren't you?"

"We were headed back to Washington when we ran into that storm."

"How did you manage to get this far off track? You are way down in Fairbanks!"

Chris was feeling a little uncomfortable. "Sir, is there any kind of transportation we could use? We left four co-workers on the plane with the temperature dropping. They won't last the night."

"Yes, we have a snowmobile in the back of the building and you're welcome to use it."

"Thanks sir!"

"You are welcome to stay here until the storm breaks."

"Just what kind of place is this, sir, if you don't mind my asking?"

"It's a research center for the Army! We're on classified business and that's all I can tell you!"

Jack felt that was more than he needed to know. They would have to be very careful not to overstay their welcome. They headed to the crash site to pick up the rest of the crew. It would be dark soon. They definitely didn't want to get lost out here. Jack had let their new friend drive since he seemed to know the area better. Jack showed him where the plane had gone down. They would spend the night and leave first thing in the morning. He hoped the phone would be working by then and

Letting Go

they could call for another plane. Their new friend was named James.

"Where is everyone, James?"

"Gone home for the holidays. I will take my holiday Christmas. This building has twenty four hour security."

James seemed friendly enough; still we all stayed pretty close together. Jack knew Jean was hysterical by now. If only his cell phone would work!

"Who was it Beth?" Jean asked. Beth had turned red. Jean had plates in her hand and when she read Beth's face she dropped the plates. "What is it Beth? Its Jack isn't it?"

"Please Jean, sit down."

"No Beth, what's happened to my husband; he's dead isn't he? Please God, don't let him be dead!"

Beth tried to calm Jean down before continuing. By this time her parents was at her side. "Please Jean, you have to calm down and let Beth finish. Think of the baby!"

"All they know is the plane went down near Fairbanks. They had a mayday call from Jack's plane then nothing!"

Jean fainted and was caught by Jack's father and her father. If her father wasn't already holding on to her arm she would have fallen hard. They carried Jean and laid her on the couch. "Someone please dial 911," her mother instructed. She was having a hard time keeping calm. Beth dialed 911 and the ambulance arrived in fifteen minutes. Jean was just coming around when they got there.

She had awakened calling for Jack. "Jean, please, we don't know what happened. They are probably ok." Jean wasn't listening, she kept repeating Jack's name. Beth called Jean's doctor. She would meet them at the hospital. Jean was admitted for a few days for observations. Jack's parents had stayed at the house with the girls, while Beth rode in the ambulance with Jean to the hospital. Jean's parents followed in the car.

Jean's doctor came in and examined her and the baby. She explained to Beth and her parents that Jean needed to stay calm. She had given her something to make her rest. Beth wished she could have called Brad; she needed him right now. She got up the courage to call him, this was an emergency. Jean needed him! Brad answered the phone on the second ring. "I'm sorry to bother you on Thanksgiving, but Jack's plane is missing in Fairbanks, Alaska and Jean is in the hospital. I need for you to try and find him and bring him home. Please!"

"I'm on my way, Beth! What hospital?"

"She's in the one in Potomac, Maryland. I can't really think right now! Please hurry Brad!"

"I'll be there in half an hour. Thanks for calling me, Beth."

Beth knew she would feel better once she saw Brad even though he would be there for Jean, not her. She really didn't want to take him away from his family at Thanksgiving but she needed to find Jack. Jean wouldn't survive if something had happened to him. She knew the pain Jean was feeling, she truly loved Jack and if she lost him she would welcome death. Beth had tried to talk to Jean in the ambulance. She kept telling her she had to be strong for the baby that she would pull through and so would Jack, at least that's what Beth hoped. Please hurry Brad!

Brad had moved out the home he shared with his wife two weeks ago. He was still fighting to see his son. She had refused to let him see him ever since he filed the divorce papers and moved out. The divorce would be final in six months since they hadn't slept together in over a year. That was one law in Virginia that he liked. Ellen had tried everything she could think off to get back in his bed. Brad was sure he hadn't seen the last of her tricks. He had been granted visitation rights to see his son on weekends but Ellen would always have an excuse for taking him out of town. When the divorce was final they would share joint custody. He had not asked for anything except his clothes and freedom. He would give her everything except his son! They would have to share him.

Brad reached the hospital in less than thirty minutes. Beth was waiting at the entrance of the corridor. She ran into his arms and let the tears fall. She hadn't meant to cry but somehow she was crying for herself as well as Jean! She had missed him and needed him! Brad's arms were strong and he held her close. She had longed for this moment! It was sad that he was here for Jean

Letting Go

and not her. She pulled away and wiped her eyes. "She's not doing well, Brad, she needs to know that Jack is ok."

"Will you please go with me to Fairbanks and help bring him home?"

"Yes Brad, I will do whatever it takes. Where do we start looking?"

"Where is Jack's private plane kept? We can use it if he left it in the hanger."

"He used the bigger company plane! Jack keeps it at some airfield in Maryland."

"I know this guy that owes me a favor. He can fly us there."

"Can we leave tonight, Brad?"

"Sure. What about the girls, are they fine?"

"They're with Jack's parents at the ranch. I need to call them and let them know what's going on!" Beth went back into Jean's room. They had a monitor on her and the baby. I could hear its heart beat. It sounded so far away! Jean would have to get control of herself. She owed that much to her miracle baby. Beth reached over and kissed her friend's forehead and while touching her stomach she said "Little one, Uncle Brad and I are going to bring your daddy home! I need you to hang on in there for mommy and daddy." She then turned and walked out of the room.

Jean's father had stepped out to get coffee. "Where are you two going, Beth?"

"Mr. Campbell, you remember Brad from the wedding?"

"Yes I do! What up?"

"We're going to get Jack and bring him home. When Jean wakes up I want her to look in her husband's face!" She reached over and kissed Mr. Campbell on the cheeks and left. She was positive they would find Jack alive.

When they reached the airport the weather report for Fairbanks had just came in. The airport was closed due to the weather! They would have to land in Juneau. That was as close as they could get. That was twenty miles east of Fairbanks. Beth didn't care, she knew he was alive. The man Brad had called met them at the hanger. Brad made quick introduction while moving toward the plane. Brad explained the details further about the mission. Beth was a little nervous. Glenn was quite young. Brad seemed to sense Beth's uneasiness. "He's very capable of flying this small plane Beth. He's an instructor at the Air Traffic School in DC."

"Thanks Brad! I'll get us there and if Jack's alive we won't come back without him!"

"Thanks a lot Glenn. That's what we both wanted to hear!"

Jack and his co-workers were led to several carts that were used for beds. Each one of them was exhausted, they needed rest and food. They were grateful for everything; James had saved their lives! Jack didn't think he would be able to sleep. But he was out the moment his head hit the bunk. The walk from the plane had taken a lot more than he realized from him.

They all had awakened to the smell of bacon and eggs. Jack made his way back to the kitchen by following the smell of breakfast.

"Good morning sir! How did you sleep?"

"Very well, thank you! Are the phones working?"

"No, I'm afraid they are still out. You are welcome to try them again. I tried them a few minutes ago."

Jack walked over and pressed the receiver down. The line was still dead. "Is there an emergency radio here? What happens in cases like this?"

"Well, Mr. Morris..."

"Please call me Jack."

"Jack we usually wait the weather out. It's not often we get plane crashes around here, people know when to fly. No offense to you!"

"None taken."

"It's rare we see anyone up in these parts. We have a ranger station about ten miles north of here. We can make a run for it after breakfast if you don't want to wait on the phone."

"I say let's do it! Can we all fit in your snowmobile? I'll make it worth your time."

"That's not necessary. You better get your friends moving; storms come up really fast around these parts. We can't waste any time, we need to get on the road immediately."

Letting Go

Jack needed to get word to Jean that he was all right. He knew she would think the worst. That had always been the case with her. She was always talking about him being a gift from God. I guess she was figuring that God might want his angel back! Jack had to smile at himself for thinking of something so foolish at a time like this. She worried way too much!

Beth and Brad landed at the Juneau airport. Brad checked with the air traffic control tower to see if they had heard any news about the plane. He also had someone call the Fairbanks airport to see if they could locate where the last transmission came from. They would have to rent a snowmobile to travel to the Fairbanks airport from here. They would need an escort with a good sense of direction. The weather was getting worse so they would have to leave the area soon. Beth was ready to head out! She wanted to find Jack and get home. Beth called back to the hospital to check on Jean. She was still resting. Beth knew she was running out of time! She was happy that Brad was a take charge kind of guy. He had made all the decisions for them. They were on their way to a research center. It was located in the middle of nowhere. The escort was keeping in touch with the tower. There was another storm on the horizon. They would have to find shelter soon.

"How long have you two been married?"

"We're, not married."

"Well he's married, I'm divorced."

"I'm sorry, you two looked as if you were married."

"It's perfectly ok, sir."

Brad didn't try to explain things any clearer. He had filed for his divorce. He would wait on telling her. He would come to her when he was free. He just wished it were now. She was lovely and even in this harsh winter storm she took his breath away! Brad had to keep his wits. She was depending on him and he would not let her down. They would find Jack and bring him home to his wife.

"Brad, what's on your mind?"

"I was just thinking of Jean and Jack. Jean has been through so much with Charles leaving her and now she has everything she ever dreamed of. If she lost Jack, she would lose herself! I would hate to think of what it would do to her spirit. They're so in love!"

"I know, Brad, that's why we have to find him and soon."

She was hoping they weren't lost. You couldn't see anything for the snow! The young man pulled up to a building that stood out like a sore thumb. You could barely see it for the snow was much thicker than it had been when they left! "There's another storm headed this way. It should pass us in a couple of hours. We need to get inside fast." The radio was blaring out instructions about the storm. Brad grabbed Beth's hand and made a dash for the door. "Let's hope whoever is inside has seen or heard something about the plane."

"We heard all the phone lines were down in the area. Cell phones weren't even working out here! Where is everybody?"

"Everyone has probably gone home for the holiday. They probably won't return until Monday."

The door was open and they walked in as if they lived there. There was smell of bacon was in the air. "Someone has been here lately; I can still smell the food. Where would they go to try and get out of this place? Why would they leave the door unlocked? You can't be too safe out here."

"I'm sure that was an oversight. But right now I'm not mad at them!" The weather was getting a little ugly out there.

"You're right, someone will be returning here soon."

"I'm sure your friends made it to some place safe before the storm hit. The wind chill would drop to ten below in just seconds they would have to move fast. If they were out there walking they wouldn't survive the night! Why would they leave here and where would they go? I'll bet a thousand dollars they headed to the ranger station and they're probably not walking!"

Beth wasn't going to think of Jack as stranded. He was fine, she was sure of that! "Ok guys, we might as well get comfortable. We will be here a few hours."

"Miss, you might want to get some rest. The road up at the ranger place is going to be rough."

"Thanks, but I'm fine and I'm really good at taking care of myself!" Beth said the words with more anger than she felt. She just wasn't happy at the moment. Brad was at her side before she

Letting Go

could say anything else. "I'm fine, Brad, I don't want to rest. I want to stay alert. We may get a call or something."

"Beth, remember I tried, the phones are all out! Please Beth, you have been up over twenty four hours straight and you're exhausted. I will stay up so try and get some rest. If there's any news I will wake you, I promise."

"Brad, this is a strange place and I'm just not sure it's safe here. What kind of research center is this that people leave the door open? Any crazy person could wander in here."

"Beth, we're in Alaska. There are no crazy people wandering around here. It's too cold!" He made her smile! "Come on I'll walk you back to the carts and stay with you while you rest."

Beth felt better knowing Brad would be there watching over her. She hadn't realized they were holding hands until she came to a stop. It just seemed like such a natural thing to do. "Brad, how are things at home, if you don't mind me asking?"

Brad wasn't prepared to discuss them at this time and he didn't want to lie so he just said, "They are fine, Beth. Let's talk when we get back home." He left it at that. Brad was looking into her eyes and saw what he had seen there so many times before. She needed him, it was obvious, and he needed her. It took all his will power to pull himself away from her but he was still married! They would have their whole life to be together when this was all over. "Brad..." Beth was about to say something when Brad cut her off.

"Whatever you're going to say will have to wait until you get some rest, Beth. I'll stay right here, now lie down." Beth was resting on the cart not far from the door. He placed a blanket over her and set on the cart at the bottom near her feet. "Now, please try and get some rest!" Beth tried to speak again and Brad touched his finger to his lips to quiet her. "Get some rest and that's and order!"

Beth wanted to tell him she loved him but he didn't want to hear what she had to say. Is it because he's not really in love with her, is that's it? That's the reason! Beth turned her back to Brad so that he wouldn't see the tears running down her face. He had decided to stay with his wife! Why not? Isn't that what marriage is all about, working through hard time so the good time are even better? This was the woman he had made promises to for better or worse. They had worked it out and she was happy for him. She was crying tears of joy! She had been throwing herself at him from day one. She was in love and he could care less. She cried in silence. She would never let him know her true feelings about him again. She had made a mistake! She would fix it when they got back.

They needed to find Jack and hurry back home. She had to start putting her life back in order. She would ask for a transfer. She needed to get as far away from Brad as possible. Distance was the only answer to her prayer. Beth had fallen off to sleep. She was awakened by Brad's soft voice saying, "Beth it's time to go. The storm has passed and we need to get moving before the next one comes."

Beth moved from the cart and headed to the latrine. She needed to brush her teeth and comb her hair. Brad waited by the door for her as she walked back into the main corridor. "Did you get some rest, Beth?"

"Yes, thanks for watching out for me!"

"My pleasure. Anytime!"

Beth was cold and she was well aware of that. She wanted to show him that she didn't love him. She refused to look at him because her eyes might betray her again. Beth said very little on the way there. Brad had asked the distance to the ranger station. Beth had never seen anything so beautiful in her life! The snow was so white and thick! She had fallen on the way back to the vehicle and Brad had tried to assist her in getting up. She refused his hand and said, "I'm fine thank you!" She wanted to hurry and get there! "Can we go any faster sir?"

"I'm afraid not Miss, the snow is pretty thick!"

She found that out when she fell. It was like falling on cotton balls. The weather was getting colder and the sun was going down. Beth was determined not to show any emotions, cold or not she would never let Brad comfort her again!

They reached the ranger station around sundown, it had started snowing again. Beth was tired and hungry. She missed the girls and Jean. She needed to find a way to check on Jean

Letting Go

once inside. The ranger door was opening and a white haired man stuck his head out. "You guys better hurry inside, it's headed this way pretty fast."

Beth couldn't believe another storm was coming up so fast. It had been so calm, the sun was shinning and there was no wind, just the soft white snow falling. It reminded Beth of what it would probably feel like to be inside a snowball. Brad was reaching for Beth's hands to help her down out of the vehicle but she refused his hand and jumped. She almost lost her balance, but the young driver caught her from behind. She looked up and smiled and said, "Thank you; that could have been ugly." They both laughed and ran inside building.

Beth had thought nothing of his holding onto her and balancing her through the snow. They all arrived at the door together. Brad had mixed feeling about what was happening. He had noticed Beth's lack of conversation. He had also felt she was giving him the cold shoulder back at the center; so he was wondering what was going on in that pretty little head of hers. He would have to find out and very soon. Why was this guy holding on to her waist as if she was helpless?

"Come in, come in," the man said, opening the door wider.

Beth spotted Jack immediately and she ran to him and hugged his neck. "Jack, we've been so worried! What happened? Are you all right?"

"Yes, Beth, I'm fine!"

Brad walked over and hugged him also.

"How's my wife?"

Brad looked at Beth.

"Beth, what's going on? How's Jean?"

"Jack, she was in the hospital when we left!"

"What happened? Is it the baby? Did she loose the baby?"

"No, Jack! She's been in there every since she heard your plane was missing! She passed out when I told her. I'm sorry Jack. It's like she's afraid to wake up because she's afraid you're never coming home again. She thinks your dead!"

"How did you guys find us?"

"We flew into the nearest airport and had to drive here. We stopped at the research center and waited out one storm. Then we headed on here."

"I need to get home to my wife! We need to get out of here before the next storm."

"I have to hurry back also, Jack." Brad wasn't even aware of his words.

Beth assumed he was rushing home to be with his wife. Brad's words hit her right in the heart! She was so stupid to think this man wanted her! She was an ex-wife now! Did Brad consider her used material? He really didn't seem to mind the fact she was married before. Things had changed when she accidentally told him she had been divorced. She turned away as Brad turned to face her. She was not sure how she would control her anger. She needed to get out of here. She needed fresh air. She would not be able to face him on the plane ride home.

The storm was over and Jack was on the radio trying to arrange for a pickup once they touched down in Washington DC. Beth walked outside while the plans were being made. Beth wasn't that concerned about her health, she just wanted her heart to stop hurting.

The young man that had driven them up there came out behind her and introduced himself. He was quite handsome his name was Raymond, this was his home. He had been married before and it hadn't worked out either. He told Beth that he was engaged to marry his high school sweetheart. They would have a Christmas wedding. Beth tried to speak but the tears just started falling.

Raymond wasn't sure if he had said the wrong thing or what! "I'm sorry, was it something I said?" He wasn't sure what to do. Women didn't usually cry until after the first date! He tried to make a joke. He placed his arms around her shoulders and let her cry it out whatever it was.

Beth was ashamed she had broken down. "I'm sorry Raymond, it's just I'm so happy we found Jack that's all!"

"Look, I may be young, but I'm not stupid. I know there's something between you and Brad. A blind man can sense the tension."

Letting Go

"Whatever it was its over! He's a happily married man that can't wait to get back home to his wife! So you see there's nothing going on between us."

Raymond was still holding her close when Brad exited the door. He stopped dead in his tracks! He wasn't sure if he should rip his little head off! He wanted answers and he wanted them now! Beth managed to pull herself together before Brad made it to where she was standing. "What's was that all about, Beth?"

"What, Brad?"

"What I just witnessed between you and Raymond!"

"It was nothing! Excuse me, sir, but don't you have to hurry home to your wife?" Beth walked past him and Raymond helped her onto the vehicle. She would never feel anything else for him but contempt!

Raymond was a good distraction for Beth; he knew she was in pain and it had nothing to do with the rescue. He tried to cheer her up as best he could. Once they reached the airport Beth felt she would not be able to handle the ride home. She stayed close to Raymond until they arrived. She would have to go the balance of the way alone. Brad was angry for some reason. She couldn't understand how he could be jealous of her when he had Ellen at home waiting on him. Brad was the one rushing home to be with his wife. Why snap at Raymond about the luggage, he was just trying to help. He hadn't realized that everything was already on the plane. Beth had to get away from this man. He wasn't worth any more of her tears.

Jack had called the hospital once we reached the airport to check on his wife; she was resting. Jack asked for them not to disturb her, he would be there soon. He spoke to his parents back at the ranch. They assured him that Jean and the baby were both fine. Jack was so thankful he would never be able to thank Beth and Brad for coming for him; he owed them his life and the life of his family. How do you pay someone for giving you your family back?

Beth avoided Brad at all costs; she occupied herself with Jack and his co-worker. They had discussed the crash and the oil wells. Jack was happy that Beth and Jean were best friends. They were closer than sisters; he would have to do something for them when he got settled.

Jack wanted to see them together, he knew how much Brad loved her. They had talked about it countless times. But Brad was a man of honor; he wanted to free himself before he committed himself to Beth. Beth had to say goodbye to Brad. She stood out by the plane once it had landed. She had to end this once and for all! Brad was busy getting their bags off the plane.

He was still angry with her for letting another man touch her waist. He had to control his temper. She didn't belong to him yet!

"Brad," Beth called, "I just wanted to thank you for going with me to find Jack. There are no words for what you've done!"

"It wasn't for you Beth, I'm very fond of Jack and Jean, and I know how much they love each other. They're very lucky to have someone like you in their lives, you're a true friend. You risked your life for your friend."

"I never thought of it as a risk. I guess I knew you wouldn't let anything happen to me. Thanks Brad, you're a true friend also."

Beth started to walk away and Brad reached for her hand. "Beth, please don't leave without telling me what was going on between you and Raymond back in Alaska!"

"Nothing, Brad! I was upset and he was comforting me, why were you so upset, just a whole lot of crazy stuff. I had made a mistake and it hurt, more than words could explain. Brad, shouldn't you be getting home? Your wife will be waiting on you."

"Beth, please, it's not like that."

"No? Then please tell me how it is, Brad. Can you please enlighten me?"

"I need time, Beth. Can you give me a little time?"

"No, Brad! Time is what I don't have. I'll see you around!" She turned and walked away. This would become one of the worst days of her life. She would have to "Let Go." Jean always said if it was meant to be then God will bring him back to me.

Letting Go

Beth headed to the hospital with Jack. She wanted to see Jean and be there when she saw her husband. Jack ran through the hospital, he was not going to waste another minute. He pushed open the door and hurried to her bed. Beth made it just in time to see Jean open her eyes and see Jack's face. "Am I dreaming or are you here?"

"I'm here sweetheart. What happened to you honey? Are you all right?"

He was kissing her tears and she was thanking God for bringing him home! "Did you get hurt? I heard the plane crashed and that you were missing Jack. I was lost without you! I tried to eat but I couldn't. I didn't want to live without you."

"I'm here baby! Now you need to get your strength up so I can take care of you."

"Jack, please promise me that you will never ever leave me again!"

"I promise. I'll always take you with me, how's that?"

"I can live with it!"

Jean couldn't believe it. All this time she had been praying for God to send her husband back to her. "Thank you Lord. Thank you for sending him home so I can keep a close eye on both your angles." She would always be grateful to God for sending her a true angel. "How did you guys get here?"

"Beth and Brad came looking for us. They found us, Jean. I owe Brad and Beth my life. They didn't just save me they saved my wife and child. They will always be dear to me, Jean."

"Hey, guys!" Beth yelled from behind them. "I was only looking out for my girl's god parents. You're my family also! I needed my best friend back and my best friend needed you back! I did what any good friend would have done. I love you both."

Brad came in to say hello to Jean and to make sure she was truly ok now that Jack was back. Jean reached out her hands to Brad and he leaned over and kissed her forehead. "Thank you! Because of you and Beth I have my husband and we're a family again. I owe you two a wedding and when the time comes it will be on us. Jack and I will send you two off on the best honeymoon money can buy."

Beth was speechless and so was Brad! Thank you was all they could think of to say. Brad shook Jack's hand, hugged him and started to leave.

"We'll talk later," Jack said.

"Sure, call me," Brad said as he turned to look at Beth before leaving.

She turned her head away from his stare. When she finally looked up all she would remember seeing was the back of his head as he walked out of her life! How could she live without this man? Better yet, how would she get through these next few minutes knowing she would never see him again? He was on her mind and in all her thoughts! He had taken possession of her heart! Would she be able to get it back in one piece? She knew the answer before she even asked. Brad was not a keeper. She had made the right choice and she would keep moving forward.

Beth had to hurry home to her girls. They hadn't asked many questions when she left. She just told Marie that she was going to get Uncle Jack and bring him home. "That's good mom. Maybe Aunt Jean will feel better."

"I'll see everyone later. I'll get a cab home, Jack." Beth would start working on her life again. When she arrived at the ranch the girls were already in bed. She would let them sleep and leave in the morning.

Charles had turned on the late news and heard that Jack Morris's plane had been reported as missing and that there were no known survivors! He needed to call Jean to see if there was anything he could do. Charles called the ranch and was told that Jean was in the hospital. He drove there immediately, not knowing what was going on, after all she was still one of his close friends. He would always think of her in that manner. If she needed him he was there for her. He had explained the situation to Amy and she was fine with it. Amy wasn't threatened by Jean and Charles's friendship; after all he was with hers now. Jean was the past.

Charles arrived at the hospital and checked at the front desk to locate her room. Since visiting hours were over he would need permission to go up. "What relationship are you sir, to Mrs. Morris?"

Letting Go

Charles explained that they were married once. He was given the room number and he headed off to see Jean. When Charles reached Jean's room he walked in. There was a nurse taking Jean's blood pressure and listening to her pulse. She had some kind of monitor hooked up to her stomach. She looked fine, Charles thought, for some reason she didn't look like a woman who had just lost her husband. Maybe she didn't know!

Jean asked, "Charles, what are you doing here?"

"I saw the news and heard that your husband's plane had crashed and they hadn't found any survivors. I'm sorry Jean! I called the ranch and they said you were here. Is everything all right? Is there anything I can do Jean?"

"Charles! Jack's plane did crash but..." just as she was about to tell him Jack was fine, Jack walked into the room.

"Honey..." He stopped and noticed a man holding his wife's hand.

"Charles, this is Jack Morris, my husband. Honey, this Charles. He heard about the plane crash and came over to see if there was anything he could do for me. I was just about to explain when you walked in that your plane did crash but no one died."

"I'm sorry man. I was just concerned about Jean and the baby, that's all."

"I can assure you my wife is in good hands and I would appreciate it if you would let go of hers."

Charles hadn't realized he was still holding on to Jean's hands. He dropped them as if they burnt him and backed away. "Well, Jean, I guess you won't need any help after all."

"Charles, how's your new baby? Jack and I are hoping for a son in about five months. Thanks again Charles for coming but as you can see I'm well taken care of."

Jack reached out to shake Charles hand and thank him for coming also. "Thanks man, it's good to know my wife will always have people looking after her if anything ever happens to me." Jack leaned down and kissed his wife lightly on the lips.

Charles apologized again and left the room. He walked into the hall and stopped. How could he have been so quick to act? She was his ex-wife. He had no right to come here but he wanted to see if she needed him and to let her know he would always be there for her and her child.

Charles remembered his life with Jean. She was happier now than he ever remembered her being with him. She had everything she ever dreamed of, a baby that's due in five months. Charles was thinking back to the last time he and Jean were together. They had made wild passionate love. It was around six months ago he thought but he had to be mistaken; she was with Jack. Was it his child or was it not? Charles had to know for sure. There was a slight chance this baby could be his and he would have to find out. He would have to talk to Jean as soon as she was out of the hospital. It would be hard trying to see her with her husband around. He seemed very protective of her. Charles would have to leave it alone for right now. He had five months to check into Jean's due date. He would not take no for an answer! This could very well be his child!

He was quiet when he returned home. He was thinking about Jean and the baby. Amy asked about Jean and the condition of her baby. "She's fine and so is her husband. Everyone survived the plane crash." He never mentioned meeting Jack or the other information he was looking into. He needed to contact Beth; she would have answers for him.

Ellen Gets Desperate

Beth was in a rotten mood these days. She seemed to be walking close to the edge of insanity. She missed Brad something terrible but it was all her fault. She knew before she started that there was no future in a married man. This is what she could write a book on. She would have to do that one day. It would be titled, "There's no Future in a Married Man, Only Pain and Suffering!"

Brad had gone straight to his soon to be ex-wife's home. He wanted to see his son if he wasn't in bed. He knew she was determined to fight him in court for full custody. Ellen met him at the door. "What do you want Brad?"

"I would like to see my son if he's still up!"

"He's not here. He's staying with his Aunt."

"I will be here tomorrow Ellen."

Brad turned to leave and as he was leaving he heard his son's voice coming from behind his mother. "Where are you going, daddy?"

"Hi, son, I was going to get something out of my car."

"Did you come to see me daddy?"

"Yes, I did! Go and get your coat so we can go and get a goodnight treat." The moment his son was out of ear shot. Brad whispered in Ellen ear, "Be careful of this game you're playing."

"You better be careful and hurry and bring my son back. It's much too late to be taking him out. You could come back tomorrow and get him."

"I'm taking him now!"

Brad couldn't imagine how he married such and evil woman. Was this his punishment for not loving her when they got married? He took his son to Baskin Robins for ice cream. He was the joy that kept Brad glued to his ex-wife. His son also made a list of things he wanted for Christmas. Brad missed seeing his son! But living in a loveless married is not a healthy relationship to raise a child in. Children should be surrounded by love and parents that respect each other. He couldn't believe he was remembering the talk he and Beth had on being married. She had also said that people sacrifice their happiness for their kids everyday. She's right; kids can be loved by one parent as well as two. Brad wanted his life to be close to what Jean and Jack had. He could have that and more with Beth.

Ellen was standing at the door waiting for Brad. She didn't want him spending too much time with his son. She would find out who he was sleeping with and put a stop to it. He was her husband and she would never let a little divorce stand between them. Her son was her security.

Ellen had already gone to check out a fertility sperm bank. She wanted a second child and since Brad refused to sleep with her it was going to be hard getting pregnant the conventional way. She had to hurry if she was going to hold on to her husband. Her appointment was in two weeks and she would need money a lot more than she had; she had taken out a second loan on the house already. Ellen found it so easy to sign Brad's name to the loan papers and mail them back to the company. She would be pregnant and no one would believe that Brad was not the father. It was easy to fool him; she had done it so many times before! She would see to it that he did the right thing. The same as he had done when they got married. She had gotten pregnant by someone else before she and Brad were married. Brad will never know that Jamie is not his son. She would die with that secret!

Brad let his son out and watched him take the steps two at a time. He was growing so fast. He would never turn his back on his son no matter how stupid his mother got.

Ellen asked Brad if she could speak to him after work tomorrow to discuss their son. Brad's initial thought was to say no but he needed to be civil to this woman. "All right Ellen, I'll meet you at Hardies on Main Avenue at four."

"Thanks Brad. It's about us and Jamie."

"There is no us, Ellen!"

Ellen left work early. She had to work fast because she needed time to go by her house and change clothes.

Letting Go

Brad arrived at the restaurant at four. Ellen was sitting at one of the tables in the back. "Can't we go somewhere less crowded?"

"No! This is fine. Please get to the point."

"Jamie is having a hard time with your being gone! He wakes up with nightmares almost every night. He cries for you, Brad!"

"Ellen, are you sure this isn't about you and not Jamie?"

"I'm not lying Brad, our son needs us to be a family."

"It takes more than my coming home to make us a family Ellen. That's not going to happen. The divorce will be final in a few months. You need to start getting used to living alone."

"Brad, I love you! You're my husband! You can't just walk out on your family like we don't exist."

"Ellen, first of all, I would never have been your husband if you hadn't of tricked me into marring you. I've tried to get past this whole ordeal and continue with this so called marriage, but life is too short to live in these conditions."

"What conditions? Brad, I love you. What is so bad about that?"

"The truth is, Ellen, I don't love you. I tried to forget what you're done to me in the past but I won't be able to forgive you for what you."

"Brad, please, let's give it one more week! I will make you forget that I ever lied to you. I'll be the perfect wife. I'll stop following you and listening in on your phones calls. I'll stop everything and be the best wife any man could ever ask for. Just give me a chance Brad."

"I'm sorry, Ellen the divorce is already being processed and I won't change my mind again."

"Then don't, Brad! You'll be sorry you can be sure of that! I'll find out who she is and when I do you both will pay! I'll ruin your career! I'll tell everyone you're having an affair and that you're leaving me for another woman! How will that make you look?"

"Go ahead Ellen, they already know I'm getting divorced. I told the General to be expecting a call from you. The guards have already been warned and you are to stay clear of where I live and work. Do you understand me, Ellen? No more games!"

Ellen stood up with such force she knocked the chair over she was sitting in! She had every set of eyes on her in the restaurant.

Brad knew this was a mistake. He should never have agreed to meet with her. He would have to bring his lawyer from now on. She needed counseling!

Ellen left the restaurant angry. There was no reasoning with this man. He had no idea about who he was messing with. She was not the kind of woman that let her man leave without a fight! She would know who this lady was before the week was out Ellen swore.

Brad had to pull himself together before leaving the restaurant and he wanted to make sure Ellen wasn't following him. He needed to see Beth. He wanted to warn her about Ellen. If she found out about Beth she would make her life a living hell, even if there was nothing going on between them. She would take one look at Beth and know she wasn't the kind of woman that had one night stands. She would know it was serious.

Brad called the store to make sure Beth hadn't left work. She was still there. Brad entered the store at closing time as Beth was in her office making out a report of the day's sales. "Hi, Beth!"

She knew the voice; she didn't even have to look up. "Hello, Brad, I didn't ever expect to see you again."

"I know. I'm here to warn you about my soon to be ex-wife."

"What are you talking about "warn me"? Why would she even think that there's something going on between us Brad? You're warning the wrong person."

"I just want to protect you, Beth! I feel she will try to hurt you."

"Aren't you being a little overly protective?" Beth found it amusing that he felt so strongly about protecting her. "Ok, Brad. Brad what do you want me to do? I'll stay in lighted areas when I walk outside. The girls and I will be extra careful when we are out at night. I'll look both ways when I cross the street."

Letting Go

"Beth, this is very serious. Ellen can be very dangerous when she feels threatened."

"I'm not threatening her! I'm not seeing her husband, or anyone's husband for that matter. Brad, please leave so we can close up."

"No, I'll wait and walk you out."

"No, Brad! That's not necessary. I'll walk out with my employees. Please don't let them see how worried you are about me. They will think your wife is psycho!"

"She is! That's what I'm trying to tell you! Beth, promise me you will be careful."

"I promise!"

Brad left so Beth and her employees could finished closing the facility. She didn't give it a second thought until they started walking toward their cars and suddenly a car came from no where, speeding through the parking lot. It was very dark and the car never turned its lights on. They jumped out the way to keep from being run over. They couldn't believe what had just happened.

Beth ran to her car and so did everyone else. She yelled out to her employees, "We will discuss this tomorrow!" Right now I need everyone to go straight home. She decided to call Brad's cell to let him know what had happened. He told her Ellen must have followed him there from the restaurant tonight. "Brad, do you mean to tell me she follows you?"

"Yes, she does and I'm sure she was the one that tried to run you guys over tonight."

"Now she knows where I work. Brad, what are we going to do?"

"Beth, please calm down. You are driving and when you get home you don't want to upset the girls!"

"The girls will have to be made aware of this woman. Brad, do you think she would try and hurt my kids?"

"I don't know, Beth. I can't really say."

"Brad, can you meet me at the park? I'll have Carol stop by the center and pick up the girls. Brad will you be able to meet me?"

"Sure, Beth, I'll see you in a few minutes.

Brad was trying to settle on the giant's head in the park. But he kept sliding off. She remembered how she and Jean had talked about "The Awakening." It seemed to make you want to dig him up. They both loved coming here. She had always loved this spot. Brad was down by the water when she walked up behind him. He was startled. "I'm sorry Brad; I didn't mean to sneak up behind you."

Brad gave her a long hug. "Do you see what I'm talking about now?"

"She's dangerous Brad. She'll be coming into the store soon and no one knows what she looks like."

"I'll bring a picture by so everyone will know who to look for. The best thing we have going for us is she doesn't know who I was there to see. You need to stay clear of her."

"I will Brad, but I'm not going to run and hide! I haven't done anything wrong! She is barking up the wrong tree. What makes her think you're having an affair?"

"She wants me to give our marriage another chance but I know it's over, it's been over for years. I filed for a divorce two months ago. Now she thinks I've fallen in love with someone else and that's the only reason I left her."

"You never told me you had filed for a divorce."

"I didn't want you to think it had anything to do with you."

"Did it? Was I the reason, Brad?"

"No Beth. I did this for me. I want more from my life than living like a monk with a woman that I'm supposed to love. We have not made love in over a year. I have no desire to be with her. She will never accept that but I've never lied to her. I've always told her the truth about how I felt about her."

"She's still in love with you, isn't she, Brad?"

"I suppose so."

"I know she is. Why else would she act so crazy if she wasn't? What's your plan Brad?"

"Beth, please tell me I need to know how you leave someone who won't "let go." She has to let go Brad, sooner or later she will let go!"

They walked and talked until it was late. Beth finally pulled herself back to reality. "I will keep my distance, Brad. I don't

Letting Go

want any trouble from her. Will you please try and clear this up before someone gets hurt?"

"I wish I had never brought you into this, Beth, but I can't change the way I feel about you! We don't always make the right decisions but if God allows us a chance to make things right and we don't, we've failed again. I will make things right Beth, you'll see!" Brad reached for her hands and touched them to his lips.

Beth was getting used to the hand kisses; they had become his trademark, especially when it came to saying goodbye to her. She left on another sad note.

Brad drove back to his apartment. He would see Ellen first thing in the morning. She would have to be stopped and he was the one to stop her. She had tried to run over Beth and her co-workers. She was someone to be feared! Brad opened the door to his apartment and Ellen was sitting on the couch in his living room. "How did you get in here?" His anger was flaring.

"I picked the lock. It's amazing what you can do with a credit card."

Brad tried to keep his cool. "You need to leave now Ellen, before I call the police!"

"To say what, Brad? That your wife won't leave you alone?"

"No, Ellen. I'll tell them that you tried to run down a couple of ladies with your car tonight. Does that sound familiar? If they check your record they are going to see you already tried this once before."

"They never saw me!"

"Yes, they saw you all right. They even got your license plate number." Brad was bluffing but that's all he had at the moment and she didn't know that! He had to try and scare her so she would stay away from them.

"You're lying! They didn't see me! I had my lights off!"

"So you just admitted that you tried to run those ladies down."

"I'm not worried about you, Brad! It's your word against mine. They're not going to believe you because you're sleeping with one of them."

"I'm not sleeping with anyone. Ellen, why are you following me and where is my son tonight while you're out playing detective?"

"He's in New Jersey with my mother."

"Ellen, please leave and never ever try this again. I'm going to the courts tomorrow and have you barred from the development so this won't happen again. I will also give your picture to the gate guards so they will not let you enter the post."

Ellen got up to leave. She turned around and looked at Brad. "I will find out which one of those Bitches you're sleeping with. It's just a matter of time."

The next few weeks Ellen stayed clear of the Exchange. She knew she couldn't chance going back there too soon. After several weeks she felt it was time to pay the ladies a visit at the Exchange Store. Ellen used an old pair of uniform pants to make her plan work. She walked up to the customer service counter and asked the sales associate is she could assist her in finding a matching jacket. Julie was a very friendly associate. Ellen also noticed she was about six to seven months pregnant. She knew this was not the young lady.

Ellen made small talk while Julie tried to help her. "Is there anyone else that may be able to assist us since you're not sure if the colors match? Maybe we could have another set of eyes look at them?"

Julie was sure it matched perfectly. Why was this lady questioning her? Julie called for Sofia who was a Jamaican with a deep accent.

"Yes, girl, what is it?"

"Sophia, please take Mrs. Jones out to the sunlight to match this pants and jacket."

There were no rings on her fingers and she had a lot of spunk so Ellen thought she might be the one. But how could she know for sure? She would just have to ask questions that were non-threatening to make sure. "I'm going to a company banquet with my husband. He asked me to pick up a few things for him. I noticed he needed new pants."

"Yes, ma'am! That's nice. My boyfriend is in the military."

"What's his name?" Ellen asked.

Letting Go

"His name is..." Just as Sophia was getting ready to tell her Beth called her to the phone for a call. "Excuse me ma'am. I'm expecting a very important call today. I'll be right back."

Ellen was sure she was the one. She would have to listen and wait. Beth said, "Ma'am, I will help you if you don't want to wait."

"No, that's ok. I'll wait on Sofia to come back."

Ellen only noticed Beth in passing. She was poised and beautiful so she was sure she was happily married. She was definitely not the one.

Sofia returned to Ms Jones. "I'm sorry, it was a very important call."

"Is everything ok, Sofia?"

"Yes, just fine thank you. These pants are a perfect match Ms Jones; I'll get someone to ring you up."

"Julie, can you please ring Ms Jones up? I have to leave early. I have to meet my boyfriend at the courthouse. Thanks, Julie."

Julie came over to ring continued to ring Ms Jones up, but at the end of the sale she realized she didn't have her credit card. Ellen had no intention of purchasing any trousers. She was there for information only. "I'll be right back. Could you hold my purchase for me? I'll be back in half an hour. Will Sofia be back today Julie?" Ellen asked.

"I don't know ma'am. Sophia was just talking about her boyfriend and then she had to leave," Julie said. "Sophia told us it was love at first sight! I told her that kind of stuff only happens in movies. He is supposed to be some high ranking person on post. We haven't met him yet," Julie said.

"That's nice," Ellen commented. Ellen had enough information; she didn't need to know anymore. Sofia was the one sleeping with her husband, Ellen thought. She would have to follow her and see if it led to Brad.

Beth exited the office at the same time Ellen was leaving the store. Beth realized she was not purchasing the pants that Julie and Sofia had spent hours matching up! "Is everything ok, Mrs. Jones?"

"Yes, I'm fine, thank you! I'm going to my car to get my credit card." Ellen was trying to hurry but Ms Customer Friendliness seemed to be holding her back. "Look, would you please step aside? I'm in a hurry thank you!" Ellen snapped at Beth.

Beth excused herself and moved to the side so Ellen could pass. How rude, Beth thought.

By the time Ellen made it to the parking lot Sofia was gone! She was probably going to meet Brad. She would just have to come back tomorrow. Ellen had that manager to blame; she had been stopped by her. She was only days away from finding out about Brad's new love interest; she had a plan for tomorrow.

Brad had left a message on Beth's answering machine. He wanted to see her tonight. If possible, Beth was to meet him at the park. When Beth arrived at the park she ran into Brad's arms, they were happy to see each other. They parted as quickly as they hugged. "I'm sorry Brad, I shouldn't have done that. It's just that I haven't heard from you or seen you for two weeks. How are things going with Ellen, is she still looking for me?"

"Yes I'm sure she is! So please Beth, don't let your guard down because she is not the type to give up."

"Thanks Brad! I'll remember that!"

"I wanted to tell you that I have to go away for a few days on assignment. Do you think you'll be ok while I'm gone?"

"Why wouldn't I be?"

"Ellen and I will sign the divorce paper on my return, and if she refuses to sign I'll take her to court."

"Brad, I will miss you! Have you told her you're leaving yet?"

"No. I'm going over to tell her tonight."

"Where will you be going Brad?"

"I'm going to Fort Steward to do some training. Beth, if anything goes wrong please call me. I'll catch the next plane home."

"I'll be fine Brad. She's probably forgotten all about the store. She's been watching it and hasn't seen you come in there anymore. What happened to the picture of her?"

Letting Go

"I went home and realized I had no pictures of her in my new apartment. I couldn't take a chance going into her place and getting caught. I will try and get a picture from Ellen's place before I leave; I will have to be real careful. I was hoping that I scared her enough when I told her the ladies had her tag number and had given it to the police on base. Believe me she hasn't forgotten about you."

"This may sound strange coming from me because most men have a hard time expressing their feelings but even before we made love I knew being with you was my final destination. No one will ever touch my heart the way you have. I love you! Beth, I think you already know that I do. I will do want ever you ask me to do as long as you tell me we will be together in the end. I've never lied to you about anything. My future lies with you if you will have me once I'm free."

"Brad, we're not discussing our feelings until things change."

"I know, but I had to tell you just in case you had forgotten."

"How could I forget the feel, the touch, the kiss and our love making? You showed me what my body was made for and how to enjoy the pleasure your body had to offer. You took me on the ride of my life! You took my body and made it come alive. No one has ever taken me to my final destination more than once on the same ride. Brad, I know you love me, as I do you, but we should never act on our feelings again." At that moment he pulled her into his arms! His mouth was taking everything she had promised not to give! They were both breathless after tearing themselves away from each other. They needed each other but both of them had made promises to wait it out. Brad kissed her once more before leaving. Beth couldn't believe he had traded her hands for her lips and she would make that trade any day of the week.

Brad arrived at Ellen's around nine; he was hoping to get there earlier but things got a little hot and heavy with Beth.

Ellen was surprised to see Brad at her door. Did he know she had been to the store? Was he now following her? No, he couldn't have found out so fast. She never used her real name.

She used Ms. Jones. She would wait for him to say something before she started defending her actions.

"Ellen, may I come in please?"

"Why are you here Brad?"

"I wanted to inform you that I'm leaving town for several weeks and I was hoping to see Jamie before I left. I would also like to ask you to stay away from those ladies at that store. When I get back our divorce will be ready for our final signature. You will be a free woman Ellen."

Ellen wasn't even thinking about anything Brad was saying. She knew he was going away with that lady from the store. She would put a stop to that first thing in the morning.

"Ellen, can I see Jamie? Where is he?"

"He's at my sisters. You can pick him up over there."

"Why is he never with you Ellen? You are always giving him to someone else to keep. When I get back I will take him and free you up even more."

"Ok, what ever, Brad!" She practically closed the door in his face.

Ellen had to hurry. She had an appointment with her doctor about artificial insemination but she would have to take care of little Miss Sofia first. She was running off with her husband! Ellen entered the store exactly at opening. Ellen was the first customer in the store.

Beth was walking back to her office when Ellen stopped her to ask for Sophia. "She should be here at any moment, Ma'am, could I help you with something?"

"No, I'll wait... Maybe you can help me! You have an associate named Sophia. She's not married is she?"

"Excuse me?"

"She's not married is she?"

"Ma'am, we aren't allowed to discuss our employee's personal lives. You will have to ask her those questions."

"I believe she's sleeping with my husband and I'm here to confront her."

"Ma'am, I think you've made a mistake. You need to leave our store. This is not the place for what you are trying to do! Shouldn't you be taking this up with you're husband?"

Letting Go

"Well, I just wanted to tell her that I'm pregnant and that I'm going away with him tonight for several weeks. We're going to Paris and Greece for our second honeymoon and to visit friends."

"Why are you telling me this, Ma'am?" Sophia was just walking in. "I think you had better leave, Ma'am."

"I'm not leaving until I speak to her!"

"Let's take this into the office." Sophia said her good mornings. "Sophia, this lady is here to accuse you of sleeping with her husband." Beth was sitting across from Sophia. She was there to make sure things didn't get out of hand.

"I'm sorry Ma'am, but I don't know your husband. What did you say his name was?"

"His name is Brad Walker!" But you said your last name was Jones. So, I lied sue me! Ellen said.

"I'm sorry, Ma'am I don't know a Brad Walker."

Beth couldn't believe her ears! This was Brad's wife and she was here accusing Sophia of having an affair with her husband. She couldn't have been more wrong! Beth wanted to say so but under the current circumstances she kept quiet. She needed to call the police and tell them she was the one who tried to run us over two weeks ago! Did she say she was pregnant and that she was leaving town with Brad tomorrow? "Mrs. Walker, since you seem to know everything about Sophia did you ask your husband about her?"

"He denied everything. He said he still loves me but she's been chasing him. He asked me to step in and ask her to leave us alone, especially with the baby coming and all."

"Congratulations. When is the baby due?" Beth couldn't help but ask. She had to know everything.

"I'm two months! My husband and I just want to be left alone!"

Sophia was in total shock! "Mrs. Walker, I'm telling you the truth! I don't know you're husband! You've got the wrong woman. I don't do married men. There's no future in them."

Those words hit Beth a lot harder than she had hoped. She had to get out of here and get some fresh air! She tried to composed herself. She had to know it all. "Mrs. Walker, what makes you so sure it's Sophia that's seeing your husband?"

"I've heard you talk about your man around here. The way you talk about your man it was love at first sight. Julie said he was some big shot on post. That's my husband! Women fall head over heels in love with my husband all the time. It never means anything to him. He's just using them for sex. He doesn't love you!"

"You know this and you're still with him?"

"I'm never leaving my husband and he will never leave me."

Sophia was getting angry. She got up to leave and Mrs. Walker stood and blocked her path. Beth moved in front of Mrs. Walker. "I think you had better leave now and take this up with your husband! If he's cheating, that's you're problem Mrs. Walker."

Ellen looked at Beth and saw she was ready to take her on! Just when Ellen was ready to make her next move Brad stepped into the office, his face full of anger. "Ellen, why are you here? I told you last night to stay away from these ladies or it would be trouble."

Beth wanted to run into his arms, but she knew that would be foolish. She needed to think with her mind and not her heart! "Mr. Walker, your wife seems to think you're having an affair with Sophia! She keeps telling her she's never met you before."

"That's right Ellen. Now please leave before I have them call the police."

"I'm not leaving until I find out the truth."

"I will also tell them that you tried to run these ladies down with your car two weeks ago."

Beth had to hold Sophia back! "You crazy bitch! You could have killed one of us! That was you? You need help lady! We are not after you're husband. Why don't you grow up? It's not the woman you should have an issue with, it's your husband. If he doesn't want you, please move on." Sophia was telling her off; she was so angry and ready to fight!

Letting Go

Brad had moved over near Beth. Without thinking his eyes met hers and he saw fire in them. He had never seen that side of her before.

"Mr. Walker, your wife gave us the good news she expecting a child. Now would you please take your expectant wife and get the hell out of my office! Mrs. Walker, if you even think about coming into this store again I'll have you locked up! You're not so stupid that you don't understand the part about locking you up are you? Mr. Walker, your wife needs to see a psychiatrist. Both of you need to have your heads checked."

Beth saw the veins in Brad's neck bulging out. He was past angry. But not half as angry as she was! The nerve! He had been sleeping with his wife all this time and now she was pregnant. How could he do this to her? How could he take her life away from her like that? Beth had trusted him with her heart. She needed to get out of here before she lost it. She excused herself and took her purse and almost ran to the door. Beth didn't believe Brad was sleeping with his wife until Ellen said she was pregnant. Like she said, he only wanted sex. She had given it too easily!

Brad stepped outside through the exit with his wife. "What were you hoping to discover by coming here? What do you want Ellen? I'm divorcing you. If you have a problem it's with me not anyone else."

Brad was having a serious conversation with his wife, Beth noticed, as she walked to her car at almost a running pace.

Beth Gives Up on Love

Brad called after her and left Ellen on the steps. She knew she had the wrong woman at that very moment. Beth, didn't stop until she reached her car. "Brad, please leave me alone. We don't have anything to discuss. Please take your psychotic wife and go wherever it is you two are going for your vacation! The Bahamas, Paris, Europe, I really don't care Brad. I don't need this drama and I sure as hell don't need you! Now please stay away from me."

Ellen made her way over to Beth's car; she had a few words for girlfriend. "So you're the one. You're the reason he wants to leave me. Well, I guess the secret is out now. If you think I'm going to give up everything I've invested in this marriage you are wrong. He's never going to be yours. He is mine and will always be mine."

"You're welcome to him! Good luck, Brad!"

"Beth, what about last night?"

"What about it? Brad, that was before I knew you were sleeping with your wife and she's pregnant," said Beth.

"If she is pregnant I am definitely not the father," Brad said. "I can promise you that. Beth you have got to trust me. I've never lied to you, not once."

"Brad, please leave me alone. Even if you're not the father the judge is going to look at this baby as being conceived during the marriage and that makes you responsible for it and her," Beth said. "There's just too much baggage to deal with, Brad."

Ellen was standing there smiling because she knew she had won! Wasn't she supposed to win, after all he was her husband?

"I wish you luck Brad, you're going to need it with a wife like that. Please don't call me or try to see me and please keep Mrs. Psycho away from me!"

Brad looked at Ellen with hatred and disgust. He was sure she wasn't pregnant. If she was she had probably hired someone

Letting Go

to sleep with her. He would put nothing past her. How could things get so crazy two days before he was scheduled to leave? He stopped by the Exchange to pick up a few things before his trip and noticed Ellen's car in the parking lot. He had been alarmed right away. Beth meant so much to him and now he had lost her forever. Nothing he could ever say or do would change things. Ellen had thrown a wrench into the wheel and it had stopped turning. He could only look at the woman he had married. What was he thinking? She had been sent straight from Hell! He would never get rid of her. She was worse than a leech. Brad turned to walk back to his car. He had to find away to make things right with Beth. Jean was the only person he knew she would listen to. He had to call her and see if she would help him.

He would have to postpone his training class. His boss would have to appoint someone else to attend in his place. His life was too much of a mess for him to leave at this time. Brad called Jean and asked if he could stop by the ranch. Jean had been excited to hear from Brad. He asked if she had heard from Beth. Jean assured him she hadn't. Brad tried to explain as much as he could on the phone. He really wanted to talk to her in person.

He arrived at the ranch on Friday afternoon. Jean was walking in the yard. The weather was always beautiful there on the ranch. Brad hugged her. He noticed how healthy she was looking. "I bet you are being spoiled rotten by Jack, aren't you Jean?"

"How did you guess?"

"I know Jack, he's the man!"

"What are you and Beth going to do?"

"I wish I knew Jean. She won't even take my calls!"

"Brad, what happened? How did your wife get pregnant?"

"She is lying about being pregnant. I don't believe she is pregnant. She tricked me into marrying her with that same kind of lie. She is trying to keep me from divorcing her. I'm not falling for that again! Jean, Beth was so hurt. You should have seen her face. I promised you that I wouldn't hurt her. I've destroyed her faith in me Jean. She will never trust me again.

She thinks the baby is mine and there's nothing I can do to change her mind."

"Brad, I want to ask you a question. Do you think your soon to be ex will try and hurt Beth or the girls?"

"I don't know Jean. I never thought she would do this so I can't really say. She's desperate right now trying to get me not to divorce her. I don't know how far she will go."

"I will send our security over to Beth's home to watch her and the girls. I'll feel better doing that."

"If you tell Beth she will refuse. You know that, right?"

"I know Brad. She won't know they are there! Can you get me a picture of Ellen to show security to make sure Beth is not being stalked?"

"I'll send it over tomorrow." Brad would enter into the house and take a picture.

"Brad, don't worry, things will work out. You and Beth are meant to be together."

Brad left feeling better than he had when he arrived. Jean would help him. She was a good friend.

Jean explained everything to Jack when he returned home. "Brad has major problems."

"Yes, he does Jean! I wish we could help them get it together."

"They will, sweetheart. It will just take a little time, trust me on that."

Jean called Charles and asked if he could check on Beth at the store once in a while. She didn't give any details about what was going on. It was Beth's business and no one else had any reason to know about it.

"How are you doing, Jean?"

"I'm just fine, thank you Charles for asking. I'm having a boy Charles! Isn't that great?"

"When are you due Jean?"

"It's going to be a Christmas baby."

"That's wonderful, Jack must be very happy."

"He's already bought everything you can think of."

"If there is anything I can do, please let me know Jean."

"Thanks, Charles. How are Amy and the kids?"

Letting Go

"Its great having kids around! I'm sorry I didn't listen to you, Jean. It would have been wonderful."

"Yes it would have been Charles."

"Jean, have you ever checked out the date when you got pregnant? Is it possible that I could be the father of your child?"

Jean laughed. "No Charles, you couldn't be the father of my child! I didn't get pregnant until I met Jack. I'm sorry Charles, I know how you're reaching at stars trying to have your own child but this is not yours. This is Jack's baby. I knew the moment he was conceived."

"I'm sorry Jean. I just had to ask."

"It's ok Charles."

"Thanks for checking on Beth, I do appreciate your doing this for me."

"Please don't mention to Beth that I asked you to check in on her."

Jean hung up the phone, not feeling as sure as she had been about her baby's father. She had had doubts before but she had soon dismissed them. This time would be no different. Charles was not her baby's father. She was sure of that. Jean didn't think any more on the subject. Jack would be home soon. She was almost nine months pregnant. He never left her for long periods anymore; he stayed close to home just in case.

Jean called Beth to see how things were going at work. Beth really didn't have much to say. She hadn't heard much from Brad or his estranged wife. She didn't want any part of that craziness. They would have to stay away from her. Beth didn't want to talk about Brad. He had hurt her deeply. Jean heard the pain in her voice. She knew Beth loved him, but was it enough to keep their love alive?

"Jean, he lied to me. He said they weren't sleeping together and here she is pregnant."

"How do you know she's pregnant Beth? She could be lying about being pregnant."

"I guess you're right. If she's desperate enough to follow him lying should be real easy."

"I wouldn't give up completely on Brad yet Beth. He loves you; I'm sure of that, but he has things that have to be worked out. His marriage has been tough from the start but he's stuck it out for his son!"

"Jean, how do you know so much about Brad's life?"

"We've talked a few times. He's a good man Beth. There's not many of those left. I don't want you to take my advice but please just think about what he's told you and the things he's trying to do."

Beth would do just that. She wasn't going anywhere, she would wait him out. It would be Christmas soon. She and the girls would be alone; she needed to concentrate on her kids.

Earl called Beth, to check on the girls. He hadn't talked to them in over three months. "What do you really want Earl?"

"I want to visit my girls."

"Why, Earl? You haven't even called them. I'm going to ask you again what you really want."

"I want the girls to meet their sibling."

"That's great. So when are you planning on bringing your wife and kids here?"

"We're going to Alabama for Christmas Eve. I want to bring them to Alabama for the holidays."

"No way! Earl, this is my first Christmas with my girls in our new home and we've got plans. You are welcome to see them, but they're not going anywhere for the holidays. That's what I'm talking about Earl you only think of your self. You call here once in three months and expect to take my kids off with you to your new family. It's not going to happen."

"Don't be bitter, Beth!"

"Bitter! I'm not bitter, you trifling little man!" She hung up the phone on him.

She needed to hurry. They were spending the holidays at Jean's and Jack's ranch. Beth had fallen in love with the ranch; it was so beautiful in the winter. The girls were always asking to stay over. She couldn't refuse them! Beth still hadn't heard from Brad. She knew his divorce was final a few weeks ago. She hadn't seen or heard anything else from Brad's ex-wife since the incident at the store. Beth noticed several key scratches on the hood of her car. She didn't make a fuss, the less attention she

Letting Go

received the better off they all would be. She had already let go of the past.

The Engagement

Brad had stopped calling and the pain had lightened up a little but he still haunted Beth's dreams at night! She needed time and plenty of it. Beth and the girls arrived early at the ranch because she wanted to beat the evening traffic. Jean and Jack were making Christmas cookies and the girls joined right in. There was plenty of laughter. Beth felt a streak of sadness at first, but the laughter was contagious. She wanted to make sure the girls had a wonderful Christmas and did not miss Earl. Jack had all the toys from the house picked up and delivered to the carriage house. They would bring them back in later tonight after the girls had gone to bed.

Beth needed to take another look at the sunset on the farm. It reminded her of Alaska. It was snowing and the sun was setting. It was the most beautiful sight she had ever seen! She walked out to the barn to check on the horses.

She envied Jean and Jack, they were so in love. Every moment was filled with love and warmth. Jean's life was a fairy tale. Beth felt blessed to be a part of their lives and she thanked God for that. She had wanted that with Brad. There she went again thinking of Brad. How would she live without him? She knew the tears would come! Whenever she thought of Brad the tears would fall; it was as if they were crying their own cry for him. She wiped her eyes and said a silent prayer. Beth was talking to the horses Jack had purchased for the girls right before summer ended. Beth hadn't noticed that she wasn't alone, that someone was coming up behind her. She had to get back to the house because it was getting late. She turned around to face the man that had been keeping her up at night for the last ten months. "Brad! What are you doing here?"

"I'm spending the holidays at the ranch. Jack asked me after Thanksgiving when we found him. He called me the other day and reminded me. I had no other plans."

Letting Go

"Where's your family?"

"My ex-wife and my son are in New Jersey with her family. She gave up after the parking lot issue. I told her I would have her locked up if she didn't leave you alone and sign the divorce papers when they came through. She still tried to hold things up but I was ready for every move she made."

"Brad, what about the baby?"

"She was never pregnant. Her plan fell through. She was trying to get artificially inseminated but the clinic called the house when I was there babysitting Jamie one day and I answered the phone. They had been trying to reach me because they wanted to confirm my statement of consent. Well, I threatened to bring her up on charges of fraud if she didn't sign the divorce papers."

"She was determined not to let go, Brad."

"What makes a woman try and hold on so tight?"

"I don't know Brad. All I know is we gamble hard and sometimes we lose everything before we would ever consider the idea of "letting go." That's enough about that."

"How's everything with you?"

"It's great. Did you see the girls?"

"Not yet. I was driving up when I saw you walk into the barn. Beth, we really need to talk but it's pretty cold out here. Can we talk back at the Main House?"

"Sure, Brad! We can talk there. The girls will be glad to see you." Brad had the look of a complete and happy man. Beth had watched him closely, he was so thoughtful. He stopped back by the car to pull out several bags of toys and presents. Beth helped him with the bags.

"Did you know we would be here, Brad?"

He could only smile as he walked past her to the door. Jean had already told him that Beth would not be going home to her family for the holidays. Who do I have to thank for this? Probably Jean. She can't hold water.

Brad made his way into the family room, calling for the kids. Marie ran into his arms first and then Michele. They had both missed Brad almost as much as she did! Michele stayed in his arms and hung on to him as if her life depended on him.

"Hey girls, I've got you guys some Christmas Eve presents. Go look in the bags over by the Christmas tree."

"Can we mom?"

"Sure guys, go!"

Brad stood up and placed Michele on the floor. She was running in the direction of the tree before her feet hit the floor. Beth knew Brad was a wonderful father. She had watched him with the girls. You would never know that he wasn't their natural father.

Jean and Jack both were happy to see Brad. They hugged him and thanked him for coming. Jean smiled at Beth. Jean noticed how she had started glowing again. She and Brad deserved to be together. Jean also noticed that Beth was watching Brad when he wasn't looking. Beth was, wearing her heart on her sleeve. It can take a lifetime to find one's soul mate and even when one finds them there are forces working against you that can take them away. Beth decided to wait on hers this time. She had tried to find true love on her own so many times before but it was always one step ahead or two feet behind her! She had "let go" and let God send her who he felt she needed and deserved. He had given her another chance.

Beth realized that prayer and faith went hand in hand. She was looking at her prince charming this very moment and it filled her with such joy. So, I just want to say prayer does change things. I'm headed in the right direction for the first time in my whole life. I will now start praying to God to help me hold on and that I never have to let go. She realized she had been silent for some time but even with all the Christmas joy she would find a quiet moment to give God thanks. The room was filled with the Christmas spirit. Beth sat on the couch next to Brad. He had both girls in his lap talking and playing with their new Christmas Eve toys. He had allowed them to open one toy each. The others would be opened tomorrow. This was what family was all about!

Brad needed to talk to Beth. "Girls," Brad said, "do you think I could speak to your mommy for a minute?"

"Sure you can, mom won't mind," Michele said laughing. "Will you mom?"

"No sweetie, mom certainly won't!"

Letting Go

"Come on guys, let's go and bring some of those Christmas cookies we made out of the kitchen," Jean said. "Come on Jack, we may need help."

Brad came over and set on his knees in front of Beth. "I want you to know I never stopped loving you. I'm aware of all the pain you've felt in these last few months. I've been in the same pain, not knowing if you would be here for me when things changed. I had prayed and hoped that you would still be free."

"Brad, I'll never be free. I may be less expensive but never free. You will have to pay and pay big. I just haven't decided how much yet."

He was so serious that he didn't realiz she had made a joke! "Ok Beth, I'll pay!"

"Brad it was a joke!" They both burst into laughter! "Brad, you have got to lighten up. I want to be a part of your life also."

Brad breathed a sigh of relief! "Beth, we are so good together. I never loved anyone as much as I love you. You're my life. You and I were meant to be together." Beth had tears in her eyes. She already knew Brad loved her! "I need you Beth! I need you to be my life partner, I want to grow old with you, I want to lie down at night and wake up in the morning with you breathing my air! We will share everything; our hopes and our dreams. I need you to be my wife, my partner and my best friend. Please say you'll marry me and make me the happiest man on earth!"

"Yes Brad, I'll marry you."

Laughter and hurrahs came from the kitchen. Everyone had been listening at the door. Brad pulled a ring out and placed it on Beth's finger. It was the most beautiful thing she'd ever seen in her life! She was filled with the joy of renewed love and hope for the future. She knew he was the one! She would hold on to him for the rest of her life. They deserved each other's love. Congratulations came from the kitchen along with hugs and kisses. Beth knew what Jean had felt the day Jack had asked her to marry him. It was a kind of completeness that one gets when one is driven by self worth! Beth didn't need Brad to complete her. She was already a complete person and for the first time in her life she put God first. She needed Brad to complete the circle of life.

Jean walked over to Beth and said, "You see? What we talked about came true. If he's the one God will send him back to you! Some things are worth waiting on. I love you Beth!"

"I love you too Jean!"

Jean felt something wet going down her legs and realized her water had just broken. "Darling, my water just broke!"

"No, Honey, we have two more weeks!"

"Well, tell that to your son because he wants to come now!"

Jack jumped up and grabbed Jean's hand. "Lets go baby!"

"No Jack, I have to change my clothes."

"There isn't time!"

"Yes there is. I won't be long. Brad, the suitcase for the baby is in the hall closest."

Beth called Isabella in from the kitchen and had her keep an eye on Marie and Michele. Jean was so calm!

"Brad, can you keep my husband from passing out while I go change my clothes? Beth, can you help me change? I will be right back. Everything is under control!"

"Hurry back, Beth!" Brad was beginning to panic also.

"Jean, we need to get moving. How are the contractions, baby?"

"They're a good fifteen to twenty minutes apart."

Jean changed her clothes and they all headed to the hospital. Brad drove while Jack coached his wife through each contraction. "Hurry, Brad!" Jack ordered.

"Jack, if we go any faster we may get stopped! Calm down Jack."

"I'm fine," said Jean just when another contraction hit! "Hurry Brad!" Jean was making the request this time. "They're less than five minutes apart. Please Brad, hurry! Jack, I don't think I can make it!"

"Yes you can. Think outside of the contraction; think about our honeymoon, think of the white snow."

Beth was getting worried! "Brad, are we going to make it?"

"We will make it, but it's going to be close."

Beth had called the hospital and Jean's doctor was on her way in. Jack had already arranged for Jean to be on a private floor away from the other patients.

Letting Go

Brad drove like a pro. The roads were icy so he had to use caution. Jean arrived in record time and was whirled into the delivery room with Jack in pursuit. He was scheduled to cut the umbilical cord. "Jack, the baby is coming, I feel it!"

"Hold on, Mrs. Morris, you are doing just fine."

Beth and Brad walked into the waiting room with a sigh of relief. "That was close!"

"Yes, it sure was! What made them move so far out in the country anyway?"

"You've seen that place. It's absolutely wonderful year round! I would love for us to live in a place like that with horses and animals for the kids."

"One day soon, Beth!" One day soon was all that Brad would say.

"Beth, we need to call Jean's and Jack's parents." Jack's parents were in town for the holidays. Beth located Jean's parent's number on her cell and placed a call to them. They would be there as soon as possible. Jack's parents were already on the way. Isabella had informed them that Jean was on her way to delivery.

Brad continued to pace the floor. "Brad, please sit down. You're making me nervous."

"I'm sorry love, it's just she was so scared and Jack was a mess."

Jack walked out of delivery and announced, "It's a seven pound boy! He came kicking and screaming with ten fingers and ten toes!"

Beth and Brad got to Jack about the same time with congratulations. "How's Jean?"

"She's fine, she did great. They're getting her ready so they can bring her and the baby upstairs." Jack passed out cigars to everyone in the waiting room. "Did you guys get a hold of our parents?"

"They're on their way!"

"Thanks guys!"

Jack Jr. was beautiful! He was named after his father. Jean was holding the baby as they walked in. "Brad and I wanted to say congratulations before we headed back to the ranch. We called your parents. They're flying in as soon as they can get a flight and Jack's parents are on the way here."

Jean asked the nurse to place Jack Jr. in his crib. He would have a full time nurse while in the hospital and when he returned home. Jack's parents came in and they were admiring their grandchild. Jean was so full of joy. "Beth, I have a son! He's perfect! He looks just like his father!" They all hugged and kissed goodnight. They would see them back at the ranch. What a way to begin Christmas! Beth would have to hurry home and tell the girls they had a little cousin. "Beth, I wanted to tell you, and Brad that I'm so happy you two got together. You're perfect for each other."

"Thanks, Jean, for making this the perfect Christmas. I got engaged and a new nephew all on the same night. It doesn't get any better than this."

Brad commented, "Yes it does, you just wait and see! Jean, you need to try and get some rest after everyone leaves."

Jack was bringing his parents and his sister over as Beth, and Brad, were leaving. Jack and Brad hugged and Beth kissed him on the cheeks and said "goodnight daddy I'll see you later." They spoke to Jack's family as they left the room.

Beth couldn't help but smile, she would love to give Brad a child. They had plenty to discuss as they drove slowly back to the ranch. There was no need to rush. The hard part of the night was over. They were engaged to wed and Jean had given birth to a healthy baby boy. Everything was right in the world. Beth and Brad checked in on the girls, they were sound asleep. They would tell them about the baby in the morning. That would be an extra Christmas present.

Brad asked Beth to spend the night with him. They had a lot of catching up to do. Beth was ready, but it would take a hundred years and she would still be playing catch-up! They entered Brad's bedroom. The housekeeper had already placed her bags in Brad's room by accident. "How did she know?"

"Beth, everyone knew you were mine. All they had to do was look into my eyes when they were looking at you."

They made love in celebration of the birth of a baby and a new beginning for the two of them. Beth had been so lonely for

Letting Go

Brad's touch that when he laid her on his bed and she closed her eyes she knew she had been delivered into a new world. A world filled with new possibilities and fresh dreams. A world where you didn't have to wonder when your man left home if he would be coming back. A world of love so deep it would overflow with emotions every time you looked in his eyes. A world that allowed you to be who ever you wanted to be and not be judged. A world where there's no hurt and the only hurt would be self-inflicted. This was Beth's new world! This was the world she would share with Brad! She had been groomed her whole life for this man. Even before they met he was to be hers and she his. Every piece of her heart that Earl tore away was rebuilt! Her heart had been made new and she was stronger from the inside out and more appreciative of what true and real love was. So that when it came she would not be afraid to open her heart and accept her gift. They made love to the past and to the future. They made love for the ones who held on and the ones who had to "let go!" This man had set her free and she would give him a king's ransom for his heart to keep.

Brad couldn't remember ever feeling this type of wholeness. Beth finished his dreams. She was everything he dreamed of. He knew this was where his life would begin. The only past he would remember is his son. He would not be able to look back at the mistakes he had made.

Beth wasn't asleep. She needed to get to her room before the girls got up. It was too soon to try and explain staying with Brad overnight. She needed time to absorb her engagement and marriage to Brad. Beth knew she would be planning a wedding very soon.

Jean bought the baby home the day after Christmas. The girls begged to stay over. Brad stayed at the house with them since he had taken leave for the holidays. The days that lead up until New Years were full of joy. The new baby, the kids, it was the kind of life fairy tales was made of! Jean and Beth had a wonderful holiday.

Beth was planning her wedding for Memorial Day weekend. The excitement was growing. Jean made plans and assisted the wedding coordinator with all the details. All Beth had to do was to take care of her dress. Beth chose an off the shoulder white gown that with a ten foot train. She didn't think white was appropriate but, what the heck, this was her wedding and she would wear whatever color she desired! After all, this was to be her last wedding and she wanted to look like a princess. She picked a tiara for her final hair piece. She wanted to go out in style. Jean had insisted on paying for everything. Beth was happy. She had moments when she wasn't sure if this was real or she was dreaming. She was still a little scared. She and Brad had made such a mess out of their last marriages. They wouldn't go down that road again. They had too much respect and love for each other.

Charles had stopped by the store a few weeks before the wedding and noticed the ring. "My goodness Beth, just who are you marrying, Mr. Carat himself?"

"No Charles, his name is Brad Walker!"

"I'm happy for you!"

"Thank you, Charles. How's married life treating you the second time around? I hope what they say is true!"

"What's that?"

"That it's better the second time around! Actually, anything I do with Brad will be an improvement over my first marriage. The kids were the only joy I received from that marriage, and a well learned lesson about self worth. He taught me that no man or woman can complete you."

"Beth, do I hear a little anger in your voice?"

"There's no anger toward him, I'm just sorry I didn't learn my lesson sooner."

"Well, Beth, I can only speak for myself. Its much better the second time around! I love it, no regrets! The kids are great and I have a wonderful wife," Charles said. "We decided to try for another boy as soon as possible."

"That's great Charles. I'm happy for you."

"How are Jean and Jack doing?"

"They are extremely happy; my god son Jack Jr. is precious. He's adorable, Charles!"

"Did Jean mention our conversation about her pregnancy?"

"No, Charles, did it concern me?"

Letting Go

"No, I questioned her about the time of her pregnancy. If it was possible that I may be the father."

"Jack is the father of that child! Are you going to start trouble for them by making stupid statements like that?"

"I just thought she may have mentioned it."

"Why would she? She knew you were trying to find a way of staying in her life, that's all. Charles, stay away from Jean," Beth threatened. "You made your decision a long time ago. You chose Amy, remember? You let Jean go. Now move on Charles. That part of your life is over and that door has closed. Jean has never been as happy as she is right now. She has a man that loves her for who she is and not what she can do for him." Beth's blood pressure was on the rise. "I want to forget we ever had this conversation Charles; you need to promise me you will never bring it up again to anyone. Does Amy know what you're thinking these days?"

"No Beth, she doesn't."

"Then back off! I've seen that baby and he definitely is not yours. If you attempt to see Jean or her baby I will pay Amy a visit. I will let Amy know you are still trying to hold on to someone you let go. Don't make me do that Charles. I like you, but I love Jean and Jack and my God child! I'll fight you for their happiness."

Charles left after running Beth's blood pressure up.

"What's next?" Beth thought. "What makes people look for something that's not there? Please tell me why it so hard to let go? Even when we let go, do we truly let go? Why was Charles trying to find a way back into Jean's life if he's so happy with his own? Beth pondered those questions. She hated her job; it was not the same with Jean gone.

She wanted out!

Who's Jamie's Father?

Someone walked up behind Beth and said, "Excuse me Ma'am, could you help me?"

"Sure, what can I do for you?"

"I'm looking for Beth Taylor."

"Yes?"

"You're engaged to marry Brad Walker?"

"Before I answer any more questions you need to tell me who you are and what it is you want!"

"Well, I'm an old friend of his wife."

Beth began to back away. "Sir, I don't know why you're here, but if you try something..."

"No, please calm down. I wanted to give you and Brad a wedding present."

"What is it?"

He opened a folder and handed her what looked like a paternity test of a child by the name of Jamie Walker. "That's Brad's son's name. What is this?"

"Brad is not the boy's father, I am. Ellen was pregnant when she married Brad."

"Brad told me he had a paternity test proving he was the father."

"She lied to him."

"What about the test?"

"I changed the test. She was paying me to stay away all these years."

"How did you get this test?"

"I worked in the clinic where the test was performed. I switched the blood type to match Brad's when he was tested."

"How do we know this is not a trick?"

"Please trust me on this! Ellen and I are first cousins. I know what you're thinking, but that's not the case! When we met we didn't know we were related because I was raised here

Letting Go

and Ellen was raised in New Jersey. We never discussed family. We met when she was in college here. Once she found out she was pregnant we went to meet her family and that's when we found out we were related. So we never told anyone about the baby and I helped her set Brad up to be the father. I'm sorry for what I've done!"

"Why bring this to me and not Brad?"

"He will probably hurt me! I figured you were safer! Please, Ma'am, can you make sure he gets this? I want to see my son Ma'am! Ellen has refused to let me even see him. I want to be a part of his life and since Brad has moved on I was hoping she would finally let me be a part of my child's life. I'm able to support her and my son if she'll let me."

"I didn't get your name."

"I think you're safer not knowing. She is very dangerous Ma'am, be careful! Once Brad confronts her with this there's no telling what she may do!"

"What about you? Aren't you worried?"

"I told our parents about our son and they are looking for her to have a little talk."

Beth left work early. She needed to know Brad's blood type. They had already had their blood test for the marriage license. She would have to check it against Jamie's. There's no way he could be the father. Beth called Jean and asked her to call her doctor for confirmation.

"It's true Beth. Brad is not Jamie's father."

"What should I do Jean? How do you tell a man that his son of two years is not really his? That he was set up from the beginning."

"I guess you should keep it simple."

"He's coming by the house after work today; I'll try to tell him then." Beth knew she had to tell him. She had no choice. She would reach deep down inside herself and find the strength to do it.

Once the girls were in bed she calmly asked him over to the couch. "Brad, there's something I need to tell you."

"What is it sweetheart? You aren't having second thoughts are you?"

"No way, never. I had a visitor today. He wouldn't give me his name but he left you this."

Brad read the papers. "Do you believe this crap? If this DNA report is true Jamie is not my son."

"I'm sorry, Brad."

"This can't be true Beth. I was there when he was born and he looked just like me."

"Brad, you saw what you wanted to see! What will you do with this information?"

"Who is Jamie's father?"

"He's Ellen's first cousin."

"What?! That's sick."

"No, Brad, he said they didn't know they were related when they started dating until she got pregnant and they were going home to tell their parents. That's when they found out they were family. They ended the relationship and she paid him to never come around. That's when they set you up to take the fall for the baby!"

"If Ellen has been lying to me for the last two years about my son I will eat her alive in court. My only concern is Jamie. I can't do this to him!"

"Brad, you haven't done anything, it's his mother. How could she refuse to let his biological father see him? He's hoping now that you're divorced he may have a chance to see his son. That's why he's doing it now. What are you going to do?"

"There's a copy of his birth certificate in the safe at his mother's house. I'm going to check it out first."

Brad headed over to Ellen's. She would still be at work. He had his old keys and she hadn't changed the locks. Brad located the birth certificate. The blood type was the same. He was not the father! Brad waited on Ellen. She had lied to him all these years! Now they were headed to court to fight out the custody of his son and child support. He wasn't sure if he needed to confront her now or if should he wait until they went to court. She would only lie if he asked her now anyway. He would wait and see her in court. Court was scheduled for the following Monday.

Letting Go

Beth accompanied Brad to court but, as usual, she wasn't allowed in the courtroom since they weren't married. Brad had already given copies of Jamie's blood test to his lawyer. This would be an open and shut case.

Ellen's lawyer presented her case first to the judge. He discussed the issues of divorce and her desire to stay married at all costs. That Ellen had been the perfect wife, always willing to do whatever it took to make her marriage work. Ellen was smiling at the judge in confirmation of her lawyer's statements.

Brad's lawyer took the floor. "Mrs. Walker, you're asking for a thousand dollars a month in child support. Is that correct?"

"Yes!"

"Why so much?"

"He can afford it."

"Mr. Walker had agreed to give you six hundred."

"I want more. That's not enough to raise his son on!"

"Your Honor, this was given to me yesterday. It pertains to the young man in question. Apparently Mr. Walker is not the father of Mrs. Walker's son."

Ellen jumped to her feet yelling profanity at Brad and his lawyer! Ellen's lawyer was trying to calm her down. "Where did you get those documents?"

"There's no way he could be the father, your Honor. Mrs. Walker has known this from the beginning. She tricked Mr. Walker into marrying her by claming she was carrying his child when all along she was carrying her cousin's baby."

Ellen's lawyer asked for a recess, he needed to confer with his client.

Ellen walked out the courtroom steaming mad. She needed to get out of there. How did he find out about Jamie's father? She had kept the secret for two years and only two other people knew the truth! She would get to the bottom of this. The judge ruled in Brad's favor, no child support and no alimony. She was to locate the father of her child and reapply for child support.

Brad caught up with Ellen before she left the court house. "How could you do this to Jamie all these years? He's lived a lie and you knew the truth. How could you hurt him? What will you tell him Ellen?"

Ellen looked Brad straight in the eyes and said, "I'll tell him you died. Now get the hell out of my face. I never want to set eyes on you again!"

"I'm sorry it has to be like that Ellen. I would like to see him. I'm the only father he knows."

"Brad, I want you to forget you ever had a son. You are not his father so leave my son alone. I mean that Brad! Don't push me."

Brad knew he was skating on thin ice, she was ready to explode. He would never be able to see Jamie again. The only good thing was he's young enough to forget Brad. He would be replaced by someone new. The pain tore at Brad's heart. He loved Jamie and it would be hard giving him up but deep down he knew that was the right thing to do.

Beth was waiting on Brad outside in the car. She decided to hold her tongue unless Brad felt like talking about it. She really didn't know what to say. He didn't mention what had happened in the court. He wanted to let it pass.

Ellen was having a hard time containing her anger. She would make Brad pay if it was the last thing she ever did! She wasn't going to let him walk out on her and their son. She called her friend Zack. She made arrangements to meet him at his place. He wasn't thrilled to be hearing from her. She was trouble with a capitol T! Zack wished he had gotten his phone number changed. Ellen was a woman who liked to call all the shots. She had threatened him on numerous occasions and he knew she meant business. Zack wouldn't say he was afraid of her; she was just one of those women you never wanted to cross.

She arrived at his place around six thirty. "Hello, Ellen, it's been a long time! So what are you doing so far from home?"

"I just needed to see and old friend!"

"How's married life? Are you still living uptown with your rich officer?"

"He's not rich and we're divorced!"

"What did you do Ellen?"

"I'm here to ask the questions. You just listen! Where's that no good cousin of mine hiding these days? Someone told Brad about Jamie being Clarence's son. I need to find him because if he had anything to do with it he will regret it for the rest of his life, cousin or no cousin."

"I haven't seen him in months. Now, Ellen, why would Clarence tell Brad about Jamie? You've been paying him to be quiet all this time!"

"I stopped paying him several months ago. I told him he's not getting any more money out of me. He had to know I was serious when I told him if he opened his mouth to anyone he would be sorry."

"Maybe he wants to be a part of his son's life, Ellen. You never gave him a chance."

"He didn't deserve one; we couldn't raise Jamie as parents."

"Why not? People do it all the time."

"Where is he Zack? I know you two are close."

"Ellen, I don't know but if I find him I'll call you."

"You do that, and Zack, if I find out you are lying I'll be back to pay you a visit. I have people in high places."

"I already know you don't play Ellen. I remember what happened to that young lady Brad was dating before he started seeing you."

Ellen left without another word.

Zack remembered all too well how dangerous Ellen and her friends were. He wanted no part of her. She had made someone less attractive in no time at all. Zack knew Ellen had connections in the high crime scene in New Jersey. When Ellen met Brad he was dating Karen. Brad and Karen had been seeing each other for several weeks. They were all at a party one night when Ellen was introduced to Brad and Karen. From that moment on she had set out to trap him. That's when everything started. Karen's car was car jacked and she was beaten so badly that she suffered brain damage and was placed in a home. They never discovered who had attacked her. They all suspected Ellen had something to do with it but no one knew for sure. She wanted Brad and there was nothing or no one standing in her way. The next thing we knew she was getting married! She had already made a deal with Clarence. He would never lay eyes on the baby and the child would be raised by Brad.

Zack made several calls trying to locate Clarence. He would try one other place that they hung out. Even Ellen didn't know about this place. Clarence was there! Zack made it fast. "Clarence, man, Ellen is looking for you and she thinks you had something to do with Brad finding out Jamie is not his son."

"I told him!"

"Are you crazy? Do you want to die? What on earth made you do that?"

"I'm tired of that woman keeping me away from my son."

"If I were you, I would leave town until things settle down. She is on the war path! If she finds out, you are going to disappear forever; you know what I mean, man? We've been best friends forever and you are like my little brother, but I can't save you or protect you from Ellen. She's Satan in a dress!" They had been friends since grade school. He had promised his mother he would look after him, but what could he do? He couldn't stand up against Ellen. She had powerful friends in the underground. "Clarence, meet me under the bridge on Fourteenth Street. I will make a few calls and see if I can get you a ride out of here."

"Ok, Zack!"

"And keep your eyes open! I hope your reason was worth the price you may have to pay."

"Zack, I called my family and told them about Jamie. That I was the father and that Ellen would probably try to kill me for telling them. They are looking for her right now too."

"I hope they find her before she finds you Clarence."

"Yes, man, but it was worth it. Now everyone knows that Jamie is my son! Even if she kills me, they all will still know the truth!"

"Get to moving man."

"Zack, I had kept my part of the bargain but she reneged on hers so I made her pay for all the years she kept me away from my son!"

"Now you may be paying with your life if she catches you!"

Clarence remembered Beth. She had been nice. Brad had made a good choice and he was happy for him. The thought of any man leaving Ellen was scary. She was evil from the

Letting Go

beginning. Clarence had to pack; he had no time for day dreaming while Ellen was looking for him.

Ellen put the word out and she would soon know where Clarence was hiding. In the meantime she would deal with Brad and his little princess! Ellen knew where Beth lived, she had followed Brad there on many occasions. Tonight she would give them something to celebrate as a pre-wedding going away gift. Ellen looked at the five gallon gas can she had placed in the back of her car. This was too easy. She would be back at midnight when everyone was asleep and burn them down.

Beth had picked up the girls; they would be spending the night at Jean's. The wedding was a week away and there were still so many things to do. Beth was so excited! She had ridden into work with Brad. They would all be spending the weekend at the ranch. Jean had given them a key to the place. They loved the ranch just as much as Jean. They picked the girls up from school and headed to the ranch.

"Beth, why are you still working?"

"I told Brad that we would combine our income and buy the ranch that's for sale two miles down the road, Jean."

"Beth, let Jack give you guys the money to purchase it and you can pay us back later."

"No, Jean! Brad would never go for that, he's determined to do it on his own. It's a man thing."

"If it was me, I'd give it to you for a wedding present."

"I know you would, Jean, and I love you for thinking of it. We'll sell my house and buy the ranch. That's the plan; the house goes on the market tomorrow. Jean, you have done so much for us; look at what you're doing for our wedding. I'll be the most beautiful bride in the world."

"You should be, you deserve it after all you've been through."

"Look who's talking. We should write a book about our first marriages!"

Brad and Jack walked into the room asking, "What's so funny?"

"You don't want to know!"

Beth was holding Jack Jr. "He's really growing, Jean."

"I know, isn't he perfect?"

"Yes, he looks just like me," Jack said from behind Beth.

"You're right Jack, he does. I tease Jack all the time about little Jack's ears!"

"Jean, I'm so glad to see you so happy."

"I thank God everyday for Jack and Jack Jr. and for friends like you and Brad and of course my god daughters."

They changed the subject before the tears started falling. They both had a lot to be thankful for. The girls broke up the silence. "Aunt Jean, do you think Isabella would make us a snack?"

"If you ask her nicely, I bet she will! Why don't you two run into the kitchen and ask."

"Thanks Aunt Jean!"

"The girls are so excited about the wedding! Have they heard anything from Earl?"

"Not since Christmas. He sent the girls two hundred dollars and a Christmas card. Let's talk about the honeymoon. Where do you and Brad want to go?"

"I've never been to the Bahamas!"

"Jack, did you hear that Beth has never been to the Bahamas?"

"Well we will have to see about that."

"Jack, I'll take care of that; you guys have done enough for us all ready. We will never be able to repay you for this wedding."

"This is from our heart, Brad! I wouldn't accept a dime from either of you anyway. The girls will stay here with us. Beth, Jack will have everything ready for you two when it's time to leave. It's already arranged; the hotel and flight to the Bahamas. Just one thing Beth, don't come back pregnant."

"All right Jean!" Laughter filled the house.

The girls heard the laughter and ran into the room. They went straight to Brad. Michele asked to be picked up and Marie was holding onto his arm. "Ok girls, let's see." Brad was attempting to pick them both up at the same time. Beth had picked the perfect man. He would be what Earl never was, a father. They all fell back on the couch laughing and talking.

Letting Go

Isabella called them back into the kitchen. "Girls, I made hot cookies. Who wants to go first?"

"Me," said Michele. "No, I'm the oldest. I'm first," said Marie. "I should always be first and you should be second. Right, mama?"

Why don't both of you be first?" They ran into the kitchen.

Brad poured ice tea for everyone. Beth was glad they were staying at the ranch tonight. She had noticed Brad wasn't himself since he had to give up his son. She knew he missed him. The girls were good for him and Beth was sure they would have more kids. She would start working on it on their wedding night! Beth smiled to herself. She would give him as many kids as she could. Ellen had hurt him badly! Beth couldn't understand how someone could be so evil.

The Fire

Ellen drove back to the house around midnight. Brad's truck was in the driveway so they would all be asleep. Beth would be in bed with her husband! Who does she think she is? I'll teach her that he will never be free! They will both die together! Ellen placed a bar across the back door and jammed a chair under the front door so they could not open it from the inside. She poured gas over the entire porch and at the back door. She would make sure no one escaped their destiny. She would see to it!

Ellen set the fire and ducked back between the houses. The flames were rushing around the house. A neighbor had been out walking his dog and heard the noise from a trash can being knocked over. A spotlight went on in the back yard of the home next to Beth's.

Several neighbors were up and about. The fire was burning out of control. One neighbor had already dialed 911. The dogs started barking and howling as if to get the neighbors up! The fire was burning out of control. No one could get within twenty feet of the house. The heat was so great that Mr. Davis had noticed a vehicle parked down the street where he usually walked his dog, Chad. The car had been parked back off the main road. The only reason Mr. Davis noticed the car was because it was the vehicle he had been after his wife to buy for them. He really didn't think anything of it. He was headed back to his house and looked over and saw the flames at the neighbor's home. Mr. Davis tried to run into the house. He was calling for Beth and the girls, he knew they were in there. He thought he had seen them this afternoon. He had noticed her friend's truck in the drive way, he was there also! The fire department arrived about ten minutes into the fire, Brad's truck exploded! The Fire Department wouldn't be able to save Beth and the girl's home! The flames had devoured everything; he

Letting Go

didn't see anyone come out. His only thought was they had all perished in the fire!

Ellen drove by the burning house and she smiled at her handy work. Yes, she had paid him back so now when she tells her son his father is dead she won't be lying. That's the price he paid for leaving her! No one leaves Ellen Walker, no one unless she tells them to.

The fire department had subdued most of the flames before going around the house to see if anyone made it out. There were no signs of anyone making an exit. Mr. Davis spoke to a policeman and someone from the fire department. He mentioned the cream color vehicle he had seen parked down the road a bit, he had looked for it on his way back to the house to call the fire department but it was gone.

The policeman asked Mr. Davis if he happened to see the tag number. He had to search his memory for a moment, it wasn't as good as it used to be, but he remembered the tag because it was a word. That was what caught his attention, the word Boss1. He thought that would be a good name for his wife to have on her tags. "Thanks, Sir!"

"You're welcome." The fire department chief returned and told the cop it was an attempt to burn whoever was in the house up. All the doors were jammed from the outside.

"Sir, do you know the family that lives here?"

"Sure do! Mrs. Taylor. A nice lady and her two beautiful girls. Her boyfriend sometimes stays there."

"Do you know his name, sir?"

"No, but that's his truck!"

The police took the info on the trucks tags. The announcement was made that there were no bodies found in the house. Mrs. Davis approached to where her husband stood talking to the fireman. "They're not in town. They are at their friend's house in the country."

"Officer," Mr. Davis called as the Officer was walking away. "They're visiting a friend, sir."

"Let's keep that a secret right now. Someone wants them dead. We need to locate the family and let them know."

"Officer, I know where they are staying," Mrs. Davis said. "I have the phone number if you would like it."

"Sure Mrs. Davis, please don't mention this to anyone else."

"No, sir! We wouldn't want this person to know where they're located."

Mrs. Davis came back with the number and address. He called the number on his way out to the ranch. Jack answered the phone wondering who would be calling this late at night. It was 2:00 am in the morning.

"Sir, I'm sorry to wake you. This is a special unit from the Maryland Police Department. Please don't be alarmed. We're on our way to your ranch. We need to speak to Mrs. Taylor and her friend. We'll explain when we get there. We should be there in ten minutes."

Jack didn't have to wake Jean; she had been awakened by the phone. "What is it?"

"It has something to do with Beth and Brad. The police are on their way here to speak to them!"

"I'll get them up," Jean said, slipping on her robe and rushing out the door. "Jack, they didn't say anything about what they wanted to talk to them about?"

"No, sweetheart. We will all know in ten minutes."

Jean knocked on the door softly; she didn't want to startle them. "Brad, Beth, can you two get up and meet us down stairs?"

"What is it Jean? Is it the girls or Jack Jr.?"

"No Beth, it's a policeman from Maryland."

Beth and Brad looked in on the girls before going downstairs to the family room. There were two policemen, one in uniform and one in plain clothes sitting and waiting. "What's going on?" Beth asked, starting to panic.

The officers introduced themselves. "Mrs. Taylor, there was a fire at your home tonight. It was set and both exits out of the house were blocked. The house had been drenched with gasoline before being set on fire."

Beth turned to Brad and said, "It had to be Ellen! Oh, Brad, we could all have been killed tonight! What about the girls? She wants to kill everybody Brad! What kind of person is she?"

Letting Go

"Mrs. Taylor, do you know anyone that may want the two of you dead?"

"Yes, Brad's ex-wife."

"What type of vehicle does she own, Mr. Walker?"

"She has an SUV with the tags Boss1 on it," Brad said.

"That vehicle was seen parked down the road from your home before the fire, Mrs. Taylor. We've already put an APB out on the vehicle and someone is staking out your ex-wife's home. I need you to stay put until we find this person and bring her in for questioning. If she's the one and is found guilty, she will be going away for a long time. Mr. Walker, did you know your ex-wife had an outstanding warrant on her for questioning in another murder case? Do you know anyone by the name of Karen Waters?" Mr. Walker.

"I dated a Karen Waters before I met Ellen. But I received a note saying she never wanted to see me again and not to try and contact her because she was moving back home. I did try to call her a few times to see what happened but she never returned my calls."

"I'm sorry to tell you this but she's dead. She was beaten and left for dead. She never fully recovered and they placed her in a nursing home. She died two months later from complications. Would you happen to have any photos of your ex-wife around here Mr. Walker?"

"I've got a copy of the one I gave to the guards a while back," Jean said. "I'll get it. It was the one we got when she had tried to run you and your employees over on the post," Jean explained.

"This is not the first time she tried to hurt you, Mrs. Taylor?"

"No, sir, but we couldn't prove it because she had turned her lights off on her car."

Jean returned with the picture. "Ellen never liked taking pictures," Brad explained. "She always said that pictures had a way of looking into a person's soul through their eyes." The officer took the picture and encouraged them again to stay put until she was apprehended.

Beth was scared to death! "She couldn't stop shaking! Jean was trying to comfort her the best she could. "Brad, we can't stay here. We can't expose Jack and his family to this crazy woman."

"No one leaves. You and Brad and my nieces will not leave this house," Jack said. Jack picked up the phone and called his head of security. "I need around the clock surveillance on the ranch," he said. "Send as many men as you need."

"Jean, I'm so sorry," Brad said as if he was apologizing for Ellen's insanity. "I had no idea she was wanted by the police or that she could do something so inhuman."

"She would have killed everyone, even the girls. What kind of human being would try and kill innocent people? Jean asked."

Brad was so angry. "I have to go and find her, Jack. She will not terrorize the people I love, and she won't get away with burning your home down, Beth."

"I don't care about the house Brad, I'm just glad we're safe," said Beth. "Brad, please don't go. You have no idea what kind of person you're dealing with."

"I'll go with you Brad."

"Jack!" Jean yelled.

"Honey, I'll be fine. I'll take care of Brad and we will stop her tonight," Jack said. Jack's head of security met them at the ranch.

"Jean, I didn't mean for this to happen," Beth said.

"Don't worry Beth, the guys will deal with this problem and be back home before we know it, I'm sure of that," Jean said.

Ellen was feeling really good that she had taken out the one and only person who had ever attempted to leave her. Now, she needed to find her so called cousin, Clarence. There was a score she needed to even with him. She paid no attention to the police car following her. She knew no one could place her at the scene of the fire. She had been extremely careful not to park within view. The old guy walking his dog had already gone inside; he hadn't seen anything. Ellen drove on, unconcerned about the cop.

James had spotted her SUV from two streets over. A vehicle that size is pretty hard to miss; plus the Boss1 tags were a dead

Letting Go

giveaway. He was scheduled off in less than an hour. He would make this his last arrest before getting off duty. Nothing ever happened on his shift anyway. James called in his position and was told not to stop her, just keep a safe distance and follow her. Back-up was on its way; she could be armed and dangerous.

The Chief wanted to be present. He wanted to see the female that was responsible for such a vicious act. What kind of person would attempt to take the lives of innocent children? He would question her in-depth himself. The police Chief's car pulled in behind James. James pulled back so the Chief was behind Ellen now. He turned on the siren.

"What now," Ellen said. She wasn't speeding and her car was in perfect condition. Why was she being stopped and why were there two cars behind her now? Ellen was attempting to speed up when she noticed several other police cars approaching from the front. She stopped the vehicle and opened the glove compartment just in case she needed her piece. She had no problem using it on a cop; it wasn't registered to her anyway. She had taken it and used it on some rich guy sitting in a parked truck crying and writing letters.

She wished she had taken the time to read both letters so she could have known why he was trying to kill himself. But one was already sealed and addressed to someone name Brian. She read the one addressed to Amy; he hadn't sealed hers yet. She respected his privacy. She was wondering what had happened to that case; she never heard anything on the news or read about his death in the papers. He had begged for his life in the end. He said his wife was pregnant and they had two little girls. Ellen felt sorry for him but she needed the gun and the money he had been carrying in his wallet; plus he had been trying to pull the trigger for half an hour. She just helped him along. Now here we go again!

Officer Fields asked her to turn off the engine and step out of the vehicle with her hands in the air. "What's the problem, officer?"

"Ma'am, please just turn off your engine and step out the vehicle and keep your hands where I can see them! Just want to ask you a few questions about a fire, Ma'am. I'll ask once more, please step out."

The minute the officer said fire, Ellen reached into the glove compartment, pulled out the gun and started shooting. The Chief yelled for everyone to get down and take cover! Ellen tried to drive off. The Chief hit her in the shoulder and the truck swerved into an embankment and turned over. She wanted to get out and run but she was pinned in by the airbags. She had really made a mess of things. Why didn't she just answer their questions? They had nothing on her. She hadn't been seen at the fire or the park. The only connection was the gun and she would say she found it.

Ellen was taken to the nearest hospital to have her arm stitched; she had only been grazed by the bullet. Ellen was trying to piece together what might have happened. Maybe it was that old man and that dam dog of his. She would have to deal with him and Clarence once she was out on bail. Her main mission had been accomplished and that was to take Brad and his new family out.

She would go to jail, happy knowing they won't be living happily ever after; plus they had no proof she'd done it. Ellen had a smile on her face when she met the Chief. "I would like my lawyer called; I'm not talking to anyone."

"You don't need to talk; the evidence will speak for you, Mrs. Walker! We're booking you on four counts of attempted murder and arson and resisting a rest. We are also holding you in conjunction with another murder."

"I didn't kill him, he was dead when I got there and I just took the gun!"

The chief wasn't sure what Ellen was speaking of, but the gun was being run through ballistics to see what might turn up. "Mrs. Walker, do you know a Karen Waters? She was found beaten and left for dead. We're checking out the gun you mentioned also, thanks for the tip! Please give Mrs. Walker thirty five cents to call her lawyer. We will try and locate your ex-husband."

"I have no ex-husband, thank you!"

Ellen called her lawyer. He was a little annoyed she had called so late at night. "I'll be there first thing in the morning."

Letting Go

"It is morning you dick; now come and get me out of this place!" Ellen knew she would get out tonight; they had no reason to hold her. She would post bail and leave town.

Jack and Brad were on their way to the police department. They had been notified by his head of security that she was in custody. Brad wanted to make sure they had the right person; plus he wanted to let her see his face. Jack entered into the Chief's office ahead of Brad and asked, "Did she confess?"

"She is waiting on her lawyer before she says anything."

"Did you tell her you have an eye witness?"

"No, we don't want to overplay our hand; plus we have no idea what kind of connections she may have out there."

"Can I see her Chief?"

"All right, Brad, but keep it simple. She's being booked right now."

"Hey, do any of you know anything about a guy name Ken Robinson," the chief asked. "We ran the gun Mrs. Walker used in the shootout and it was registered to a Ken Robinson."

"He was found dead last year in his truck over in the District. It was listed at the time as a possible suicide, apparently there was a suicide note," one of the officers said.

"Keep digging. Lets see what else we can find out about this gun and Ken Robinson."

Jack was concerned that Brad wanted to see Ellen. "Brad, do you think that's smart? I'm surprised you want to see her. She thinks you and Beth are both dead. Seeing you may set her off! Let her keep thinking you are dead; then you're no threat to her. But once she knows you are alive she'll realize she's failed on her mission and she may try again."

"I know what you're saying is true Jack, but Ellen would have to have some pretty long arms to reach this far." Brad was angry with himself. He had no knowledge of the person he married; who was she? Ellen was willing to kill innocent people because she couldn't "let go." He had married a monster! Brad wanted to face her and hear her excuse.

Ellen's lawyer arrived thirty minuets later. Jack and Brad had been moved to a waiting room. They would have to wait until Ellen's lawyer finished speaking with her. Brad didn't care;

he would wait all night if he had to. Ellen was seated and smiling as if this was all a waste of her time. She would be out in a day or two. She wasn't really worried. Her lawyer wanted to know the charges.

"We're holding your client on four counts of attempted murder, arson, and resisting arrest. We're also holding her in connection with Karen Water's death. We need your client to take a DNA test. We found blood on the victim that we're hoping to match with her assailant."

Ellen was still smiling. "I'm not taking any test," she said. "How could I set a fire when I wasn't even in the area?"

"We have an eyewitness that says otherwise."

"Who?" Ellen asked.

"Your tags were identified at the scene."

"He's lying!"

"How do you know it's a he Mrs. Walker? I never said."

"You said attempted murdered. What does that mean?" Ellen asked.

"That means your plan failed, no one was home at the time of the fire."

"What?!" Ellen jumped up. "Where were they? I made sure of it!" Ellen didn't realize she was confessing. "What I mean is, I had called Brad earlier and said I would stop by there. We had a meeting."

Brad walked into the room. "Stop lying Ellen! Just tell me why Ellen! What made you want to kill me along with three innocent people?"

"Who says they're innocent? You left me, Brad, no one has ever left me before. I do all the leaving."

"Not this time."

"This is all about Jamie and his father isn't it?"

"You should have told the truth. Ellen. Where is Jamie, Ellen?"

"That's not your concern anymore. I'll be out by tomorrow and I'll take care of this mess myself."

"There's one more charge in the making, it's about the gun your client used tonight. It was used in an apparent suicide last year. The victim's name was Ken Anderson. Mrs. Walker, can

Letting Go

you finish telling us about the gun and how it came into your possession?"

"I told you earlier that he was already dead when I got there. I saw the gun and took it."

"You're finger prints were on his wallet."

"He had a couple of hundred dollars on him. It was not like he was going to need it."

Brad couldn't believe what he was hearing. "Ellen, you robbed a dead man?"

"Mrs. Walker, this is what happened." The chief was going to tell her how she killed Ken Anderson. "Mr. Anderson wasn't dead when you got there, his wallet was still in his pocket. You took the gun away from him somehow and made him give you his wallet. You then took all his cash and left the credit cards because they're too easily tracked. You threw the wallet back on the seat next to him. How am I doing so far? You then put the gun to his forehead and pulled the trigger. Isn't that what happened Mrs. Walker? Did I leave anything out? I bet he begged for mercy and you shot him anyway didn't you? You killed him in cold blood."

"No, I gave him a chance to confess his sins first, he was a coward. I read one of those letters. He was a sick man. I had watched him try and pull the trigger a couple of times. When he was about to try it again I didn't want him to fail since he was trying so hard so I helped him on his way. He would have eventually killed himself anyway. He was a married gay man.

"Thanks for clearing everything up for us. We were a little confused until we found the gun. We were trying to figure out why his wallet had blood stains on it if you robbed him after he was shot. If you robbed him after he was shot the wallet would have still been in his back pocket and free of blood stains."

Ellen was booked and held over for trial. There would be no bail tonight or any other night.

The Chief made a call to Mrs. Anderson, who is now Mrs. Brown. "Mrs. Brown, I wanted to let you know that your deceased husband did not kill himself. We have a full confession to his murder."

"Who was it, sir?"

"It's a young lady we picked up on other charges and made the connection through your husband's gun. He was murdered, Mrs. Brown. Her name is Ellen Walker."

"Why did she kill him?"

"She robbed him and then she killed him execution style. I'm sorry to tell you all of this, but you should know the truth about your husband's death. The trial is set for two weeks from now."

"Thank you for calling."

Amy was crying. Charles had been in the bathroom and hadn't heard the phone ring. "What's the matter, sweetheart?"

"Ken didn't kill himself. He was murdered by someone name Ellen Walker. Charles, all this time I've been angry and I called him a coward."

"Honey, you were being led on by the letter he wrote to you; how were you to know?"

"I need to call Brian, Charles; he has a right to know."

"Do you want me to tell him for you?"

"No Charles, this is something I'll have to do."

"I'll go and start breakfast; the girls will be up soon. Charles stopped by the crib and kissed his son. "I don't feel any different about your father, he's still a coward. Ken wasn't man enough to stay here and face his fate. He wanted his cake, and tried to eat it to. Something had to give." Charles knew his son was too young to understand what he was saying; but he felt better saying it anyway.

Amy was calling Brian; they hadn't spoken in a long time. "I just wanted you to know also that Ken had changed his mind about killing himself in the end. The chief didn't give me all the details but he did say he was murdered by a young lady name Ellen Walker. He fought to stay alive but, in the end, he lost. I wanted you to know that Ken didn't leave us; someone else took him away."

"Thanks, Amy. I feel much better now. I can finally "let him go." All this time I've blamed myself for his death and in the end the decision was taken from him. He had wanted to live."

Letting Go

"The trial is set for May first if you would like to attend. I will be there. I have to see what kind of person could take someone else's life in cold blood."

"I'll be there also, Amy."

Brian kept saying Ellen's name over and over in his head. The name Ellen sounded so familiar. He had heard her name somewhere before. Was it on the TV or what? He needed to remember where. Ever since Ken's death he'd blamed himself for his life falling apart. This was his chance to put things back together. He would start with his parents. He had fences that needed mending. He would have to drive out to Maryland to see them. His father had a hard time accepting his life style but that seemed like ages ago now. He would make things right!

Brian didn't waste any time. He reached his parent's home at 0800 a.m. They were just sitting down to breakfast. He noticed the house that used to sit on the right side of his parent's home had burned down. He was hoping that everyone made it out safe. Brian rang the doorbell. He hadn't seen his parents in over two years. Why had he stayed away so long? He knew they loved him and being gay wasn't a choice, it was his way of life. "Hello, Mother."

Mrs. Davis started crying the minute she saw her baby, Brian. "Where have you been honey? We've missed you so much."

"I've missed you too mom."

His dad was standing in the background waiting on a chance to apologize for the harsh words they had exchanged on their last visit two years ago. "Dad I'm sorry for all the trouble I've caused you two, you're my family and I love you and I'm so sorry for everything."

"Me, too son! I acted like an old fool!"

Mrs. Davis had tears running down her face; she had prayed and prayed for this day! She needed her family to be together again. "Brian, I never want you to stay away this long again. We need to stay close, life is so short one minute you're here and the next you're gone."

"Speaking of gone, what happened to the old Peterson home?"

"Arson. Some crazy woman tried to burn the whole family up in it. She is in jail right now."

"Did any one get hurt?"

"No one was home at the time. Your father has to attend court in two weeks to testify against her. The Chief called us first thing this morning saying she had been caught."

"What's her name? Maybe it's someone I know."

"I think its Ellen or Helen, something like that."

Brian was having a hard time believing that this could be the same woman. Dad you're going to testify against Ellen for burning her ex-husband's girlfriend's home down."

"That's about it."

"Mom and Dad, you two better sit down. This is the same lady that killed a friend of mine last year over in the district."

Mr. Davis asked if he was a close friend.

"Yes dad, he was a close friend. She shot him in the head after she robbed him. What kind of woman would do such a thing?"

"They say she is pretty evil; I'll be glad when this is all over."

"I don't think you have to worry, dad, when they finish with her she's going to go away for a long time."

"Your dad and I were a little worried about her coming back here and burning us down while we slept."

"Does she know you saw her truck?"

"She will when I get ready to testify against her."

"She won't be able to get out dad; plus you got me to protect you."

Brian was happy to be back with his family. He had missed them so much. He needed them after Ken's death; but he knew his father wouldn't have understood his need to mourn. He was home again and he would have to make sure this psycho went to prison for life.

The Courtroom

Brad and Jack returned home to find everyone up and rambling around in the kitchen. "It's over," Brad said to Beth.

"Thank God she's behind bars where she'll be spending the rest of her life. That's the best news I've heard all day. The only problem is we have no place to stay."

"You and I will be married in less than a month, why can't we all stay in my apartment together until our home is finished?"

"That's nonsense! Everyone will move in here. You're here almost every day anyway," Jack said.

The next few weeks went rushing by. Ellen's hearing had been set; no one were really looking forward to it they just wanted it to be over. They had all agreed to attend together. Ellen's trial was scheduled for 12:00 p.m. Brad and Jack were scheduled to pick them up on the way in. They wanted to keep a low profile because of the negative press that had been surrounding the case.

Beth wanted to support her soon-to-be husband Brad and all he wanted was for Ellen to go to jail for a long time. Beth wanted to take a look at pure evil; she had never seen it before. She had heard about people like Ellen and she wanted to look into her eyes and see it for herself. She had been having nightmares since the fire had been set. The courtroom was full; everyone was at the trial.

Jean saw Charles long before he noticed her. They had chosen seats close to the front on opposite sides of the courtroom. Charles looked very concerned and Jean understood why when Amy stood up to change positions. Jean noticed Amy was pregnant. Jean showed Beth that Charles and Amy were both here. The trial was about to start when Mrs. Davis spotted Beth and came over and gave her a hug. "Hi sweetie, how are you?"

"I'm fine, Mrs. Davis." Beth made introductions and so did Mrs. Davis. They had to take their seats and both promised to speak on their first break. Beth waved at Mr. Davis from across the room. She would have to see him before she left. Charles had spotted Jean and Jack across the way from him. He was trying not to stare at Jean but his eyes kept going to her position. Her husband was holding her hands as if in support of what had happened. Charles was glad this would be the last time they would all probably be breathing the same air. He did not like Jean being that close to him.

Ellen was escorted into the courtroom. She was still sporting a look of no concern on her face; she had touched so many lives. She noticed her cousin Clarence sitting in the corner of the courtroom with his friend Zack. She would make a mental note of that. Zack was supposed to have helped her out with everything but he was such a coward. She hated cowards: that's why she was here. She had helped someone do what needed to be done. Ellen stood up for five minutes studying the courtroom; she wanted to look into the faces of the people who were there to see her go down. She looked deeper in Brad's eyes and only saw contempt and rage for her. She matched his stare. She moved on to Beth and saw a woman that would tear her to pieces if she were within reaching distant. She would have her friends take care of her after they had a little fun first. Ellen smiled at Beth and moved her attention on to Amy. She must be the poor little sucker whose husband was gay. Looks like she moved on pretty well. Ellen wanted to yell out and tell her she had done her a favor by killing Ken. He was a coward and a low-rider and she didn't need him anyway. Her eyes rested on Brian for a long time. This man was beautiful. He was the kind of man that made you look twice. She would have to look him up when she got out; he was past good looking. Why was he sitting next to the old man that was there to testify against her? Where they related? The old man will have to die and his old busy body wife as well. He had noticed her truck on the side road. Who would have thought that he saw her truck? She was hoping they weren't related and if they were too bad! Ellen had to be pulled into her seat. She had taken a visual picture of everyone who wanted to

Letting Go

do her in; she would be back. This trial didn't mean a thing. She knew people in high places.

The trial was over just as fast as it had started. They were waiting for the sentencing which was sure to be a death sentence for Ellen. They found her guilty on each count of attempted murder and two counts of manslaughter that were the deaths of Ken Anderson and Karen Miller. "That's one crazy lady," someone yelled out in the courtroom. The judge had asked for a ten minute recess. Ellen would be sentenced today; she was sitting and waiting on a man to come back and make a decision that would change the rest of her life. What gives him the right to decide her life? The people that she had killed weren't even missed.

She had never heard anything about Karen nor did she see or hear anything on the news about Ken. So what's the big deal? She had probably done someone a favor. How did she get to this point in her life for doing good deeds? Ellen knew she didn't have a problem, people just weren't appreciative of her gifts to them. She should be given a medal for what she had done! She would have to go to jail for a few years to make the judge happy. Once she gets out she will make them all pay and pay dearly.

There was the call to order, the judge was ready. Everyone took their seats. Ellen stood up for sentencing. "Mrs. Walker, would you like to say a few words to the family of those you hurt before I sentence you?"

"Yes, your honor, I would. First I would like to address my ex-husband for trying to burn him and his new family up. I made a mistake when I didn't check to see if there were kids in the home. I had no intention of hurting them and for that I do apologize. I was also wrong for going after you, Mrs. Taylor. If your man does not love you there's nothing you can do to make him love you. It's not your fault; I should have let him go long before it got to this. Mrs. Anderson, I really wish I would have been able to save your husband; but I only helped him end his misery. He wanted to die and I helped him. He begged to live but I knew if I let him live he was going to leave you for Brian."

Amy held her head down and cried. Amy knew what she was saying was true. Ken would have left her, if he would had lived.

"His parents would have died of embarrassment. So, I helped him out of his miserable life. Brian, I took your life partner away from you and left you in pain. I know how much he loved you; I read it in Amy's letter. I'm sure he wrote the same to you. No, one has ever loved me like that; you were truly loved! In the end he wanted to be with you. He knew he would never be able to live in the open and be as proud as he wanted to be about the relationship that you two shared. Brian, Ken was a very weak man. He would have broken your spirit with his cowardly behavior and I couldn't take seeing a grown man cry. I helped him cross over. At least in the end he may not have gone to hell. When I get out of jail I would like to look you up and see if we can make a go of it. I feel I could change your mind about being gay." She then winked at Brian and keyed her eyes in on Clarence.

"Clarence, I know you told Brad about his son to free up your position in your son's life. We didn't just happen, we happened for a reason. You have a wonderful son and I want you to get to know him while I'm away. I'll sign over custody to you and you can continue to raise him. I would have never hurt you; we're family after all. Mr. and Mrs. Davis, I guess you're related to Brian, I can see the resemblance. I'm sorry for what I said or if I made you feel threatened in any way, it wasn't your fault I got caught. I did a stupid thing, please forgive me."

"Mrs. Walker, how much more time do you need?" the Judge asked.

"Not long your Honor, I'm almost finished. Finally, Brad, I took two loves from you, mine and your son's. Hell, you probably never loved me anyway. After all, I tricked you from the beginning of our marriage. I never gave you a chance. I saw you and I wanted you. I can understand Beth falling in love with you and your being in love with her. I wish you the best of whatever life has waiting for you. Your Honor, I would like to say one more thing before I get sentenced. I will never forget the lives I've ruined and the people I've left broken because of my

Letting Go

refusal to let go. There hasn't been a moment in the day when I haven't wish things had gone differently. My parents didn't teach me the one lesson that each of you were taught. That lesson was to walk away and let God take charge. I couldn't do it and I hurt the people I loved." Tears were running down Ellen's face, she knew she had them under her spell. Just a few more words and she would be home free.

"What I've done to Ken and Karen was inexcusable and I'm sorry; they're in a better place now. I have prayed to God to forgive me and he has. Now I'm asking you all to forgive me also."

Brad couldn't believe the judge was listening to this crap. Ellen had them all snowed. She was going to make who ever crossed her pay if she ever got out. She won't be able to fool him with this speech.

"I want to ask everyone again to forgive me," Ellen said one more time. "Thanks, your Honor, for allowing me to ask for forgiveness."

"Mrs. Walker, I've listen to your reasoning behind your actions and it seems to me that you were misguided as a child. Parents are supposed to teach their children right from wrong. I'm not sure where you crossed over to the dark side but you did; and when that happened you took innocent lives and you hurt people that cared for you. I have thought long and hard about your sentencing." The press was eager to hear the verdict; they were ready to print the outcome. "Mrs. Walker, I sentence you to ten years in the institute for the criminally insane; no one can do what you've done and be sane. I feel you need mental help more than hard prison at this time. We will re-evaluate your case in five years. At that time we will determine if further treatment is needed. Court dismissed."

Ellen's lawyer whispered in her ear, "That's better than rehearsed. You should have been an actress."

"I am!" She looked back at Brad and smiled! With only her lips moving she mumbled the words, "I'll see you later." He was the only one aware of what she truly meant. The cameras were flashing and people couldn't believe the sentence. She had gotten away with murder! Ellen's lawyer led her out of the courthouse and back into the holding area. She would never spend a waking moment in a real jail. They would all pay for taking her away from her family. She would see to it; that was a promise she had made with the devil Ellen thought.

Jean and Jack were standing at the entrance to the courtroom while Beth and Brad were speaking to Mr. and Mrs. Davis. Brian was their son. Beth had never met him in all the time they lived next to each other and they had never mentioned having a son. "Well, guys, was that a misuse of justice or what?" Mr. Davis asked. "The jury finds her guilty and the judge lets her off. She dammed near walked out a free woman."

"Honey, watch your language," Mrs. Davis told her husband.

"I'm upset and I have a right to be," he said.

Brian excused himself; he was going over to speak to Amy and Charles. "Excuse me Amy, could I speak to you for a moment?" Brian asked.

They were all walking down to the entrance and stood in one semi-circle. Jean spoke to Charles and he introduced his wife Amy to her and Jack. "This nightmare is finally over," Charles said.

"Not by a long shot," Brad commented. "She's just beginning."

Clarence came over and introduced himself to Brad. "I'm sorry for what we did to you. I had no choice in the matter. Ellen would have killed me if I hadn't help set you up. I do believe she would have done it after today," Clearance said. Clarence and Zack started walking away.

"Clarence," Brad called out.

"Yes?"

"She'll be back in a few years."

"I know!"

"You should take your son and get as far away as possible!"

"That's exactly what I'm going to do," Clarence said.

"Good luck, man," Brad said.

"The best thing is she's going to jail," Zack yelled back to them both.

Letting Go

Everyone had been introduced and they all had been touched and brought together by one evil Satan driven woman! She had destroyed marriages and taken lives. Ellen would always be feared and they would never let their guard down. They drove home in silence. There was nothing anyone could say. It was one of the worst cases of misused justice anyone had ever seen. They would live in fear for the rest of their lives.

The Wedding of a Princess

Beth's wedding was in two days; all she needed was to pick up her dress and do a final fitting! Jean had taken care of everything. "Beth would be the most beautiful bride ever. The past was behind them and she was headed toward the future with her new fiancée. Their new home was almost finished. They had driven over and checked on the final details of the farm. It was breath taking. Brad had insisted on a gate to add to their privacy.

The wedding started at one o'clock. Brad had agreed on a small party of fifty of their closest friends. The church was beautifully decorated. Jean had dressed all the pews in white roses and bows on each entrance of the seats. The altar was adorned with the most beautiful white lilies to ever grace our lands.

The bridesmaids were wearing silver gowns with a chiffon trail four feet long. All the groomsmen had black tuxes and silver vests.

The music began to play as Beth entered the church. She walked with the grace of an angel! She had waited on this man; she knew he was the one! She said a soft prayer as she was escorted to her destination, "Lord, I want to thank you in advance for this day just in case I get too caught up in all your blessings later. Thank you Lord for sending me my husband!" Tears were running down her face as she walked down the isle to meet the man that God had sent back to her. "I love you Lord for your goodness, understanding and forgiveness. I know I haven't always done the right thing but I've asked you for a chance to do better. I've been patient and I waited for you; I will never rush into anything. I will place you at the head of my life and in all I do! I know with prayer everything in life is possible; you've shown me that and more. I will love and keep him in my heart because I know he's a gift sent from you! I need you Lord to

Letting Go

take presence in our lives and guide us through this marriage so we will always walk in your grace. AMEN!"

When Beth reached Brad he looked into her eyes and he saw his future and the future of their kids. She was going to be his wife; for now and evermore. Even before they met their lives and future had already been written. It was up to them to live it to its fullest. God had given them both a second chance at love. This was his princess; she was never more beautiful than she was at this very moment. He reached for her hands. They had written their own vows and would now recite them.

The preacher asked Beth to go first. Brad, "I take you to be my best friend, my love, my all in all. I will keep you and follow you to the ends of time. I will forsake all others and hold you up to my God for prayer. Thank you for the love you give."

"Now yours, Brad."

"Beth, you're my strength, my reason for living. I've loved you from the moment you were born. I give you my heart and I promise not to break yours. Beth. you mean the world to me. When I wake in the morning I give thanks to God for you and when I lay down at night I will always keep you safe and out of harms way. Thank you for choosing me." He lifted her veil with tears in his eyes. There were no words to explain what he felt; this was his wife! She was the most beautiful woman he had ever laid eyes on. She had his heart; and he had hers. All he had to do was close his eyes and make a wish and it was made real. Jean had given them the start of a new future! She had made this day perfect for the both of them.

"I now pronounce you man and wife!"

Brad wiped his wife's tears and she wiped his. They kissed for the first time as man and wife; there wasn't a dry set of eyes in the church.

Jean wiped her eyes. She wanted to give Beth the wedding she had dreamed of all her life. She had planned a wedding that was befitting for a princess and her prince! Beth had never known the kind of love she and Brad would share. Her wedding would reflect her feelings and how she would live her life from now on. Beth had spent so many years unhappy, but today she would live her dream and her dream had become her reality.

Brad had become her prince and made everything real for her. Their vows were filled with all the right ingredients to make it a success. She loved and trusted her new husband and they would always be honest with each other. They would take their vows to heart. She would always give him what he wanted, and what he needed, when he needed it. They would put God first and let him lead them both. They would teach the girls how to love themselves; and to always follow their hearts and never look for any man to complete them. They would always have to complete themselves; no man can complete a broken woman. Always place God before any and all decisions and they would never go wrong. Brad would complete the family circle. They would finally have a father; one that they would come to love just as much as she did.

They made one last commitment on their honeymoon. They promised each other that if there ever came a time when they didn't love each other and wanted to be with someone else they would tell the other. She would never look in the direction of another man for anything.

Brad loved his wife from the moment they met. He knew they would end at this point in their lives. He had also prayed for her. Whenever she walked into a room his heart would alert him that she was there. That's how in love with his new bride he was. He made God a promise that he would cherish her and keep her safe. He would never lie or cheat on her if God gave him the chance to be her life partner. Today his prayers were answered! Tonight they would consummate those vows.

Brad took his new wife and they made love as man and wife for the first time! They knew their lives weren't always going to be easy and that in everyone's life a little rain must fall but he would use "God as his umbrella!" He was hoping these last few years were that of the storm and that the coming years would be the years of the calm.

Brad and Beth were living their dream life and they were expecting their first child in eight months. She was more beautiful than words could ever say. Brad thought to himself, "I love her with everything I have and I know she loves me. I will

Letting Go

cherish each moment and make it last a lifetime and even then it will not be long enough."

Ellen Plots Her Escape

Ellen knew Brad had gotten married two weeks ago she had gone to prison. She had read about it the newspaper. She had cried into her pillow saying, "What gave him the right? He was my husband. How could he marry another woman?" Life plays games and makes you do things you wouldn't ordinarily do. That's what happened to her. She had loved only two men in her whole life; one was her cousin and the other had been taken away from her by another woman. She always had bad luck with the opposite sex! She had to find a way to get her husband back. He had to know she still loved him and that they could make it work. Five years has passed and she nothing had change for her. She would make him forget all about Beth; especially if he found out that she was cheating on him with her best friend's husband.

Ellen had to find a way out of this place; she had plenty of work to do. She needed to call her doctor to see why she had been having stomach pains for the last two weeks; every since the guards raped her she had been sick. She never told a soul. She had taken care of them one by one. No one will ever find them; she made sure of that. She would be speaking to the head of the hospital tomorrow about her transfer to a minimal security clinic. Ellen wanted to move before she really lost her mind. She had asked to be transferred back to the Washington, DC area. They had scheduled it for tomorrow after her interview with the board. She had practice her lines. They had to be perfect. She had the ability to be great when it came to acting. Ellen was going to fool them the same way she fooled that stupid judge five years ago! She had paid her dues; it was time to go home.

Ellen was happy to be going home. "Brad darling, hold on, your wife is on her way. I'll see you real soon." Ellen had lost five years of her life. There were a lot of people responsible for her being here. She would hold them accountable for all of it. She had been cheated out of her son's and her husband's life. No

Letting Go

one will get away from her this time. She would make them all pay, one by one. This was not the place for her; she was not insane. Their tests should have proven that. She had been probed and stabbed on every inch of her body. She was tired and ready for a change. Her lawyer would bring her news tomorrow; news she's been waiting on for the last five years. Ellen knew she was on her way home.